The
PHOTO
THIEF

J. L. DELOZIER

The
PHOTO
THIEF

CamCat
Books

CamCat Publishing, LLC
Fort Collins, Colorado 80524
camcatpublishing.com

Hardcover ISBN 9780744307221
Paperback ISBN 9780744307269
Large-Print Paperback ISBN 9780744307290
eBook ISBN 9780744307320
Audiobook ISBN 9780744307337

Library of Congress Control Number: 2022937454

Book and cover design by Maryann Appel
Artwork by beakraus, denis13

5   3   1   2   4

To the Greatest Generation.

May we never forget.

Excess of grief for the dead is madness.

—Xenophon, 400 BC

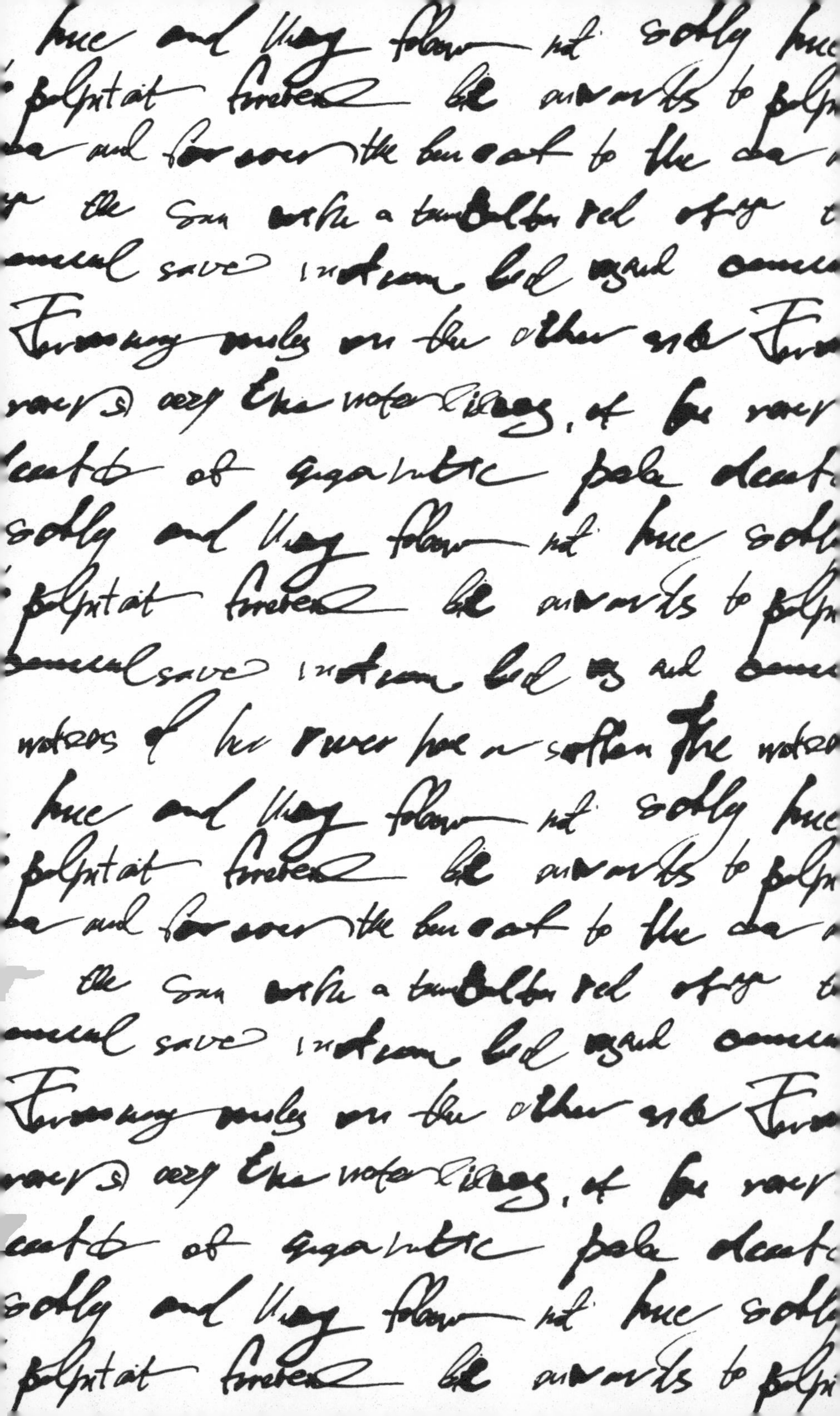

1

November 2nd
1st Journal Entry

A single black-and-white photo can damage a man's mind if the image is powerful enough. A thousand can shred it beyond repair. That's what happened to Pap, I suppose—why he simply stopped locking the photo room as if it no longer mattered. The damage to him was done. Mine was about to begin.

I didn't know that, of course, on that day six years ago when I first entered the photo room. Didn't know the images held the power to ruin me too, if I failed to answer the questions they posed—mysteries from years before I was born, pictures of grisly crimes still unsolved despite today's modern methods of investigation. I needed—still need—to quiet their voices. But the questions they ask are difficult. I promised one I'd tell her story. I did. So far, no one's believed me. That's why I'm telling you.

I was more child than teen then—twelve, sheltered by wealth and religion and just beginning to rebel against my pap's strict Catholic dogma. The photo room's dangling padlock triggered an exhilarating surge of defiance. Heart pounding, I removed the skeleton key and crept inside with no idea what I might find. I honestly didn't care. Just knowing I wasn't supposed to be there was adventure enough. Even speaking of the photo room was a punishable offense in my house back then. I never saw anyone but Pap enter or leave. That's one of the reasons the first voice frightened me so.

"I killed a man, and I'm not sorry. Everyone has to eat." Delicate yet defiant, the female voice held a hint of sly amusement, as if its owner knew my reaction in advance. I later learned her name was Ruth.

Her voice echoed from nowhere and everywhere—from within the plaster walls, the floorboards, the ceiling. A chorus of others chimed in, clamoring inside my head. Their jumbled words swelled in intensity, pounding at my skull as if trying to crack it open and set themselves free. The brass chandelier flickered and dimmed; a faint odor like that of a candlewick violently snuffed into smoke stung my nose.

I stumbled toward the door I'd closed quietly behind me, only to awaken on the room's parquet floor sometime later, lying in a puddle of lukewarm urine with no memory of how I'd gotten there. My stiff, cold muscles implied hours had passed. Golden rays from the setting sun streamed through the lead-glass windows, highlighting the fine layer of dust swirling in the air. Dozens of eyes stared blankly at me from the crinkly black-and-white photos taped to the wall. Whole families, most of them dressed in their Sunday best, bore witness to my fear and shame.

The voices were gone. The padlock was set—on the inside. I gawked at it, my confused state not allowing me to wrap my brain around what had transpired and why or how someone would lock me into the photo room, alone.

My pap pounded outside the door until the padlock swayed. I blinked, struggling to clear my foggy mind and focus on something other than my wet undies and the heavy object resting in my right palm. He repeated my name, his gruff voice growing frantic and hoarse. Even when he bellowed my scarcely used given name, I lay frozen in place—confused but calm, caged but not captive. For I knew something my pap didn't. In my right hand, I held the key.

CHAPTER

2

Detective Dan Brennan paced the pavement outside the Free Library of Philadelphia. Vibrations from a passing city bus triggered the building's revolving door to slowly spin as if pushed by a ghostly patron. Sunlight bounced off its shiny glass surface, rendering him temporarily blind. A dark cloud extinguished the glare.

He stepped toward the door, turned away, and then spun around again, nearly dropping the stack of picture books cradled in his arms. *Get yourself together, man. Just get it done.* He took a deep breath and hurtled through the door, lurching to a halt in front of the main circulation desk.

The librarian looked up from her computer. Her ready smile froze; her eyes flashed with recognition. The smile slowly disappeared. Brennan's frenzy fizzled into an awkward silence. He dropped the colorful pile onto the desk and backed away. The librarian stood and swept the books off the desk, tossing them into the return bin as if the mere sight of their childish covers was painful. "You didn't have to bring them back. Not so soon anyway. I—I know how difficult this must be—"

"They were overdue. Besides, she would've wanted me to, so some other kid can enjoy them. You know how much she loved it here. Best little library in the city." He glanced over her shoulder at the far corner, where a cozy alcove had been turned into a fantasyland for children, complete with beanbag chairs, painted unicorns, and grinning winged dragons. He had a photograph of Elle in her purple dress, the one with the polka dots she'd deemed "fa-boo-us," standing there in front of a life-sized elf, if there was such a thing.

He cleared his suddenly thick throat. "I imagine I won't be back for a while. Thanks for—for everything." He spun on his heel, sensing too late the petite figure passing behind his back. They collided, and a flurry of papers floated to the floor. He cursed aloud. The librarian's eyebrows shot skyward.

"Sorry." Brennan cursed again, silently this time, and reflexively reached to steady the shoulders of a young woman he'd seen there before. She scowled and shirked away. Her scowl vanished at his despondent expression. She looked around the room as if searching for someone. The lump reappeared in his throat, and he crouched to gather the scattered copies of vintage newspaper articles and their photos. His eyes narrowed as he examined the morbid images. Her research had drawn his attention before.

Months earlier, when chemo had cost his little girl her hair, this same young woman had been sitting at a corner table, its surface buried under mounds of similar papers. His bald daughter, entranced by the woman's long red hair, had dashed from his lap and, stretched to the max on tiny tippy-toes, fingered the woman's auburn locks. Elle and the woman had exchanged smiles before he'd led his daughter away with a mumbled apology for the intrusion.

He'd noticed the young woman several times since, but that was the only time he'd seen her smile. After observing the nature of her study, he understood why. The content never varied. A gruesome murder conveyed in the stark black-and-white print of a 1930s *Philadelphia Inquirer*. A cautionary tale of a life gone wrong. An investigation closed too soon due to the lingering Depression, and after that, a looming world war. Heavy stuff for someone who appeared to be in her late teens.

A subtle "ahem" interrupted his reflection. The young woman reached for the papers. "May I have those back, please?"

"Oh. Sure." Brennan thrust the stack into her outstretched hands. He studied her solemn expression, curious about her macabre research despite his grief, despite being on the clock, despite everything including himself. A retired colleague once told him the difference between a good detective and a great detective was the energy to question everything. Once that energy waned, it was time to turn in your badge.

The last six months of dealing with his daughter's illness had sapped his energy. Summer and autumn had disappeared in a rerun of hospital visits. Everyday activities, even getting out of bed in the morning, felt like a slog through dense fog. The days were getting darker and colder. Or maybe it was just him.

His marriage was technically the first victim, cancer's collateral damage. His work had suffered as well, and he knew it. A few times, he'd thought about transferring to a desk job. He'd even considered retiring early—really early, especially after he'd overheard a conversation about his "soft" emotions between two long-term colleagues in the break room.

After Elle died, their wives brought him meat loaf, chicken casseroles. He thought they understood. Police work could be brutal sometimes, and no one was immune to the rough patches.

The young woman, with her armful of vintage papers, sparked his curiosity back to life. He'd dealt with a lot of young adults during his career and thought of them as clueless at best and surly at worst. Then again, in his line of work, he didn't usually deal with the salt-of-the-earth types either. But this girl oozed of finishing school and Main Line money, from her formal, polite mannerisms to the tips of her retro Mary Janes. She should be sipping lattes at a Starbucks on an Ivy League campus somewhere, not researching grisly murders at the local community library, even if it was in the best part of town.

On impulse, he stuck out his hand. "Detective Dan Brennan, Philly PD."

She hesitated and took a step back. He sensed her sizing him up much the same way the local hoods did when he approached their corners. He didn't blame her.

He must've passed the sleaze test, because she shifted the stack of papers to the crook of her left arm and shook his hand.

"Cassie."

"Cassie . . . ?"

"Just Cassie." The scowl returned. She brushed by him to check out her items at the circulation desk.

He loitered until she finished and walked with her to the revolving door. "I couldn't help but notice on a couple of occasions that your research seems a little . . . dark for someone your age."

She shrugged. "School project."

"You can do better than that."

"Excuse me?"

"Your lie." He smiled to lessen the sting. "I'm a detective. Worked homicide for most of my career. I notice things for a living, which means I'm also an expert at detecting bullshit. You've been coming here at least once a week on varying days but during school hours and for a period longer than a standard school semester. You take notes in a leather-bound journal which looks like it cost more than my gun. Whatever research you're doing, it's not for school. It's personal."

"Exactly. *Personal* means it's none of your business, just like your daughter's cancer was none of mine."

Brennan winced. He'd heard the word *cancer* a thousand times over the last year, but it still hit him like a punch in the gut every damned time.

She bit her lip. "Sorry. That was rude. Please excuse me." She ducked between the glass panels and pushed the revolving door into motion. "I should get home. It's supposed to rain."

He caught up with her on the sidewalk. "Elle. My daughter's name was Elle. She thought you were a princess and the library was your castle. She loved your hair and hoped . . ." He coughed. ". . . And hoped hers would grow out red and curly like yours."

Cassie flushed and averted her eyes. "Your daughter's hair was black."

"I know." His lips curved into a sad smile. "And straight as a soldier's spine. She was young enough to believe you could wish things true."

They stood in silence until a crack of thunder made them jump. The sunshine vanished behind a veil of black clouds.

"Whaddaya know? A thunderstorm in November." Brennan frowned. "You'll have to run to beat the rain. You want me to hail you a cab or call an Uber or somethin'?" His phone jangled, and he glanced at the number. When he looked up, Cassie had rounded the corner and quickly vanished from sight. "I guess not."

The first drops of rain fell, and he ducked under the library's eaves to answer the call. "Brennan." He rolled his eyes at the curt voice on the other end. "I'm about ten blocks away. Text me the exact address. I'll be there in a few."

When gifting a shitty assignment, his boss liked to call him herself. All his assignments had been shitty lately. His old partner, Tom, retired early spring, and Elle had gotten sick shortly thereafter. Her treatments were copious and lengthy, and he'd missed a lot of work. The captain hadn't bothered to assign him a new partner yet, and he hadn't bothered to ask. It was low on his priority list.

The raindrops became a torrent. He turned up his collar and dashed to his car. His phone burbled the address. He wiped the rain off its screen and whistled. Locust and Third marked the border between Society Hill and Old City, two of Philly's swankiest neighborhoods. Maybe this assignment wouldn't be so bad after all. He could go for a simple Jag-jacking right about now—ease himself back into the workflow before handling something grittier. Grit usually meant blood. Blood meant death. He'd had enough of that to last for a long while.

He sped west past Washington Square and floored it. The short trip took forever, thanks to the oil-and-rain-slick streets and the sudden proliferation of taxis as harried tourists scurried to escape the downpour. He cursed with each sudden stop, his language growing more colorful block after congested block. He'd tried to quit swearing once, back when Elle was learning to speak. No reason to worry about that now. His vision blurred, and he cranked the wipers to high.

When he reached Third, he eased the car to the curb and lowered his rain-streaked window. The neighborhood was old—old enough that the cobblestone roads and alleys bore weathered tracks for horse-drawn trolleys. Most were too narrow for two-way traffic and many remained pedestrian only. Franklin streetlamps, rewired for electricity, lined the curbs and guarded the historic, three-story row houses that ran the length of several city blocks.

The real estate in this part of town cost more than he would earn in a lifetime—hell, in three lifetimes. He grimaced. Old families with old money made for the worst cases. Way too many secrets and a reluctance to share. Way too much to lose. Family legacies to preserve. The layers of bullshit never ended.

The house in question sat on an elite corner lot that intersected with one of the pedestrian-only alleys. The strobing red lights from a pair of police cruisers indicated the street was cordoned off ahead. He sighed and fumbled under his seat for an umbrella. He was hoofing it from here.

He approached and flashed his badge. The junior officer performing crowd control nodded, sending a stream of water flowing off his hat. "Everyone else is inside."

Brennan grinned. "Of course they are. Everyone except you. Who'd you piss off?"

"No one. At least, I don't think so. I'm new on the force. Paying my dues."

"Let me guess—your partner fed you that line."

The officer nodded again. Brennan shook his head and climbed the wide stone steps leading to the front door. Above it, a stained-glass transom glowed in shades of green and gold, lit from within by the brass chandelier hanging in the foyer. Security cameras mounted underneath the steep eaves swept in perfectly synchronized arcs. The tiny red light underneath each lens suggested they were functioning normally.

He gave a perfunctory knock, walked in, and stopped underneath the enormous chandelier to gape. It was as if he'd stepped back in time. To his right, a seven-foot-tall grandfather clock ticked the time as it had for the past hundred years. Through the mahogany pocket doors to his left, empty leather chairs faced a fireplace flanked by built-in shelves overflowing with books. The hush, broken only by the ticking of the clock, felt heavy, as if the windows, protected by thick iron bars as was typical for the neighborhood, refused to permit the slightest breeze or whisper to enter. Three generations of eyes glared at him from the oil paintings lining the papered wall of the foyer. The hairs on his arms stood on end. He was alone.

A burst of chatter from a police radio echoed down the elaborately carved grand staircase, shattering the spell. He exhaled and strode forward, breaking into an awkward jig as his wet soles slipped on the marble tile. The sturdy bottom newel kept him from hitting the ground. He grabbed the banister for support and placed his free hand on his gun. Even the house was out to get him. He hated this case already.

He tilted his head and stared up three steep stories. Thirteen steps took him to the first ninety-degree landing. He rounded the corner and stopped. Long, slender fingers dangled over the second-floor landing. Another step and the contorted body of a woman came into view. She lay faceup in a pool of congealed blood—so much blood, it had streamed onto the tread below. A pair of CSIs circled her, snapping pictures like the paparazzi.

Brennan placed his foot on the next step. It creaked, announcing his presence. The younger of the two investigators crouched by the woman's head and focused his lens on the victim's battered skull. He paused his grisly duties long enough to cock his thumb toward the third flight of stairs.

"Yo, Dan. It's been a while. I was hoping you'd get this case. Senior officer's up there interviewing the only witness. Officer Cortez, I think. Watch your step—they might be a little slick, as you can tell." His thick glasses slid down the bridge of his nose, and he pushed them in place with a shrug of his shoulder. "Welcome back, by the way. I missed our daily swim break."

"Me too, Jim. Thanks. It's good to be back." *Liar, liar, pants on fire.* Elle's childish chant echoed in his ears. Brennan climbed the remaining stairs. Pressing his back against the banister, he awkwardly skirted along the edge of the crowded landing. "What's the story?"

He studied the woman's delicate features. Mid-forties, he guessed, with green eyes and auburn hair. She was lovely even in death, if you could ignore the god-awful mess.

"Dunno yet. Pretty obvious she fell down the stairs backward." Jim lowered the camera and snapped on a pair of nitrile gloves. With delicate precision, he rotated her slim neck to display the extent of the damage. Gray matter and bits of bone had oozed into her hair, matting it into bloody clumps. "The question is whether she had help. She doesn't look much older than you, and people your age don't typically reverse swan dive down the stairs. We'll know more after the medical examiner assesses for occult injuries unrelated to the fall. X-rays, tox-icology—she'll get the full deal. Her family will demand it, I'm sure."

His lips twitched into a humorless grin. "Unless they did it, of course. Then they'll want a quick and quiet burial."

"Of course." Brennan sighed.

Jim twisted the woman's head again, and a pair of gold chains slid across her neck. The first bore a petite cross. The second held a heart-shaped claddagh locket. Brennan's stomach clenched. He'd given a similar locket—albeit smaller and likely less expensive—to his ex when Elle was born.

The camera flashed, and the gold locket sparkled in the sudden burst of light. Brennan looked away. "She looks familiar. But I guess they all do after a certain point."

"This one should." His pictures complete, Jim stood and stretched his back. "She and her husband grace the society section of the city paper at least once a month—a charity ball here, a major donation there. Her granddaddy owns it. I'm sure that helps." He grinned. "Leland Dolan. You may have heard of him once or twice."

"Jesus, is he still alive? I know he had a stroke a while back. I assumed he'd died. He must be, what, ninety by now? At least." Brennan glanced up the last flight of stairs.

Leland Dolan was a local legend. In the 1930s, he'd worked for the *Philadelphia Inquirer* as an amateur photographer and teenaged photo thief, tasked with breaking into the homes of murder victims and stealing family photographs to run alongside articles about the sensational and often grotesque crimes. The penny-per-photo salary wasn't much, but it kept him from starving until the war cured the Depression and sent him to the Battle of Okinawa.

Sergeant Dolan's breaking-and-entering skills served him well. First, he escaped from a notorious Japanese POW camp. Then, after regaining his strength, he broke back in, launching a daring, covert rescue operation that freed a dozen fellow Marines.

He returned to Philly a hero.

A media darling, Dolan used his contacts to land a job as a reporter for the *Inquirer*'s chief rival, where he earned a reputation as a hard-nosed hustler who refused to take no for an answer. Eventually, with grit and savvy investments, he bought the paper and much, much more. His empire was built on hard work and the American Dream.

Brennan straightened his damp tie. "I shook his hand once at a Veterans Day ceremony back when I was still in blue. We had a brief conversation. You know what he told me?"

"Can't venture a guess."

"He told me the next time we met I'd better have polished my shoes."

Jim smirked at the worn black leather on his colleague's feet. "I wouldn't worry about it. He's old and probably senile by now."

"Who said I was worried? There's nothing wrong with my shoes. They're just getting broken in. Besides, he has more important things to worry about than my footwear. Like a dead woman on his stairs." Brennan hopped over the corpse and plodded up the final flight to the third floor.

The grandfather clock in the foyer tolled the hour. Its resonance filled the stairwell with a mournful dirge, the notes keeping pace with Brennan and his slow ascent to the third floor. The air grew steadily warmer and more humid; beads of sweat dampened his forehead. He swiped them away with the back of his hand. Jim was right—he needed to get back to his daily swim in the precinct's pool. His health had suffered along with Elle's.

He paused at the top to catch his breath. A long hallway, darkened by cherry paneling and dressed in a threadbare carpet, ran the length of the third floor. The heavy doors at each end were closed. One was padlocked. But the door straight ahead was ajar. Brennan peered over its threshold and was punished by the smell of stale urine and old flesh.

He nudged the wooden door the rest of the way open with his foot. It creaked on its hinges, a cry of solidarity, perhaps, with the room's elderly occupant.

Officer Cortez looked up from her notepad and nodded. "Detective Brennan. We were just finishing up."

She crouched next to an unshaven man hunched in a damask-covered chair. A side table held a stack of newspapers and an old-fashioned radio. A wheeled walker rested in front. She raised her voice. "Mr. Dolan, this is Detective Dan Brennan. We're going to step out so I can brief him on what you've shared with me thus far. He may need to ask you a few more questions. Is that okay?"

The old man straightened to stare at Brennan's face. His eyes narrowed, and he allowed his gaze to drift to Brennan's feet as he sagged into his former position. "Do whatever you need to do."

The bastard remembered him. Of course he did. Leland Dolan's eyes had lost their sparkle, thanks to discs of milky-white film—not cataracts, but *arcus senilis*, a sign of extreme age, a coroner friend once told him. But behind those cloudy green eyes, the veteran's shrewd mind had not diminished. Self-made men, particularly one with the steely determination to refuse "help" from Philly's Irish mob, never forgot anything: favors cast, debts owed, even shoes unpolished. That kind of ferocious instinct didn't dull with age. Still, it'd been twenty stinkin' years. Cut a guy a break, already.

The senior officer motioned for Brennan to follow her into the hall. She flipped her notebook to the first page.

"The victim is Erin Dolan McConnell, age forty-four, Mr. Dolan's granddaughter. Every morning around nine, she helps him shave and dress and walks him to the elevator to go downstairs for breakfast. A private-duty nurse takes over Mr. Dolan's care after lunch."

"Elevator?" Brennan peered down the dimly lit hallway.

"The paneled door at the end is an elevator in disguise." She sighed as Brennan walked the length of the hall to see for himself. He slid his hands over the door's surface. It rattled, the metallic sound muted by the heavy wood veneer. His fingers probed the wall to its right until he found a seam. With a tap of his gloved finger, the burled panel slid open to reveal a single button.

"Guess it only goes down." He punched it, and the cherry doors separated.

Released from its façade, the cage of wrought-iron bars shuddered and lurched, its intricate decorative scrolls parting with a clang to reveal a service elevator large enough to hold a grand piano and then some. Brennan poked his head inside. The thick bars tapered to a gilded domed ceiling; the wide-plank floor was waxed to a high sheen. "I think this thing's bigger than my bathroom. It's definitely cleaner."

Cortez shook her head. "Satisfied? I could've saved you the time. We already processed it."

"Find anything?"

"Nothing worthwhile." She glanced at her notes. "As I was saying, Erin was late this morning. By ten, Mr. Dolan was starving and, from the sounds of it, irritable. He was about to call Erin on her cell when he heard a scream, followed by a terrible crash. He found her lying at the bottom of the steps and called 9-1-1. When we arrived, he was sitting on the step next to her holding her hand. He'd slid down the stairs on his butt to reach her."

"Why didn't he take the elevator?"

The officer scowled. "How would I know? Maybe he couldn't walk the length of the hall fast enough with his walker. Maybe he panicked."

"The man broke *into* a POW camp. He doesn't seem the type to panic."

"That was a million years ago, and he wasn't trying to save his granddaughter back then. People react differently when it's their family, their blood, at stake." She snapped her notebook shut. "Ask him yourself. I'm done here anyway. I'll start my preliminary report and email it to you once I get back to the station."

Brennan nodded, his mind already abuzz with questions. A surge of anticipation, more powerful than any caffeinated beverage, honed his focus. He'd forgotten how good it felt to work an interesting case. And any case featuring the renowned Leland Dolan was automatically interesting. A tap on Dolan's door yielded no response. Brennan pushed it open and lingered at the threshold, waiting for Dolan to acknowledge his presence. The old man, lips pursed and breathing heavily, had moved from the armchair to the seat of his walker, which was now positioned in the middle of the room. He'd been working his way toward the door.

Brennan shut it behind him. "I would recommend you stay here until . . . until the investigators finish clearing the scene. If you need something, I'd be happy to get it for you."

Silence.

He cleared his throat and spoke louder. "I want you to know how sorry I am for your loss."

"Is that so?" Dolan's speech held a slight slur, a remnant of his prior stroke. His milky eyes met Brennan's, and his thin lips curled as if he'd planned to add something snide but thought better of it. His gruff voice trembled. "Thank you." He looked down, hiding his face.

"Is there someone you'd like me to call to come sit with you?" Brennan strained to recall everything he knew about the Dolan family tree. He remembered the old man's wife had died of breast cancer shortly after the Veterans Day shoe-polishing incident. Her funeral had been the social event of the season. But as far as children . . .

"God only granted me one son. The Vietcong took him away." Dolan answered the detective's unspoken question. "He had one daughter. She's lying downstairs."

"There has to be someone you'd like me to call."

"Her husband, Ryan, is a hotshot surgeon at Jefferson Hospital. But I'm sure he already knows." Dolan's voice hardened, triggering Brennan's radar.

"Why's that?"

"Because your officer sent someone to the hospital to tell him."

The old man raised his face. His stare—as cold and unblinking as those in the family portraits—gave Brennan a chill. "You can tell a lot about a man from simple things like the way he stands, the roughness of his hands, the words he chooses—even the shoes on his feet." His eyes drifted south. "I can assess a man's character in thirty seconds flat. You believe that?"

"Yes, sir, I do."

"It's a survival skill. Helps in the boardroom too. Just like recognizing faces. I never forget one, even if I want to." Dolan leaned forward. "I remember you."

Brennan shifted on his feet. His worn soles squeaked.

The old man's lips twitched in a faint smile. "You come from humble stock, Detective Brennan. Nothing to be ashamed of. I did too. You earned your promotion the old-fashioned way, through hard work. I can respect that. You're good people, as we used to say. A little softhearted for my liking, though."

"Thank you, sir." This conversation had veered way off course. Brennan attempted a redirect. "Do you have any theories as to what happened here today?"

"I don't need any goddamned theories. I know what happened to my Erin."

"What?"

"Her husband. The bastard killed her."

CHAPTER

3

By the time Brennan finished documenting Dolan's tale of infidelity and murder, the pair of CSIs had finished processing the scene and a hydraulic stretcher occupied most of the second-story landing. He leaned against the wall beside Dolan's bedroom door and waited for a path to clear. The stifling air grew suddenly cooler; the hair clinging to his damp forehead fluttered. Someone had finally turned on the AC. He scanned the plaster ceiling for vents. If present, they were as expertly disguised as the elevator.

The gurney shuddered as the EMTs hoisted the body into place. Beneath the metallic clatter and the EMTs' quiet conversation, Brennan detected a faint tinkling. He tipped his head and focused. Music. A piano, maybe. He leaned closer to Dolan's bedroom door.

The elusive melody swelled at random intervals, wafting throughout the hallway from the elevator to the padlocked room at the opposite end and back to where he stood between the door and the top of the stairs. Then it was gone, stopping as abruptly as it had begun and taking the cool air with it. Brennan frowned and brushed the hair off his forehead. Nice to know that transistor radio, almost as old as Dolan himself, still worked. They don't make things like they used to, people included.

The crowded landing cleared, leaving two EMTs and just enough room for Brennan to escape to cooler quarters. As he eased past, he stole a final glance at the victim's gray face. An EMT zipped the body bag, sealing Erin McConnell inside an impermeable coffin of thick, black plastic.

His brow furrowed. He'd seen her face before, and it wasn't from the society section of the newspaper. The oil paintings. He jogged down the steps to the foyer. Three generations of Dolans—men with grim smiles and women with hauntingly sad eyes—maintained a silent vigil over the entry. He paused in front of the most modern of the three.

Erin, surrounded by a halo of light, stiffly cradled a rosy-cheeked infant in an elaborate lace christening gown. Her husband hovered at her back, his smug expression partially hidden in the shadows. His hands squeezed her delicate shoulders with enough force to wrinkle the fabric of her emerald-green dress. In a few strokes of oil, the artist had captured the essence of Erin's marriage. The painter's talent failed to surprise. Leland Dolan could afford the best.

The rattling gurney at his rear urged him to move along. Brennan stepped into the rain. Officer Cortez lingered on the stone steps.

He raised an eyebrow. "You're getting wet. I thought you were heading to the station."

"I was." She nodded, and he followed her line of sight.

Across the narrow street, a bedraggled figure—shoulders and chin hunched, clothes drenched—stood shivering in the rain. Pulses of red light bounced off the wet cobblestones and sliced across her face, highlighting a pair of impossibly wide eyes, pupils dilated despite the glare from the cruiser's strobing LEDs. Strands of auburn hair clung to her face, but she didn't bother to brush them away.

"I thought she was just rubbernecking and yelled for her to move along." Cortez moved to the side to allow the gurney to pass. "She acted like she didn't hear me. Girl's not right. I was about to go check on her, see if she needs assistance."

The laden gurney clattered down the weathered stone steps on its way to the ambulance, and the girl finally blinked. Her mouth widened to match her eyes. Her lips moved but produced no sound.

The puzzle pieces locked into place. Green eyes. Curly red hair, like her mother's. Brennan waved both arms, trying to redirect the girl's attention from the gurney's morbid contents. "Cassie. Cassie McConnell."

Arms outstretched like a zombie's, Cassie stepped into the uneven street. As her foot left the curb, her eyes rolled and she collapsed, arms and legs flailing. Her back arched; her head pounded the wet cobblestone. Once. Twice. The rhythmic thrashing continued.

Brennan winced at the loud cracks of bone on stone. He dashed across the street, cradled her head to absorb the blows, and yelled over his shoulder to Cortez. "Get the paramedics. She's having a seizure."

CHAPTER

4

Jefferson Hospital's emergency department underwent extensive renovations in the 1990s, prompting employees and locals alike to refer to the inaptly posh unit as "Trump Triage." But the brass handrails quickly lost their gleam, sullied by thousands of dirty hands, while on busy Friday nights, the white marble floors collected lurid splashes of red.

During the slower midweek mornings, maintenance workers struggled to lift the stains. They ran their industrial-grade polishers up and down the halls, buffing away the bloody evidence of lives lost. Brennan, absorbed by their Sisyphean efforts, loitered in the waiting area, lost in the hypnotic whirr of the buffer's circular brushes. An hour passed before the ER's glass doors whooshed open and Cassie's father arrived on scene. Beyond a smattering of steely gray at his temples and what appeared to be a recently acquired tan, Dr. Ryan McConnell's appearance had changed little from the time of the family portrait hanging in the Dolan family mansion. A short woman in a black suit and sensible heels—a hospital administrator, Brennan surmised—struggled to keep pace.

Next to her, a uniformed officer nodded at Brennan and subtly rolled her eyes.

The officer gestured toward Brennan. "Dr. McConnell, this is Detective—"

"Where's my daughter?"

The officer glanced over her shoulder at the array of rooms positioned in a semicircle around the nurses' bay. "I don't know."

"She's in room six. I checked on her a few minutes ago. She has a . . . hematoma, I think the ER doc called it, on the back of her scalp, but no cuts or internal bleeding. She's stable and sleeping off the meds they gave her. He says she'll be fine." Brennan extended his hand. "Detective Brennan, Philly PD. I was assigned to investigate your wife's death. I'm so sorry for your loss." He paused, anticipating the usual polite murmuring of thanks. None ensued. He cleared his throat. "I know this has been a terrible day, but given the circumstances of your wife's death, I have to ask you some questions."

The administrator mumbled an excuse and hurried away. Dr. McConnell gave Brennan's hand a perfunctory shake. "You can ask your questions later. I need to check on Cassie." He strode to the nurses' station and demanded to speak to the emergency-room physician monitoring his daughter's care.

The officer shook her head. "Have fun with this one. If it helps, he's been in the operating room since seven this morning, so he wasn't home at the time of death. The administrator confirmed his schedule, but she deferred any further questions to the hospital's lawyers. He's already contacted his personal attorney as well. Acting a wee bit guilty, if you ask me."

Brennan shrugged. "We're not sure his wife's death is even a crime. She could've fainted her way down the stairs. Besides, calling a lawyer is par for the course with these types. I swear they talk to their lawyers more than their wives."

The emergency-room physician patted his colleague on the shoulder, and McConnell walked toward room six. Brennan crossed the hall to join him. McConnell frowned, but before he could speak, the curtain jerked open with the harsh clack of metal on metal. A nurse exited, thermometer in hand. Cassie's red hair glowed like a crown of fire against the stark white sheets. Nodding, she moved her lips almost imperceptibly as if in silent prayer and stared heavy-lidded at the pale green wall dividing her room from the next, ignoring the men as they entered. A thin shriek, tremulous with age, emanated from the room next door.

"She suffers," Cassie murmured.

"Probably has a kidney stone." Her father flashed a tight smile. "Glad to see you're awake. I was beginning to worry."

Cassie jerked, shifting her attention to her father. She scowled and opened her mouth, then bit her lip as if having second thoughts.

The screaming intensified. "Cassandra! Cassandra, help me! Where are you?" The elderly woman's shrieks degenerated into a constant moan.

Brennan and McConnell shared startled looks.

A younger voice attempted to soothe. "Mom, I'm right here. You're okay. I'm here." The door to the room slid shut, and the voices disappeared amid the buzz of the busy department.

"Popular name," McConnell muttered.

The wall-mounted surgical light flickered. Cassie closed her eyes. "What happened?"

"You had another seizure."

"I know that."

McConnell's eyes narrowed at his daughter's prickly tone.

Cassie heeded the subtle warning by softening her voice. Challenging her father in public was apparently a mortal sin. "I meant, what happened to Pap? He was fine when I left this morning." She picked at the tape securing the IV needle to her right hand.

She doesn't know. Brennan pictured the glistening body bag, raindrops coating its dark surface like a fine veil of tears. It made sense for Cassie to assume it contained her elderly great-grandfather. Brennan would've assumed the same. He glanced at Ryan McConnell's impassive face.

The surgeon clasped his daughter's hand in his. She twitched at his touch, and her heart monitor's steady beep increased to a frantic rate. "Cassie, your pap is fine. It was your mother." He took a deep breath. "She fell down the stairs."

Cassie's face blanched, and she sagged into the bed. "No. That's not possible. You're lying to me again. You know I can tell. Why do you always lie?"

The heart monitor flashed an alarm. Cassie's pupils dilated, and Brennan tensed. She'd worn that same dazed expression before starting to seize.

Her gaze drifted to her father's face, her emerald eyes focusing on his cool baby blues. She whispered her words hoarsely, as if each syllable required tremendous effort. "Ruth will tell me the truth."

McConnell dropped Cassie's hand and silenced the alarm. "You're upset and confused. So am I. It's a normal reaction." His steady voice and clinical assessment belied any such emotion. "I've canceled my OR schedule for this afternoon. As soon as you're cleared for discharge, I'll take you home. We'll get through this together."

Cassie ignored him and rolled onto her side to curl into the fetal position. Brennan observed the exchange from a respectful distance, troubled more by the strange father-daughter dynamic than Dr. McConnell's composure. He'd expect a surgeon to have nerves of steel and a calm façade, thanks to years of experience at breaking bad news. Brennan had been on the receiving end of such news once, when Elle's tumor was found to be inoperable. That doctor's voice was calm too, although her kind eyes had misted with tears. McConnell's eyes were dry.

The surgeon gestured for Brennan to follow him into the hall. He drew the thin curtain separating Cassie from the chaotic emergency room. "Are you sure your questions can't wait? I just told my only child that her mother's dead, for Christ's sake."

"I know, and I completely understand. But Mr. Dolan and Cassie were the last two people to see your wife alive. Memories fade quickly and for good reason. I'm obligated to ask a few basic questions. If I don't ask them now, I'll have to do so later while you're preparing for the funeral. There's never a good time in a situation like this. Better to just get it over with."

McConnell drew a shaky breath and ran a hand through his wavy hair. "Fine. But make it quick. I'm going to speed up Cassie's discharge and get her out of here. She's had dozens of seizures in the past. There's nothing special about this one." He stormed down the hall to the nurses' station.

Except for her mother's death, of course. Brennan watched a gaggle of nurses, male and female, fawn over the handsome surgeon while expressing their condolences. Even amid tragedy, the man oozed the charismatic assurance typical of those born to lifelong privilege.

Behind the ugly blue-and-white curtain, an IV pump beeped and whirred. Brennan pushed the curtain aside just in time to see Cassie, her focus restored, deactivate the pump with a jab of her slender finger. She pulled the needle out of her arm and applied pressure with her opposite hand.

He stepped into the room. "I don't think you should be doing that."

"Yeah? See those two tiny bags of fluid? One's lorazepam. They always order lorazepam. I'd bet the other is phenobarb."

"Okay."

"Lorazepam's always enough. If my mom's with me, that's all I get. But if my father arrives first—and since he works here, he usually does—he insists on the phenobarb cocktail. He likes me nice and snowed."

"Why?"

"Maybe because I'm less likely to say or do something embarrassing. You should ask him that question, not me." She rubbed her droopy eyelids. "It'll probably get worse now that mom ... mom's ..." Her voice quavered, and she looked away. "I met you at the library today. You're a detective."

"Yes. Yes, you did, and yes I am. I wasn't sure you'd remember."

"I remember everyone I meet. Coincidence is strange, isn't it?"

"Very strange. We've had a lot of it today, haven't we?" Brennan pulled the room's lone chair closer to her bed. "Cassie, I've been assigned to investigate the circumstances surrounding your mother's death—"

"My father said she fell down the stairs."

"That she did. But sometimes there's more to the story, and sometimes there isn't. Do you feel up to answering a few questions?"

"I'm postictal, you know."

"Which means what?"

She recited what sounded like a textbook definition. "Postictal: the altered state of consciousness after an epileptic seizure lasting between five and thirty minutes, but sometimes longer in the case of more severe seizures, like mine. Marked by drowsiness, confusion, and other disorienting symptoms. My father would be quick to point out it makes me an unreliable historian. In your profession, the term would be 'witness.'"

"Huh. Is that right?" Brennan pretended to ponder the information before leaning forward in his chair. "I'll take my chances. You seem pretty reliable to me." He lowered his voice. "Do you know of anyone who might want to hurt your mother?"

Cassie sighed and rested her head against the pillow. "Like my father's girlfriend, maybe?"

Brennan blinked and pulled his phone from his pocket. "That's a good start. Do you know her name?"

"Amber Servello. She was my tutor. I attended a private Catholic school until my frequent seizures became too severe. I made the nuns nervous. I've been homeschooled for the past six years. Even though my mom has—had—degrees in teaching and English literature, my father thought I needed a 'proper' tutor. By proper, he meant young, blonde, and stacked. She lives in Fishtown somewhere."

"You said *was*. She *was* your tutor."

"I've known she's been banging my father for over a year, and it made me so angry. I turned eighteen six months ago and graduated a month later. After that, I refused to even look in her direction. Petty, I know, but I put her out of a job, and I love it. They can hook up at her place, and they are, based on my father's recent run of long hours. He's a liar and a cheat. My mother deserved better." Cassie's eyes brimmed with tears. "She was too loyal for her own good. Too good for him, that's for sure."

"Your grandfather doesn't seem to like him either."

"Great-grandfather." For a fleeting moment, Cassie's troubled expression relaxed into a smile. "Pap's an excellent judge of character."

"He told me the very same thing." Brennan returned the smile.

"Pap knew about my father's affair with Amber. I'm surprised he didn't kill them both. Pap had quite a temper when he was younger. Now that he's old and has had a stroke, everyone just calls him feisty. He hates that." Her smile faded. "He thinks my father married Mom for the Dolan family money."

"Do you agree?"

"I don't know. How could I?" She closed her misty eyes. "It doesn't matter what I think. My mom was happy, or at least she pretended to be. My father's happy with his fancy toys and mistress, and he ignores me when he can, which works for me."

"What about you? Are you happy?"

"I can't drive, attend school, or have a social life. The flashing lights at a nightclub would kill me. I'm on seizure meds that would drop an elephant, and now that my mom is dead, I'm stuck in a moldy old mansion with a megalomaniac father and my ninety-eight-year-old great-grandfather. What do you think?"

Brennan wasn't sure why he'd asked, other than a professional inclination to extract information whenever possible. He'd seen Cassie often enough, unsmiling, scrutinizing the library's archives with grim determination, to predict her answer. And that was before her mother's unexpected demise. He pulled a business card from his wallet and slid it between her fingers. "If I can do anything to help, or if you think of anything you'd like to add, give me a call." He slid the curtain open and paused with casual deliberation. "I almost forgot. Who's Ruth?"

Cassie's eyes flew open. "Ruth?" She rolled onto her side, stretching her monitor leads to their limits, and buried her forehead in the pillow. "I don't know anyone named Ruth. The lady in the room next door is dying, I think."

Brennan ignored her obvious deflection. "You said Ruth would tell you the truth. If that's the case, I'd like to chat with her too."

"Postictal. Unreliable witness. I warned you, remember?" She burrowed her face deeper into the pillow. Her free hand fluttered in obvious dismissal. "I need to sleep off these stupid meds."

He stepped into the hall. The blue strobe light above the door to the next room flashed. A voice boomed through speakers mounted on the walls. "Code Blue, ER, room seven. Repeat: Code Blue, ER, room seven." The nurses' station emptied as the emergency-room physician and his team rushed past Brennan into the neighboring room, yanking the curtain shut behind them.

Cassie spoke over the din. "We'll see each other again, won't we, Detective Brennan?"

"I suspect we will." Across the bustling ER, Brennan locked eyes with Ryan McConnell. "In fact, you can count on it."

5

November 4th
2nd Journal Entry

W hen I was thirteen, Ruth decided I must've been named after the Greek oracle Cassandra. Horrified to learn I knew nothing of mythology, she taught me how the young priestess fell asleep in Apollo's temple and awakened to find serpents licking at her ears. Those flicking tongues gave her the gift of prophecy. Apollo cursed her to a lifetime of disbelief. When she shrieked warnings of horrors to come, her father labeled her mad and locked her away. The horrors she predicted came true.

"So you see, Cassandra, why you must never tell anyone about me and our little temple. They'll call you crazy. You'll be committed to an asylum where they'll shock you until your teeth rattle around in your pretty little head. Do you know what else they do to girls in those horrible places?"

I didn't. She told me. Her report, historically accurate or not, gave me nightmares that persist to this day.

Now you know why I don't talk about Ruth. I tried once, before Ruth issued her warning. I told my mother about the photo room's voices; she refused to believe. Pap refuses, too—at least out loud. I hear the strain in his voice, the inflection he uses when he's lying. I see something in his face, something that looks like fear. He believes more than he'll say.

I broke my own rule at the hospital. I slipped and spoke Ruth's name. I was fuzzy from the seizure and the drugs and the shock of my mother's death, and I can't remember exactly what I said. A lie, I'm sure. Family secrets are meant to live and die with the family.

But Ruth doesn't lie. Father—he likes to be called "Father," like some kind of masculine deity—pushed my mother down the stairs. Ruth confirmed my suspicions once I got home from the hospital. Now you and I have to prove it. It won't be easy. Father has many faults, but he's not dumb.

My special talent will help. I mentioned it once already, if you were paying attention. I never forget a face or voice. My brain notices and catalogs details—all of them. A neurodiversity-affirming therapist once called me a "hyper-observant super-recognizer." It's a real thing. Look it up on the internet if you'd like. Sometimes it's useful, like when I awoke in the ER. Father spoke; I heard his guilt in every subconscious inflection. Then, once my vision cleared, I saw it in his face.

When he grabbed my hand, that sealed the verdict. It wasn't his fake smile. I'm used to that. His smile never reaches his eyes, not when they're focused on me. But to hold my hand? Something had to be terribly wrong, something more than just another seizure. A shiver of jitters joined the pounding in my head, and I wanted to puke. But I know better than to embarrass my father in front of anyone. My seizures embarrass him enough.

Pap agrees Father is to blame and believes you can prove it. He knows who to trust. "A survival skill learned early and practiced often," he likes to say. If he trusts you, so do I. We're two of the same, my pap and I. He calls me his doppelgänger. It's German, I think, for "shadow." Or "ghost."

And as for Ruth, I trust her too. It's sad to say, but she's the only friend I've ever had. The fact that she's dead doesn't matter. She has no reason to lie.

I still find it hard to say her name out loud. It catches in my throat, and her warnings of cursed prophecies and ghastly asylums ring in my ears. *They'll lock you away, Cassandra* . . . But what if I write what I cannot say? Maybe then, despite my name, Apollo's curse will have no power over my words. Magical thinking, I know. But what about this is real?

CHAPTER

6

The rain cleared by the weekend, allowing Erin Dolan McConnell to be buried on a crisp autumn day. But the sun's golden rays lacked warmth, and a stiff wind off the Delaware River to the south, sent fallen leaves swirling erratically over graves and headstones, a Saint Vitus's dance of faded color that hinted at the bitter winter to come. Bare branches clacked like old, dried bones, and melancholy hung in the air.

Five days from death to funeral had to be some kind of record. Brennan and Pete, the medical examiner, went way back. Brennan knew his methods. Pete was habitual to the point of neurosis. The autopsy would've been done within twenty-four hours and the tox screen sent for processing. But those screens can take up to a month to come back, depending on the backlog. Pete always awaited the results before issuing his report. No report meant no burial. But this time, Pete didn't wait.

Brennan shivered under his heavy suede jacket. He leaned against his car—one in a row of many—at the edge of the expansive private cemetery. In the next vehicle over, a paparazzo eager to give grief a face leaned from the driver's window and focused his telephoto lens. Brennan had left the soaring Cathedral Basilica of Saints Peter and Paul before the funeral mass's grand recessional, intent on securing a prime spot with a view of the Dolan family crypt, a giant hunk of moss-tainted granite as bleak as Dolan Mansion itself. Now, as the priest droned an additional graveside service, Brennan wished he'd stopped to take a leak and grab a cup of caffeine. He badly needed both.

With a final shake of the thurible and a sprinkle of holy water, the service ended. A dozen tearful hugs and handshakes later, the attendees began ambling to their cars. Leland Dolan sat as upright as his age and wheelchair would allow, accepting the crowd's condolences with a curt nod of his head. Cassie, her curly hair secured in a demure braid, stood like a statue by his side, holding her great-grandfather's hand.

Behind them, her father whispered to a man wearing an exquisitely tailored black suit with a green pocket-handkerchief. They shared an unmistakable genetic resemblance. The man reached forward, spoke in Dolan's ear, and placed a bejeweled hand on Cassie's shoulder. She shrugged it off and wheeled her pap out of reach.

Brennan frowned, zoomed his cell phone's camera to max, and nodded. He'd have recognized Beck McConnell's craggy face even without his years working Homicide. The long-time head of Philly's Irish mob chose to stay quiet from a media standpoint, but his operations were nonetheless efficiently brutal and well-known to every detective in the Philly PD. A quick internet search confirmed Brennan's suspicions. Beck and Ryan were brothers. His investigation had taken a hard turn down Mafia Lane, and the pool of potential suspects just got ass deep.

The detective shook his head. Dolan had steadfastly refused to go to bed with the mob, so the mob bedded his granddaughter instead.

Brennan could only imagine her grandiose but undoubtedly tense wedding. Must've been a ripsnortin' good time.

His phone's ringtone, a civil-defense siren, blasted an incoming text. He cursed and juggled it with cold fingers, searching for the volume. He glanced guiltily at the surrounding vehicles and then across the broad swath of grass at the dispersing crowd for hostile glares or snickers. Cassie, cell phone in hand, stared him straight in the eye from fifty yards away.

She gave her phone a subtle shake, and he looked at his screen.

Come to the wake.

He squinted into the sun. With the pageantry of the over-the-top funeral and the emotional crowd swirling around her, how had she noticed his presence? Granted, he wasn't exactly hiding, but still, he was just one face amid a gaggle of news reporters and paparazzi.

His phone, now on mute, vibrated a second alert.

She'll be there.

His numb fingers fumbled out a response.

She who? Amber? Or Ruth?

He shielded his eyes from the glare and watched her craft her response. Before she'd finished, however, her father intervened. Between their hand gestures and his stormy expression, Brennan surmised Ryan McConnell objected to Cassie texting at her mother's funeral.

Cassie shoved her phone into a tiny black purse and propelled her pap toward an idling stretch limo not far from the family crypt. The driver hurried to help Dolan transfer into the backseat and expertly folded the wheelchair into the trunk.

Cassie threw a final look over her shoulder at Brennan before joining her pap in the backseat. The limo's tires crunched over the gravel pathway, winding around neglected headstones and crumbling crypts, none nearly as grand or well-maintained as the Dolans'. Ryan and Beck McConnell led the funeral parade in a limo of their own. A flotilla of luxury cars snaked through the cemetery's wrought-iron gate and onto the city street, passing the row of humbler parked vehicles and their owners.

While the photographer's lens clicked at a furious rate, Brennan imagined he saw Cassie's head turn as if she were staring at him through the limo's darkly tinted window. Or maybe it was Dolan. Their shadowy silhouettes blurred into one shapeless soul.

His phone buzzed.

Pap wants you to come.

He groaned and shoved the phone in his pocket. The matter was settled. Nobody refuses Leland Dolan. Brennan was attending the wake.

B rennan hoofed it after gridlock forced him to park ten city blocks from Dolan Mansion. He arrived at the narrow stone street to find a valet directing a seemingly endless stream of limos to disgorge their well-heeled passengers and then keep moving to a designated parking area on the fringe of Society Hill.

What a difference a week and a large dose of unwelcome attention make. Brennan shook his head at the striking transformation. The day Erin Dolan had died, thunder rolled and low-hanging clouds skimmed the historic neighborhood's brick chimneys. Then, Dolan Mansion had stood as stern and foreboding as its elderly namesake. Sheets of rain streamed from its steep, slate roof, and if not for the gentle flicker of light through the transom, the house would've disappeared behind a hazy film of gray, like an overdeveloped photo on an underlit day.

Today, the mansion blazed brighter than the Fargo Center on a hockey night. Orange, green, and red light glared through three stories of stained glass. Muted strains of funereal music escaped into the frigid air with each whoosh of the door, its brass knob polished to a brilliant sheen. Matching boxwood topiaries, pruned to perfection, flanked the entry. Only one window, high on the third floor, clung to its morose mood, its dark glass unaffected by the drama below.

He merged with a group of blue-haired ladies but was stopped on the threshold.

"May I have your name, please, sir?" The tuxedoed doorman grasped his leather-wrapped clipboard like a matron clutching her pearls.

He was not on the list. Of that, Brennan was certain. He contemplated flashing his badge but opted for discretion instead.

"Dan Brennan."

While the doorman flipped and frowned, Brennan peeked through the sidelights. Scores of guests filled the foyer and library. They chatted in hushed tones, many sipping from tiny porcelain cups while others lingered over trays of tea sandwiches and hot hors d'oeuvres.

Dolan sat in the back of the room next to the fireplace, his gaunt frame enveloped in an oversized vintage chair with nailhead trim, its supple, worn leather as weathered as he. Cassie stood guard at his right elbow, her face a tight mask but her eyes alert as always. Her gaze met Brennan's immediately, as if she'd been watching the door and awaiting his presence. She leaned to whisper something in Dolan's ear, and he nodded.

"I'm sorry, sir." The doorman gave his papers a final shuffle. "You're not on the list."

Brennan feigned surprise. "Really? I was invited by Mr. Dolan himself." He stretched his right arm overhead and waved across the crowded room at Dolan. The old man responded with a slow wave of his own, gesturing Brennan in.

The doorman hemmed and hawed. "Dr. McConnell was very explicit about sticking to the list. But I guess if Mr. Dolan says so . . ."

"He says so. It's his house, you know." Brennan brushed past, weaving a path through the congested, overly warm room. A dozen different exotic perfumes and colognes swirled into one nauseating scent, and the heat increased as he approached the roaring fire. He tugged at his coat buttons, suddenly grateful he'd remembered to iron his shirt and wear dress shoes.

A waiter bearing a tray laden with exotic pastries cut into his path. A suffocating throng eager for their share instantly formed. Brennan squared his shoulders for some heavy contact. Before he could steamroll through, his phone vibrated with a text. He glanced at the sender and raised his eyebrows. Pete must've marked the lab order as urgent. This was fast service, even for an old friend.

Prelim tox screen + for benzos and barbs. Check email. Full report in 2–3 weeks.

Brennan's stubby fingers tapped a reply.

Got it. Thanks.

He crammed the phone in his pocket and, sensing a favorable shift in the herd ahead, elbowed a path to Leland Dolan.

Even the mourners kept their distance from the intimidating old man. As Brennan broke through the crowd and covered the short gap to the fireplace, Dolan extended a veiny hand. "Detective Brennan, wasn't it?"

Brennan nodded. A trickle of sweat ran down his back. "Yes, sir."

"Thank you for coming. Although I suppose now you'll want to poke around the place."

"It's your granddaughter's wake, Mr. Dolan. I can do that another time. Besides, I don't have a warrant."

"You don't need one. You have my permission to scour the entire house if you want. We have nothing to hide." He patted Cassie's arm. "Do we, Peach?"

A shrill giggle pierced the muted murmurs of conversation. In unison, the guests turned their heads to the front of the room, where, framed by the colorful lead-glass windows, a young blonde stood too close to Ryan McConnell. She brushed her fingertips over his forearm. He scowled and took a broad step back. With a pout of her glossy pink lips, she huffed away.

Dolan's murderous glare could've scared a drunk dry and turned a serial killer into a saint. Cassie's expression was only slightly less hostile.

The old man gripped the frame of his leather chair and struggled to stand. "How dare he? How dare he invite her to my granddaughter's funeral? I'll—" His chest shook as a coughing fit rendered him mute and breathless. Wheezing, he collapsed into the plush seat.

The coughing attracted Ryan's attention. His eyes narrowed as he observed Brennan's presence, and he turned his back to accept the fawning attention of the nearest guest.

Brennan smiled wryly. "I'd say your grandson-in-law isn't happy to see me."

"He can go shit in his hat." Dolan patted his blue lips with a fine linen handkerchief. "Give the detective a tour, Peach. Show him everything he needs to see." His milky eyes met hers. "And nothing he doesn't."

CHAPTER

8

To avoid pushing through the crowd, they exited the library through a barely visible pocket door to the right, its burled wood seamlessly matched to the room's mahogany paneling. Cassie beckoned him to follow. She slid the pocket door shut on its silent hinges, and the library's heady mix of body heat, mindless chatter, and expensive perfume instantly vanished.

The dark mahogany disappeared behind a wall of icy blue damask, as lustrous as fine silk. Brennan stepped into a formal living room or sitting room, as the hoity-toity types used to call it. Maybe they still did. Hell if he knew. But based on the pristine condition of the oriental rug underfoot and the unblemished velvet sofa, no one sat in here, ever. The room was frigid in more ways than one.

The sweat dampening Brennan's neck turned chilly, and he swiped a palm across his nape, leaving a trail of goose bumps. He faced a gilded cage. The elevator.

Cassie stopped in front of the iron bars. "I told you she'd be here."

"Who?" *She'll be there.* The text. Brennan peered through the elevator's ornate door. The lift was empty.

"Amber, my father's girlfriend. I don't think he invited her, though. He's a dick, but he's not stupid. I predicted she'd show up on her own. Has to stake her claim, you know. I thought the two of you should meet."

"Don't worry; she and your father are the last two people on my list to interview. They haven't returned my calls, or I would've done so already." Brennan shivered. "Nice room. Would be nicer if it had heat."

"The radiators are turned off. Most of this house is for show. We don't bother heating the rooms we don't use." She looked around, her gaze settling on the rose marble mantel as if seeing it for the first time. "It is nice . . . in a Brontë sort of way."

"I'll have to take your word for it."

"I told you my mother had a degree in English literature. She loved books and added hundreds to my pap's collection. Since I barely leave the house, I've read every book in her library, some of them twice—*Wuthering Heights* included."

She pushed the up button, and the elevator door rattled open. "A barless prison is the cruelest kind, my pap always says." Her cheek dimpled. "But I think he's referring to a different kind of bar."

He pictured the times he'd seen Cassie at the local library. She always had a stack of vintage newspapers and magazines in her hands, but never a book. "If this is a prison, it's a damned swanky one. Besides, I've seen you at the public library—which happens to have hundreds of books, by the way. They even have ones on subjects other than murder and mayhem."

"What fun is that?" A faint smile flitted across her face. "I'll have you know my favorite book of all time is a good old-fashioned ghost story. Sort of. *The Haunting of Hill House* by Shirley Jackson. Ever heard of her?"

"Should I have?"

"Yes." Cassie stepped inside the elevator. "We don't typically have guests, and I don't usually give tours. What would you like to see first?"

"How about we start with your mother's bedroom or her bathroom? Wherever she kept her pills."

She frowned. "What pills?"

"She didn't take any medications?"

"Not that I know of. A vitamin, maybe. She was a health nut. Vegan. Exercised two hours a day. We ate nothing but organic, especially after my seizures started. As if kale could cure epilepsy. The seizures annoyed my father, but my mom—they horrified her." She raised the pitch of her voice, presumably to match her mother's. "They're just so *ugly*." She jabbed the button for the second floor.

Brennan hurried to join her. The iron bars shut with an ominous clank, and the cage convulsed into upward motion. "I got the impression you loved your mother."

"I did love my mother, and she loved me. But appearances were very important to her. When I was young and perfect, she paraded me in front of her society friends like a prized bichon. That changed six years ago. Since then, I've been hidden from view. A shut-in." The elevator stopped with a sudden jolt. "I can't blame her. My seizures are terrifying. Every household has a skeleton in the closet or a monster under the bed. I guess I'm the Dolan family monster. Pap is the only one who disagrees."

The doors parted. Cassie's ballet flats whispered across the hallway's padded carpet. She stopped at the staircase's second-story landing and rested her hand on the thick banister. "My parents' bedroom is at the end." She nervously glanced up and down the steep staircase. "I'll stand guard."

Brennan hesitated. Without a warrant, any evidence he collected might be inadmissible in court, even with old man Dolan's permission. And if anything went missing, like a medicine bottle or a piece of

Erin McConnell's undoubtedly expensive jewelry, Ryan could accuse Brennan of theft.

Cassie prodded him with her voice. "You won't get another chance, you know. My father will never permit a search, and my Uncle Beck owns enough judges to block a warrant."

She was right. No one in Philly bribed more local judges than the Irish mob—except maybe the Italian mob. And the McConnell clan had deep pockets.

Brennan glanced over his shoulder and covered the distance to Ryan's bedroom in a few long strides. He left the door wide open, in case Cassie opted to monitor his search from afar. But, head tilted high, her gaze remained fixed on the stairs.

Brennan snapped on a pair of gloves from his coat pocket and focused on a quick search of the closet, bathroom, and bedside tables. Rows of designer suits and Italian leather shoes—a single pair of which would've demolished Brennan's budget for a month—filled Ryan's closet. Nestled in a back corner, a black-and-neon-yellow case leaned against the wall. He knelt to examine the label, which featured a heart pierced by a bolt of jagged lightning. AED. PROPERTY OF JEFFERSON HOSPITAL.

Ryan had his own personal defibrillator. Not surprising, given Dolan's age and poor health and Cassie's epilepsy. The question was whether Ryan swiped it from the hospital. Brennan took a picture and moved on to the bathroom.

The medicine cabinet held an assortment of supplements whose labels flaunted exotic names and promised everything from a clean liver to strong nails. The only prescription bottle he found belonged to Ryan. Viagra. He chuckled, then grimaced. The resulting mental image was one he could've done without. The childproof cap popped off with an easy twist. He examined the dozen or so pills in the vial. The tablets all appeared to have the same oval shape and robin's-egg-blue color. His older colleagues often joked about "the little blue pill," so he was fairly certain these were indeed Viagra. As for the herbal and vitamin bottles, he was well aware from prior investigations that their labels might not match the actual contents.

He carefully positioned the bottles back in their exact spots, unwilling to remove them for further analysis. Ryan would surely notice their absence, especially if his social calendar included a hot date with Amber. After ensuring he'd left the room as he'd found it, he closed the door with a firm click and rejoined Cassie by the stairs.

She stood ramrod straight, staring at the empty third-story landing. "Did you find anything interesting?"

"Not a darned thing." He made a big show of turning his pockets inside out to prove he hadn't copped anything.

"That wasn't necessary."

"Maybe not for you, but it was for me. Now where?"

"Depends." Cassie's eyes narrowed. "Why did you ask about medications? Something showed up on Mom's autopsy, didn't it?"

A dawning realization hardened her already somber expression. She did a one-eighty and rushed to yank open a door at the opposite end of the hall.

"Search my bedroom. My pills are on the bathroom vanity. Take pictures of them if you want, but leave the bottles. I can't go without my meds." She stepped aside so Brennan could enter but lingered in the doorway.

Uncomfortably aware of how dicey the situation would appear if anyone saw them together in her bedroom, he shooed her into the hall. "I don't need to confiscate your pills. From a legal standpoint, I can't without a warrant. From a personal-gain standpoint, I'd have to be a pretty poor excuse for a human being to steal medications from an epileptic patient. Besides, I doubt there's a black market for stolen seizure drugs."

"There's a black market for everything, Detective. You know that better than I. In the wrong hands, my meds could be used for bad things. My mom . . ." Cassie, her expression distraught, pressed her hand over her mouth.

"If they were, it's through no fault of your own. And we have zero proof of anything yet. My investigation is just getting started, thanks to your father's lack of cooperation. Speaking of which . . ." Brennan raised his right hand in the air. "I, Detective Dan Brennan, do solemnly swear not to touch a single pill if you promise to guard the stairs again."

The tension in her face relaxed slightly. She nodded and returned to her post by the banister. Brennan felt her gaze on his back, watching him as he methodically studied her sanctuary.

A scruffy, button-eared teddy bear, more vintage treasure than toy, sat high on a shelf. It was the room's only embellishment. No boyband posters on the sage-green walls. No fuzzy stuffed creatures on the neatly made bed. Not a hint of anything neon or goth or sparkly anywhere. He'd seen frillier cells in the state penitentiary. Not that he was surprised. The teen studied cold cases for fun.

As promised, a trio of amber-colored pill bottles lined the bathroom vanity. He inspected the labels and snapped photos of each. Keppra, lorazepam, primidone . . . The medical examiner's text had indicated benzos and barbs. Brennan was no pharmacist, but he knew enough to suspect these were the same medications in Erin McConnell's bloodstream. He'd confirm it with Pete when he returned to the office.

He held one of the bottles to the light. Fingerprints would be nice. He debated asking Cassie to dump her pills into other containers so he could confiscate the bottles but ultimately decided against it. Ryan's or Erin's prints could easily be explained away and proved nothing. If he ended up needing prints, it'd be better to wait for a warrant.

The rest of the room was bland, all curved edges and unbreakable objects, with a platform bed so close to the ground Brennan doubted his forty-year-old knees would allow him to rise in the morning. He closed the door quietly behind him. Cassie met him at the elevator. As he approached, she searched his face with her eyes.

"Well?" She pushed the up button.

"I can't form an opinion until I read the details of the tox report. We're just getting started, remember? Between your father's lack of cooperation and his, um, shall we say, connections, I've had to tread lightly."

Preoccupied with their thoughts, they rode the elevator in silence until the door opened with a cheery ding. The third floor greeted them with a shimmering wall of heat.

Brennan loosened his tie. "I know heat rises, but this is ridiculous. Is it always like this?"

"Mostly. Pap likes it warm. It's an old-person thing, like their body odor. Did you know old-person smell is a real thing? It's caused by a chemical called nonenal that lingers on fabric, especially in enclosed spaces. I read about it in a crime report. Some clever detective with a good sense of smell used it to solve a kidnapping once."

"I'm pretty sure that clever detective was not me."

The elevator door closed, disappearing into a camouflage of burled wood. Cassie stopped several steps short of Dolan's bedroom door. "I'll wait here."

He held his breath and made it quick, breezing through the closet and the bathroom, where he snapped photos of the old man's bottles of medicine. One stood out. Donepezil. His pop had taken it for a year or so in a vain attempt to slow the Alzheimer's ravaging his brain. It failed. Brennan had helplessly watched his hearty and jovial dad become confused and anxious, then paranoid and hostile, and finally catatonic, refusing to eat until he slipped away, a shell of his former self.

Dolan seemed nothing like his pop. But then again, in the early stages, his pop had been adept at hiding it too, until a neighbor found him wandering outside one cold, dark winter morning. He'd seen something, he said. Heard something too. "Confabulation," the doctor called it, stating hallucinations were common with Alzheimer's. In retrospect, that day marked the beginning of the end.

Brennan shook his head and briefly rifled through the clutter crowding the room's only dresser. Sympathy cards, old receipts, outdated business magazines . . . At the bottom of the pile, a Purple Heart rested in its clear acrylic coffin. Brennan wiped the dust from its spider-webbed surface with his sleeve. It looked as if someone had stomped it with their heel. A source of bad memories, he imagined, but one too precious to toss in the trash. He understood perfectly.

A rattling noise, akin to the jingle of vintage keys on a heavy brass ring, interrupted his thoughts. He buried the Purple Heart back in the mound of debris. As he closed the door to Dolan's bedroom, his peripheral vision caught a metallic glint from Cassie's right hand. His stomach tightened, a reaction inappropriate to the situation—at least, he hoped—but involuntary nonetheless.

He kept his voice light. "What've you got there?" He nodded at the clenched fist tucked close to her right hip.

Her fingers slowly unfurled, revealing an ornate brass key tarnished with age but with enough residual sheen to glimmer in the overhead light. It rested in her palm like a dragonfly preparing for flight.

"You have one more room to see." She pointed down the hallway to her left, where the threadbare carpet ended in front of a heavy wooden door. A Victorian padlock, its yellow brass hidden under a thick layer of green patina, dangled from a latch on the door.

"Do you always carry that key around with you?" Brennan asked, eyeing the pockets of her black dress.

"Yes."

He took quick stock of his position. This had to be the room with the mysteriously dark window—the one he'd noticed from outside. Curiosity piqued, he followed her down the hall. The air grew blissfully cooler as they drew near. Based on the chilly living room, he assumed Dolan was frugal—most people who grew up in the Depression were.

He couldn't blame the old man for not heating an unused room on the third floor, one that was kept closed off from the rest of the house. Closed off to everyone, it seemed, except Cassie.

She inserted the key and removed the hefty padlock with both hands. "Would you mind getting the door?"

Brennan turned the knob and pushed. The door resisted. He pushed harder. It swung open in a fury, so fast that he held his breath, certain the brass knob would punch a hole into the wall behind. It stopped just short, and he exhaled.

A rush of cold air chilled the sweat beading his upper lip. Fractured beams from distant headlights penetrated the lead-glass windows and sent menacing shadows convulsing around the room. As his pupils adjusted to the dark, the shadows coalesced, revealing themselves to be nothing more than sheet-covered furniture.

Chairs positioned in front of a fireplace dirty with ashes. A hulking white behemoth in the shape of a baby grand. Another in the shape of a harp.

"A music room?" Brennan ran his hand along the papered wall inside the door.

The padlock rattled in Cassie's hand. "Maybe once upon a time. Now it's a photo room."

"Not sure I know what that means." Brennan stepped aside. "Since I got the door, maybe you can go first and get the light for me. I can't seem to find the switch."

"Of course." Cassie crossed the threshold, flicked the light switch with her elbow, and painstakingly deposited the padlock on the parquet floor several feet from the door.

He shot her a quizzical look.

She brushed her hands on her skirt. "I got locked in here once. I'm more careful now."

"Must've been terrifying, especially if you were still a kid."

"You have no idea."

He followed her into the center of the room. "Actually, I do. When Elle was two, she managed to lock herself in our bathroom while Julia, my ex-wife, went to answer the phone. I was downstairs when Julia started screaming. All I could imagine was Elle getting ahold of my razor, or drowning in the bathtub, or drinking the drain cleaner from the vanity cabinet . . ."

His fingers crumpled a handful of the dusty white sheet covering a wingback chair. "I had to break down the door to get to her. I found her sitting, happy as a clam, on the bathmat with toothpaste smeared everywhere."

Cassie smiled. "Sounds like it was more frightening for you than it was for her."

"Without a doubt." He relaxed his grip on the sheet. "I'm sure your parents were equally terrified until they discovered where you were hiding."

"My pap found me." Her smile faded. "It was six years ago, and I'd just had my first seizure. I wasn't supposed to be in here; I knew that. But he'd left the door unlocked, and the temptation . . ." Her voice quavered.

She paused, clasping her hands tightly at her waist, as prim and world-weary as a woman six times her age. "He suffered a stroke a few hours later. And don't bother telling me it wasn't my fault. Things would be much different had I never succumbed."

"Cassie, your pap's in his nineties. Strokes happen. It doesn't take much stress to push someone that age over the edge." Brennan glanced around the sparsely decorated room. "I can't imagine there's anything in here relevant to your mother's death. Let's go."

"Turn around."

He turned away from the chair and fireplace ahead, away from the piano and harp lining the east wall, until he faced the door through which he'd come. The ten-foot-high wall was covered floor-to-ceiling in dozens, maybe hundreds, of black-and-white photos.

He blinked and stepped closer to the odd collection. Technically, the wall was covered in paper, its embossed ivory stripes tinged gray with age and soot. But vintage photos, from tiny tintypes of loving couples to large family portraits, plastered its surface, scarred from remnants of yellow tape that had curled and yielded to age. Random gaps where photos were lacking indicated the pictures had been arranged and rearranged at the whim of an invisible hand. Cassie's, perhaps?

"Interesting choice of décor. I now understand why you call it the photo room." Brennan caught the young woman's enigmatic expression. A cluster of four photos achieved special prominence thanks to their eye-level, dead-center position on the wall. The surrounding photos kept a respectful distance, radiating outward in concentric rings. The overall effect was dizzying—a black-and-white vortex spiraling ten feet high and twice as wide in a room already governed by shadows and ash.

He stretched out his right hand, inexplicably drawn to a portrait of a young bride standing glumly next to her equally cheerless groom. "She looks unhappy."

"She should be. She's dead. They're all dead."

"Of course they're dead. Based on their clothing, I'd guess most of these were taken in the 1920s." Brennan plucked the picture from the wall and held it close to his face. It smelled faintly of vinegar and must.

"Thirties, actually. You were close."

"You sure about that?" He flipped the bride's photo and examined the yellowed back. ~~October 1936~~. *June 1945*. No name given.

Cassie nodded. "I know because Pap stole them. Most are labeled with the dates the photos were taken and sometimes with the family members' names. The handwriting varies, so I suspect they were dated by their photographers."

"Your pap stole these? There must be over a hundred of them."

"One hundred and seven, to be exact. Pap wasn't born rich, you know. A few of these photos he took himself, but most he stole for the newspapers." She lowered her gaze to the floor. "When I said these people were dead, I meant they'd been murdered. I've researched them all. About a tenth of their cases remain unsolved."

Brennan frowned. "I remember reading how he worked as a photo thief during the Great Depression, but that was in the thirties. This photo has two dates. October 1936 is crossed out, but the second date, June 1945, would imply it was taken shortly after he returned from the war." He squinted to read the faded print. "The handwriting's similar, but it's not exactly the same. Different authors, I'd guess."

"I know. My research . . . So far, I've cracked six of the unsolved murders, but they were all from the margins." She pointed to the last of the concentric ring of pictures. "The four photos in the middle remain a mystery. They're the only ones to have a second date on them: different months in 1945. Pap was home from the war and working his way up as a news reporter by then. He married my great-grandmother in 1946. I doubt he was stealing photos at that point. I don't understand it myself."

"Did you ask him about it?"

"No. I'm not supposed to be in here, remember? He wouldn't tell me anyway. I tried to bring it up once, but he cut me off and kicked me out of his room. He never talks about those days. Mom called it PTSD, but I like the old-fashioned term better. 'Shell-shocked.' It sounds violent, like it is. Less sanitized."

"Let me get this straight—since he wouldn't help you, you snuck in here every day for the past six years and researched all of these yourself." He swept his arm toward the wall. "For what? Giggles and grins?"

"Yep. Well, not every day, but yes. What else have I had to do?"

"Solve an eighty-year-old cold case by reading moldy newspapers at the library, apparently."

"I solved *six* eighty-year-old murders at the library. You should pay better attention."

Brennan raised an eyebrow. "Okay. So tell me—what happened here?" He pointed to a random photo on his left. The scene depicted was a happy one, featuring a jaunty-appearing young lad wearing striped suspenders and a huge smile. His parents hovered over his shoulder. At his feet, a laughing toddler splashed her hands in a washtub.

"That's Gil. His dad used to beat his mom, and Gil got tired of it. At least, that's what the newspapers said. He chopped him up with an ax and fed him to the family hogs."

Brennan whistled. "Cold."

"They hanged him for it. He was fourteen." Her voice shook. "They used to do that back then, I guess."

"Nothing mysterious about that murder, huh?"

"Except Gil didn't do it. His mom did. He took the blame for her. Can you imagine letting your son hang for you? But she had a baby to raise, and Gil loved his little sister . . ." She lapsed into silence.

Brennan studied the other photos and imagined the horrors lurking behind their glossy surfaces. A wall full of murder victims. He shook his head. "Your pap saved their pictures for eighty years. Why?"

Cassie ignored his question. "I was hoping you could help me solve the puzzle of the four photos with the dual dates. I watched you interact with your daughter at the library. You have patience, and you seem like a good detective. My pap thinks you're a good man too, and he's never wrong. Prove my mother was murdered, help me investigate these four cases, and I'll turn over the six I've already solved. I'd planned to give my research to the police eventually anyway, as soon as I found someone who'd believe me. You can take the credit if you'd like. I don't care about that."

"Then why do it, if not for some sort of recognition? You're young and rich, and murder's a nasty business. Why expose yourself to the horror? It's a hell of a hobby."

"It's more than a hobby. Pap saved the photos for the same reason I study them." Cassie's left eyelid began to twitch, and she blinked rapidly. "We're compelled. I don't expect you to understand, but you'll find my research is solid. I have a seizure disorder, but I'm not dumb, and I'm not delusional."

"Nobody said you were."

"You're wrong."

A faint female voice wafted from afar. "Cassie?"

Brennan jumped. "Did you hear that?"

The voice grew louder, more insistent. "Cassie, where are you? I'm worried about you."

Cassie's lips curled into a cool smile. "Amber, my ex-tutor. She's probably hoping I'm up here dying of a seizure. One less obstacle between her and my family's fortune. We need to go."

She slid the wedding photo from Brennan's grip and tacked it on the center of the wall next to the others. Her slender fingers lingered over the bride's white dress. "I'll be right there," she yelled down the hall.

Brennan retrieved the padlock from the floor on his way out the door. He slipped it over the latch.

"I'll do it." Cassie brushed him aside. "You take the elevator. I'll take the stairs." She clicked the lock into place and gave it a firm tug.

They walked the hall together until they reached the staircase. She paused. "Do you believe me?"

"That Amber's a conniving gold digger?"

"About the cold cases. That I solved them."

"I believe it's *possible* you solved them. You're observant, dedicated, and smart. But I'll withhold final judgment until I review your research."

Cassie's eyes misted with tears. She nodded and gripped the sturdy wooden handrail, its once-glossy finish dull and patchy from a hundred years of use. "The woman in the picture . . ." Her voice was thick, and she paused to swallow.

"The unhappy bride?"

"Yes. Her name is Ruth."

November 6th
3rd Journal Entry

"Cyanide tastes like marzipan if you close your eyes." That's the second thing Ruth said to me when I dared to return to the photo room. Over a month had passed in a blur of doctor's appointments and hospital stays for my newly diagnosed seizure disorder. Even as a heavily medicated twelve-year-old, I somehow knew my seizures were never going to respond to standard medical treatments. Instead, there was something I was meant to do. Something that could only be found in that room.

I gaped at Ruth's picture on the wall, certain the voice had come from the image of the gloomy bride but not understanding how. She mistook my confusion for ignorance.

"You've never heard of marzipan? It's an almond-flavored confection—a coveted delicacy until the war made anything Eastern European seem unpatriotic. Apparently, it's fallen out of vogue. As has cyanide, or so I've heard."

The room started to change in ways I can barely describe, zooming in and out like a camera struggling to focus its lens. The air turned cold enough for me to see my breath, and I debated turning tail to run. But my feet were glued to the floor.

Ruth, in muddied black-and-white like her photo on the wall, stood an arm's length from my face. She smiled and cocked her head, apparently delighted to have an audience.

"Cyanide wasn't so hard to obtain back in my day. Any tradesman could get a license for it. My first husband was a jeweler. He thought I was too dumb to understand what the vials in his workshop contained, or what they could do. I opened them one by one until I smelled almonds. That's how I knew I had the right one. Then all I had to do was wait for the right moment. One night, he returned from the bar so liquored up he could barely stand. But as any drunk will tell you, there's always room for one more."

One corner of Ruth's painted lips twitched, and the windows frosted with ice. "I told the police I'd awakened in the middle of the night to hear him seizing. There'd been a rash of alcohol poisonings from bootleg liquor over the prior month, and since half the town had seen him stumble from the bar, no one questioned a thing. I think they were just happy to be rid of him. He treated everyone except his customers like ignorant mules. But he treated me the worst, especially after I . . . we lost the baby."

Ruth's expression once again grew glum. The room darkened with her mood. "I hid the cyanide for future use. It came in handy with my second husband. By then, I'd burned through the money I'd earned by killing husband number one. But using the poisoned-drink trick again seemed boring. I had a hankering for something more creative. So I whipped up a batch of cyanide-laced marzipan. It was really good too. I taste-tested it—before adding the cyanide, of course."

She chattered on, describing in detail how she'd managed to kill off two more husbands over the course of the next few years. "You must think I'm a terrible person, but I'm not. I was literally starving when I married my first. My father and brothers—I was nothing more than their slave, their cook, their washerwoman. Abusive bastards, the whole lot of them. They were the terrible ones, not me. Besides, I know someone far worse." She paused, awaiting my response, but I had no idea what to say.

"I'm sorry," I blurted, not sure what or who I was apologizing for.

My feeble attempt at sympathy seemed to satisfy her. A sad smile clouded her face, strengthening her resemblance to the desolate bride in the photo from so long ago. She turned toward the photo wall.

"I was hunted by a mass murderer—sorry—serial killer once too. Isn't that what you call them these days?" She touched three seemingly random photos on the wall. They glowed with an unknown force that dissipated in seconds, leaving their edges to glisten with a fine layer of frost. "So were they."

"I can hear them," I said, as if confessing a sin.

"I know. They can be a rowdy lot. Always clamoring for attention. I can teach you how to control them if you like." She stroked a finger across her own photo, pausing over her husband's face. It disappeared in a mound of frost. "I know who murdered everyone on this wall, except for these three. And myself, of course. None of us can see our own killer's face. A quirk of the afterlife, I guess."

"Maybe the four of you were killed by the same person."

"Perhaps. A serial killer, as I said." Ruth smiled. "You're a smart one, aren't you, Cassandra?"

"Cassie."

Emboldened, I rose to my tiptoes and pulled the nearest photo from the wall. A burly middle-aged man stared at me with piercing, cold eyes. His voice, deep and menacing, whispered in the back of my brain. It grew louder. Closer. Angrier.

Panicked, I flipped the photo over, severing the connection. I drew a shaky breath. ~~September 1936.~~ *July 1945.* "Why are there two dates?"

"You'll figure it out." Ruth's icy breath whispered in my ear. "That's Paul. Don't tell him I said so, but he was an evil man. Nasty. Someone shot him in the face. Whoever it was deserves a big, fat kiss." She giggled, and the room grew warmer.

I taped the photo back in place and reached for another, but Ruth stopped me with an impatient wave of her hand. "Enough murder and madness for one day. Let's get to know each other." She drifted to the piano and patted the bench, indicating I was to sit beside her. "Do you know 'Clair De Lune'?"

Astonished to learn I hadn't been taught to play—apparently, classical mythology and piano were essential education for proper young ladies of the era—she proceeded to teach me. On more than one occasion, Pap, alerted by the faint music drifting down the hall, chased me from the room. He always locked the door behind him. With Ruth's assistance, I always managed to return.

She entertained me with vibrant tales of life in the early 1920s, before a second world war and a great depression tarnished hope for the future. She told me the stories of the three victims whose killers she could not see. Our friendship grew while she distracted me from the myriad painful tests and medication side effects I endured during those early years of my seizures, when their control worsened before it got better. When I was pulled from school and lost contact with society. When my "real" friends drifted away.

Six years later, hers is the only voice I can hear. Her presence has gotten stronger, her voice louder. She says I give her strength. I think she takes it. She's always hinted my friendship serves a greater purpose. Now that I'm older, my mission is clear: find her killer, living or dead. And although she denies it, I can tell by the chill in the room. Her patience has waned.

CHAPTER

10

Brennan lingered at the top of the stairs, trying to remember every instance where Cassie had mentioned a woman named Ruth. He replayed the past week in his mind. The hospital when Ryan McConnell had told her of her mother's death. *Ruth will tell me the truth.* But then she'd denied it.

Ruth *will*, not Ruth *had*. Her name *is*, not *was*. There was a whole lotta weirdness going on. A thin line of sweat ran between his shoulder blades, reminding him the third-floor hallway was far too warm, especially after the chill of the unheated photo room. Cassie had dashed down the steps before Brennan could formulate an intelligent question. He listened to her voice from below as she blithely lied to her ex-tutor about her reason for being on the third floor.

"Pap needed his inhaler."

She probably managed to pull one from those bottomless pockets of hers, the pockets which also held the strangely shaped key. No picking that lock. Not that he planned to try, although he wished he would've written down the exact dates from the back of Ruth's picture. Something, 1936. June or July, something, something.

He glanced over his shoulder at the padlocked door. Overhead, a bulb blew, popping and sputtering into a long, slow hiss. The remaining bulbs flickered.

A ballet of shadows danced down the hall before dissipating under the door and through its keyhole as if sucked inside by the spiraling vortex of photos. A black hole of energy in a room in which there should be none.

The padlock swayed, and Brennan blinked, unwilling to trust his eyes. Maybe he was the one who was swaying. The carpet was unevenly worn and laid over floorboards likely warped with age and settling. His stomach churned from the crooked floor plus the heat and the flickering lights—the funhouse effect, he'd heard it called. He'd be wise to head downstairs where it was cooler. He'd snag one of those fancy cookies, settle his stomach, and be on his way. He had an autopsy and a tox screen to review.

Good times.

The elevator was waiting for him.

He exited into the formal living room and slid the pocket door open just enough to slip into the library without anyone taking notice. Anyone except Leland Dolan.

Cassie had returned to stand by her pap's side. Their eyes followed him as he worked a path through the well-heeled crowd. He paused in the foyer to snatch a shortbread off a harried server's tray. He nodded a good-bye to Dolan; the old man nodded back.

From across the room, Cassie scowled as a warm hand latched on to Brennan's elbow.

Amber Servello cocked her blonde head toward the front door. "Are you leaving too, Detective? I've been dying to talk to you. And it looks like I'm gonna need a ride home."

Brennan and Amber ducked out the door together. A gust of crisp autumn air ruffled his hair and provided welcome relief from the stifling intimacy of the mansion's library. Once they'd descended the stone steps and traveled out of earshot of the curious doorman, Brennan paused.

"This seems as good a place as any to have our chat. First off, how do you know who I am?"

"Ryan told me before he kicked me out the door. He said I shouldn't have come. Said I made him look bad in front of the police." She rolled her kohl-lined eyes. "The McConnell family's all about appearances, you know. The sad part is, I was just checking on Cassie. She has seizures, and sometimes stress makes them worse. Poor kid. I'm Amber, by the way."

She stuck out a perfectly manicured hand. "I used to be Cassie's tutor before she graduated. I was more of a nanny, really, but Cassie didn't like that word. She's eighteen going on forty, in case you hadn't noticed."

"I'd say she's handling the situation better than any eighteen-year-old I've ever met."

"I'll take credit for that."

Brennan raised his eyebrows but held his tongue. "You said something about a ride?"

"Yeah, if you don't mind. I took a cab here, but if you're heading toward Fishtown . . ."

He was not heading toward Fishtown.

The working-class Irish-Catholic neighborhood had seen a decade of rapid gentrification. It was now a mix of trendy art studios and hip bistros, making Brennan more uncomfortable there than in the drug-ridden streets of North Philly's Badlands. But Amber needed a ride, and he needed to rule out a suspect. A match made in heaven, especially if she was pissed at Ryan for kicking her out of the wake. Hell has no fury . . .

"I love Fishtown." He pointed down the street. "But I'm parked hell-and-gone from here, at least a mile away toward the river. You up for the walk?"

"Absolutely." She flashed a grateful smile.

Her leather ankle boots had treacherously high heels, but she handled the cobblestone streets like a pro. They covered the ten blocks in no time. The passenger seat of his dinged-up Dodge was strewn with empty coffee cups, random notes, and crumpled-up napkins. Brennan tossed them in the back and brushed a fine layer of crumbs off the nylon and onto the floor.

A splash of bright green caught his eye. He pulled a small picture book out from where it lay wedged next to a crayon under the seat. *Goodnight Moon.* Damn. He missed one. Now he'd have to make another trip to the library. He gritted his teeth and threw the book in the back with the rest.

"Sorry about the mess," he muttered, as he held the door. Ryan McConnell's car probably smelled of fine leather, not crayons.

"No worries. I appreciate the ride. The bus is just so . . ." She wrinkled her upturned nose. "You know."

Common? Brennan slammed her door and slid behind the wheel. "I'm not sure that I do."

He turned in his seat. Amber was anything but common. Gorgeous, in fact, but not in an old-money, refined kind of way like Erin McConnell. This blonde definitely had dark roots and brassy undertones. Brennan would bet his badge she'd ridden the bus more than a time or two.

"Slow," she said, with a limp swish of her hand. "The bus is so slow. Stops every two or three blocks. Takes forever to get to Fishtown."

Brennan merged into heavy traffic on I-95. Their conversation lapsed until he took the Girard Avenue exit and the congestion thinned.

"You said you were dying to talk to me." Brennan drummed his fingers on the wheel as they idled at the first of many red lights. "Yet you haven't returned my calls, and you haven't said a single word."

"Turn left. There's a coffee shop on the next corner. It's a block from my apartment. You drove; I'll buy." She tugged at the hem of her black skirt, too short for a Sunday wake and an inch shy of being demure.

He eased the car to the curb. She didn't wait for him to open the door. "We order at the counter," she said, over her shoulder. "You find us a seat. Whaddaya want?"

"Coffee, black."

"Dark roast, you mean?"

"The darker, the better." The café was exactly as Brennan expected it to be—sleek and sterile with a too-cool-for-school vibe that made him feel like a curmudgeonly frump. Which maybe he was.

He puffed out his chest and claimed the only empty table. The orange plastic disc with aluminum legs wobbled as he approached, implying a good hard sneeze could do it in. "Handmade from recycled water bottles," a sticker proudly proclaimed. He doubted it. The hunk of junk was probably slapped together on an assembly line in China. With toxic glue.

Amber returned with two artisan-painted mugs and set his on the table. He held his breath as the steaming liquid sloshed back and forth on the unsteady surface. Hot coffee was a terrible thing to waste, especially a brew this expensive.

She cradled her mug and gingerly sipped a frothy mixture of foam and pink turbinado sugar from its porcelain edge. "I guess you're wondering what I have to say."

"You guessed right."

Another sip, another silence. "I can also guess what Cassie's told you about me—all the nasty things she's implied. I want you to know they're not true."

"You're not having an affair with her father?"

"Okay, that part *is* true," Amber conceded with a half smile.

"For how long?"

"Two years. Although it's not really an affair anymore, is it?"

He held up his hand. "This is the part where I advise you to consider withholding further comment before consulting a lawyer."

"Why? I wasn't there when Erin fell down the steps. I have an alibi and everything. Besides, I haven't set foot inside Dolan Mansion for months until today. Not since Cassie turned eighteen and decided she didn't need me anymore. Which I think she's regretting, by the way."

I think not. Brennan hid his grin with a swig from the mug.

Amber set her cappuccino on the table. A splash of muddied foam trickled down the mug's glossy surface. "Look, Detective, I care about Cassie. I truly do. When Ryan hired me, she was lonely and fragile, both mentally and physically. I protected her. And although you may find this hard to believe, she used to like me too. Then she changed."

"How so?"

"She stopped caring about her lessons. She became withdrawn and often was downright hostile, which she blamed on her meds. I'd find her whispering to herself, full-on conversations she'd never share. She lied to me more than once and would disappear for hours on the third floor, where I was forbidden to go. By the time I left, she was spending most of her time up there with her pap. You know what I think?"

"Tell me."

"Old man Dolan poisoned her mind. He's crazy or senile or both. I used to catch him staring at us from the doorway during her lessons. Just standing there, leaning on his walker, watching me." She shuddered. "He's out of his mind. If anyone killed Erin, it was him. That's what I wanted to tell you. I watched over that child. Now she has no one. She's alone in that house. With him."

"She has her father."

Amber laughed. "Ryan's not exactly the paternal type."

Brennan leaned back in his chair and chose his words carefully. "I can think of no logical reason why Leland Dolan would kill his only granddaughter."

"Crazy doesn't need a reason. Crazy is as crazy does. Surely you've seen that before."

Their table rocked, clipped by a dude sporting a man bun and a crossbody messenger bag. Amber jumped to her feet, narrowly avoiding a lapful of coffee. "Moron." She righted her tipped cup and dabbed ineffectually at the pool of liquid flooding the orange table.

Brennan threw a wad of napkins over the mess and wiped it clean. "I think we're done here." He guided her out the door to the relative quiet of the pedestrian street. Four o'clock and the sun had already begun to set. He hated fall.

As if on cue, a gust of cold wind sent litter and leaves alike skittering down the street. He assessed her thin leather coat and offered her his more substantial one. She refused with a dismissive wave of her hand. "I'm only a block away."

"I'll walk you to the corner." He eyed a young man leaning against the brick wall of the bank across the street. A lookout for sure, probably for the local drug lord. But Fishtown was also home to Philly's Irish mob, with whom Ryan McConnell was intimately connected. Which led Brennan to his next question.

"You surprised me, Ms. Servello." He casually kicked a pebble down the pockmarked sidewalk. "All this talk about Leland Dolan when I thought you wanted to chat about Ryan and his family instead. Did you ever meet his big brother, Beck?"

Amber's eyes narrowed. "Once or twice. I'm smart enough not to talk about him in public. But I will say this: Ryan is handsome, charming, and quick to spend his money. Generous. He's also spineless and surprisingly tender—too soft to work in the family business and too soft to have killed his wife. His brother bullied him terribly. Still does."

"Pillow talk?"

"Something like that."

"You have an interesting way of defending your boyfriend, Ms. Servello."

"Call me Amber."

"Amber, then. Ryan can't be that much of a wimp. He got through medical school and a surgeon's internship. I hear they're no walk in the park."

"I'm guessing his family bought his admission, but that didn't guarantee he'd graduate. It certainly didn't guarantee his success. Why do you think he married Erin? He needed a secure income to maintain the lifestyle to which he was accustomed. One little brotherly spat, and there goes his financial support. Nobody likes a mooch, least of all Beck McConnell." She rounded the corner and stopped to pull a keychain from her designer leather purse. "And that's all I'm gonna say about the McConnell boys. Thanks for the lift."

"Thanks for the coffee." Brennan handed her his card. "In case you think of something else I should know. Oh, and one more thing, Ms. Servello."

"Amber."

"Amber." He smiled. "I'm gonna need that alibi."

CHAPTER

11

Beer bottle in hand, Brennan sat in the living room of his gloomy apartment and watched the Flyers skate a hockey puck up and down the ice. On nights like tonight, when preoccupied with a case, he often muted the sound and listened to his thoughts instead. His brain and his gut instincts competed for attention. Typically, his gut spoke louder.

His buddy Pete, the medical examiner, had texted him an hour ago. They scheduled a meeting for early tomorrow morning to discuss Erin McConnell's autopsy and tox screen. Until then, he was in a holding pattern, with murderous accusations flying faster than a ninety-mile-an-hour slapshot, but no hard data to prove that Erin's death was anything more than an unfortunate accident.

He disabled the mute, determined to drown out the Dolan family drama with the crunch of bone-jarring body checks and the mindless chatter of the color commentator.

Ten minutes into the second period, his phone signaled a text.

Meet me at the library tomorrow at 2? I have something to show you.

Score! The Flyers buried the tying goal while he was staring at his phone. He cursed and slammed his beer onto the coffee table. Hoping for a replay, he tapped out a response in between glances at the TV.

What is it?

You'll see.

Brennan sighed. Cassie, isolated in Dolan Mansion with just her pap and her asshole father, needed someone to talk to. That much was clear. And admittedly, her fascination with the stolen photos and the grisly unsolved murders behind them intrigued him. But he had an active case on his hands and a career to salvage.

"Be a good steward of your energy," the police department's counselor advised during one of his "strongly suggested" sessions with the employee assistance program. Those paternal pangs he felt every time he looked at Cassie's sad face? The counselor would call them "transference," another useless nugget of psychological information he'd learned and could've lived without. Not one word lessened his grief.

After completing the free sessions, Brennan had declined to schedule any more, daring his boss to mandate him. She didn't. Now it was up to him to prove he was 100-percent back on his game. He liked Cassie, but he couldn't bleed for her. Couldn't afford those pangs.

His fingers hovered over his phone's screen. He still had Elle's library book languishing in the backseat of his car. He could kill two birds with one stone and never have to set foot in that library again. Be proactive. His counselor would be pleased.

OK. See you then.

A rustling from down the hall caught his attention, and he quickly muted the TV. The rustling became a tapping, random at first, then rhythmic—designed, it seemed, to compel him to investigate. He strained to identify its source. Elle's bedroom. He flinched. Not Elle's room. It was the guest room now. Another of the counselor's suggestions for moving on.

The bedroom door was open, the way Elle always liked it. Brennan grabbed his gun and crept the length of the narrow hall. In one practiced move, he rounded the doorjamb, flicked the light switch, and aimed his gun at the noise's origin.

Silhouetted in the cool, pale glow of the crescent moon, a solitary crow rested on the ledge outside Elle's window.

"Hey, buddy. Long time no see." Brennan lowered his gun and opened the window until only a thin screen separated him and the bird, its feathers as glossy and black as Elle's hair. The bird held his position with nary a flinch.

"You want some bread?"

The crow cawed a throaty yes.

"Of course you do, you little mooch. I'll be right back."

He retrieved a slice of stale bread from the kitchen and ripped it into chunks. The bird bobbed its ebony head in anticipation as Brennan raised the screen a few inches and scattered the bread onto the ledge.

The crow dropped a shiny object from its beak before pecking at its dinner. It finished its meal in minutes and stared at Brennan as if awaiting his next move. When Brennan didn't stir, the bird nudged the token under the screen with its beak, blinked its beady brown eyes, and flew away.

A gust of cold wind fluttered the gauzy curtains. He plucked the object off the ledge and closed the window. Somehow, most likely via a constant stream of bread and crackers, his toddler had made friends with a crow.

One summer, curious about the animated babble coming from her room in the wee hours of the morning, he'd walked in to hear them "talking" through the screen. Julia, his ex-wife, had freaked out when he told her about the sweet and magical friendship. She forbade

Elle from interacting with "those dirty birds," so the crow's frequent visits became a father-daughter secret. The visits stopped the day Elle died, as if somehow the crow knew. Brennan liked to think the bird had flown away with her, accompanied her on her journey. Apparently not.

Brennan moved to toss the crow's gift in the trash, but paused, too curious to chuck it without taking a peek. Elle had amassed quite a collection of whatever the crow managed to scavenge, from bottle caps to bus tokens, and saved them in the ballerina jewelry box on her dresser. He opened his palm. Tonight's gift, a two-inch round disc of aluminum, appeared to be a button or a pin. He flipped it over and froze. His daughter's face smiled back at him.

His abs tensed as if he'd been gut punched. He clenched the pin in his fist and rushed from Elle's bedroom—the guest room, goddammit—and into his own room. The same picture, embraced in a heart-shaped frame, rested on the bedside table.

It was his favorite photo of many. With her chubby hands clutching a book and clad in her polka-dot best, Elle sat earnestly reading to the elf at the library. He and Julia made pins with the photo and distributed them to family, friends, and the staff at the oncology ward to wear as a show of support for Elle. Everybody loved them. Even her crow.

Brennan slammed the pin down next to the picture frame, rattling it and the pile of loose change scattered across the wooden table's surface. He paced the suddenly claustrophobic room and tried to remember his counselor's advice for when he was "triggered." Slow, deep breaths. Yes, that's good. Get another beer. No, not good, but who the hell cares?

He shut Elle's door with a determined click, stalked to the kitchen, and grabbed a cold one. He'd catch the last period of the game and hopefully fall asleep in front of the TV. If not, there was always room for one more beer.

CHAPTER

12

Brennan arrived at the morgue carrying an extra cup of black coffee and a half dozen jelly-filled doughnuts. Not exactly the breakfast of champions. But he and Pete had been friends since Pete was just the assistant medical examiner and Brennan merely a patrol officer. He knew there was nothing Pete loved more than jelly-filled doughnuts. Not even his wife.

A sullen assistant released the lock and buzzed him in. Juggling the box and two cups, Brennan hurried through the automatic door and immediately regretted not zipping his coat beforehand. Cooled to a constant forty-five degrees, the frigid air triggered immediate goose bumps. But the temperature was only one part of the morgue's chill-inducing effect.

The gymnasium-sized room lacked windows, and the overhead fluorescent bulbs flickered a stark, blue light. White tiles lined the walls and floor. Hulking stainless-steel refrigeration units dominated the center of the room, which, for the moment, thankfully smelled of antiseptic. A dozen rolling metal gurneys sat empty.

Brennan exhaled and loosened his death grip on the doughnut box. He'd timed his visit right.

Business was slow.

In the far corner, transparent acrylic panels defined a rectangular space Pete called his office. Brennan tapped awkwardly on the glass with his elbow.

Pete looked up from his cluttered desk. "Let me help you with that." He grabbed a cup and the box of doughnuts and sniffed appreciatively. "Mmm, raspberry jelly. My favorite."

"You can smell that through the box?"

"My nose is a finely tuned instrument. I missed my calling. I should've been a sommelier or perfumer."

"Instead, you dissect cadavers. Not a good combination." Brennan raised his cup in a mock salute. "Cheers."

"I can turn it off if I want to. It's called mouth breathing." Pete crammed most of a doughnut in his mouth. "Besides, that's one of the reasons we wear face shields and surgical masks." He slurped unsuccessfully at a giant blob of jelly, which dripped from his bottom lip onto the papers scattered across his desk.

Brennan grinned. "You're a mess. You know that?"

"But I'm a talented mess." Pete wiped his mouth on a paper towel and dabbed ineffectually at his red-stained papers. "Which brings me to your case. Erin Irene Dolan McConnell, age forty-four." He tapped his computer keyboard, and her naked body appeared on the screen.

Brennan shifted his feet and looked away.

Pete washed down another doughnut with a giant swig of coffee. "First, the easy part. I asked for a stat prelim report on the tox screen, essentially looking for illegal or unusual substances. It came up empty for anything strange but did show significant levels of two compounds: barbiturates and benzodiazepines, both widely available by prescription. It'll take weeks for the complete report to come back, but it looks like the benzo was tentatively ID'd as the sedative lorazepam, known on the streets as a downer."

"I'll bet you another dozen doughnuts the barbiturate is phenobarbital."

"What makes you say that?"

"Educated guess."

"Then I decline your wager. Doughnuts are far too precious to waste." Pete zoomed the screen's image to focus on Erin's upper torso. "Now for the hard part. The cause of death was obvious: blunt-force trauma to the back of her head from a fall, possibly due to excessive sedation from benzodiazepines. That's what I said in my report. But there's an anomaly."

Pete fiddled with the settings, slowly upping the contrast until two rosy blotches appeared on Erin's chest. "Burns. They're a little blurry but perfectly symmetrical. So faint I missed them at first. Initially, I wrote them off as a superficial sunburn."

"It's November, Pete."

"I know. But there are these amazing devices called tanning beds, Dan. Perhaps you've heard of them. Or she could've jetted off to Bermuda for a long weekend. I'm sure the McConnell family can afford it. But the more I stared at them, the more they looked like handprints, which raises the possibility that the victim was pushed." He flashed a sheepish grin. "You see them too, right?"

"Yeah, I see them. But there's no bruising over the rib cage. For someone to have pushed hard enough to leave a pair of prints, there should at least be a bruise." Brennan leaned closer to the monitor. "I hate to say it, but I agree with your sunburn theory. They look like first-degree burns."

"Because they are burns. I did a skin biopsy and examined the sample under the microscope to be sure. One-hundred-percent consistent with thermal injury—not impact or pressure phenomena. And if you think that's weird, this next picture is gonna blow your mind. The markings are far from superficial."

Pete clicked the mouse. The next image featured an identically positioned set of marks on the victim's back.

Brennan frowned. "What the hell?"

"Indeed. At first, I hypothesized the prints had nothing to do with her fall—assumed someone had been pushing her around for a while. But she had no healed bone fractures or other evidence of long-standing abuse. The burns are fresh. And to make things even weirder . . ."

The next photo looked like a slice of overcooked beef. Pete smiled at his friend's perplexed expression. "The muscles and other tissues under the prints show evidence of thermal damage too."

"Could a defibrillator cause this? Her husband's a physician, and I found one in his closet. He wasn't home when she fell though, and there was no defibrillator at the scene." Brennan tried to imagine elderly Leland Dolan carrying the device down the stairs in a futile attempt to resuscitate his granddaughter, then lugging it back up the stairs before the police arrived.

"Highly unlikely. It's a through-and-through injury like a gunshot wound, except instead of a bullet, the assailant used heat or electricity. To replicate those marks, someone would've had to shock her chest, then flip her over and shock her back. Even then, I'm not sure you'd get a deep enough dermal injury to match my tissue findings. It's like she was touched by the steaming hot hands of death, or something."

"That's flat-out insane." Brennan shook his head. "Maybe we're just imagining the marks are handprints. What do they call it? You know, when people see faces on Mars or Jesus on a piece of toast?"

"Pareidolia. That might explain it. But the marks are so dainty and perfectly symmetrical . . ." Pete shook his head. "I've never seen anything like it, and I've seen some weird shit in my day. If there's a more scientific explanation, I doubt I'll find it. At this point, I'm working off of pictures and tissue samples. The family wanted her buried posthaste."

The refrigeration unit's condenser fan kicked on. A series of loud clangs echoed around the cavernous morgue, followed by a high-pitched whine that set Brennan's teeth on edge. "We could always have her exhumed."

Pete winced. "*Exhumed* is a dirty word in my business. We prefer the term *disinterment*. No matter what you call it, digging her up means I didn't do the job right the first time. And the law hates it, especially when dealing with a family like the McConnells. There has to be—and I quote—'exigent circumstances that disinterment is within the interests of justice.'"

"You lost me at *exigent*."

"It means hot hands of death ain't gonna cut it. Usually, it takes a bulldog of a defense attorney to push for a disinterment. And to have a defense attorney, you need to arrest a suspect. Which, last I checked, you hadn't."

"Hmph. No wonder Ryan McConnell wanted her buried so fast. Which reminds me—I can't believe you submitted a report without the final tox screen."

Pete flinched. "I know, I know. I was under direct pressure from above. I made it as basic as I could and emphasized I'd amend the report later. I had no proof this was anything but accidental, nothing to justify a refusal to release the body."

Brennan succumbed to the sugary lure of a jelly doughnut. "Is that it?"

"Yep. Positive tox screen for prescription meds, weirdly shaped burns. That's it. The rest of the autopsy was as bland as a day-old bagel."

They munched in silence. Pete polished off two doughnuts for every one of Brennan's until they were staring at the bottom of a jelly-stained, crumb-filled box. The medical examiner tossed the empty box into the trash and leaned against his desk. "What are you gonna do now?"

Brennan folded the screenshot of Erin's chest and shoved it in his pocket. "I still have to question Erin's husband, who, as I mentioned, happens to be a surgeon. It'll be interesting to hear what Dr. McConnell has to say about the burns."

"You're gonna tell him?"

"Sure. Why not?"

"Just remember, pal, we both have reputations to uphold."

Brennan grimaced. "You have a reputation to uphold. Mine's pretty well shot at this point."

Pete stood tall, his expression suddenly serious. "Cut me a break, Dan. Everyone in this office and all the CSIs love working with you. You're as methodical and hardworking as they come. We know what you've been through lately. One solid high-profile case and your mojo will come roaring back."

"I have mojo? I had no idea."

"Knock it off. This is your case, Dan. A high-strung socialite chugs too many drugs and takes a dive down the stairs. Period. Let it go. Our bosses are happy, the rag mags are happy, and you're happy to have an easy one under your belt. On to the next. I've been telling myself the same thing."

The sugar gritting Brennan's teeth tasted cloyingly sweet, but it felt like sand. He stared morosely at the bitter dregs clinging to the bottom of his empty cup and wished for one dark swallow more, a few drops to swill the sweet away. "She had a daughter, Pete. Her name is Cassie. And she's anything but happy."

CHAPTER

13

E lle's illness had taught Brennan many things, one of which was gratitude for small blessings. He was grateful the Free Library's usual librarian wasn't on duty when he dragged himself yet again through the revolving door to return Elle's borrowed copy of *Goodnight Moon*. He was grateful that at two o'clock on a dreary Monday afternoon the facility was devoid of patrons. And he was grateful to have a legitimate excuse to delay briefing his boss, who texted a demand for an update on the case. He was questioning the victim's daughter.

Libraries have a distinct smell, like that of dusty parchment paper from fine, old books mixed with a hint of fresh ink from the newly shelved periodicals. Brennan stopped inside the door and took a deep breath through his nose. The odor triggered a wave of memories.

Cassie, wearing her usual studious expression, sat in her usual corner table strewn with folders and loose papers. All seemed normal and right. If Elle were holding his hand, he could've easily chalked up the past six months to a bad dream.

She glanced up as he approached and waved him into a chair. "I wasn't sure you'd show."

"Why wouldn't I?"

"You're a busy detective. I'm sure you have more important people to meet with than me."

"I keep my appointments." A plain manila file folder sat apart from the rest, directly in front of him on the oak table. Brennan opened it and winced. "I know I've said this before, but I'll say it again. You have a hell of a hobby."

The homicide scene depicted in the photo was graphically brutal, even in black-and-white. He thumbed through the remainder of the file, which contained an assortment of photographs, newspaper clippings, and other miscellaneous scraps of paper. A pale orange ticket stub from 1930 captured his interest. He gently pinched it between two fingers and read the faded text aloud. "*All Quiet on the Western Front.* Holy cow. I bet this thing is worth beaucoup bucks."

Cassie slid the top photo out of the folder. She pointed to its most prominent feature, a bullet-ridden young man draped across the hood of a hulking Plymouth. In the background, an old-time theater's flashy marquee advertised the iconic film. "That's Henry. He was a rumrunner during Prohibition."

"He had excellent taste in movies. How'd you get these?"

She shrugged. "Most of it comes from public records and newspapers."

"Most, but not all. Like this ticket stub. If it was at the crime scene, it's evidence. If it's evidence, it's part of the official police file. Cold case or not, the hard copies of those files are never released to the public."

"Officially, this isn't a cold case." Cassie rifled through the file until she found a mug shot of another considerably shadier-appearing young man. "The police claim Henry double-crossed his supplier, who ordered him killed. The man they convicted died in prison thirty-five years ago."

"You're avoiding my question."

"Except Henry didn't double-cross anyone. He was actually an undercover officer who discovered the local police department was getting paid to turn a blind eye. He was killed by a member of his own team."

"You're still avoiding my question."

Cassie shut the folder with a quick flick of her wrist. "Look, Pap donates a lot of money to the department's widows-and-orphans fund, okay?"

The curious librarian looked up from her computer, and Cassie lowered her voice. "The point is, Henry was a good man."

"More like a kid, from the look of that baby face."

"That kid had a wife and a newborn son."

"Both of whom are probably dead by now." Brennan leaned back in his chair. "Is this all you wanted to show me? Or is there something else?"

She stared at her interlaced fingers. "Any updates on the investigation into my mother's death?"

Brennan pictured the pale red marks burned into her mother's skin. "None that I care to share."

"Why not?" Her stillness contrasted sharply with the tension in her voice.

"Because it wouldn't be appropriate." Brennan softened his voice. "Let me finish my job. I promise I'll tell you everything once I'm done."

An old-fashioned clock ticked on the wall, adding emphasis to her lengthy silence. Finally, Cassie retrieved a huge leather tote emblazoned with splashy initials from the floor. She placed it on the table between them. "This was my mother's. I claimed it before my father could give it to Amber."

"Thanks, but I'm not really into purses."

She laughed, and her pensive mood vanished. "I would never have guessed." She pulled a pair of manila folders from one of the tote's deep pockets. "I told you I'd solved six murders on my own, but I needed your help with four others. These are two of those four case files."

She dropped the files on top of Henry's and stacked the five other folders scattered across the table. "Keep them too. I shared Henry's with you because it's a good example of my research. They all are. Read them through. I think you'll see that my methods are valid and my conclusions are sound. Then take a look at the two unsolved cases and let me know what you think. Maybe we can meet again in a few days to discuss them. Somewhere other than the library next time. The Mütter Museum, maybe. It's creepy and peculiar, and I love it. Ever been there?"

"No." The museum of medical oddities, reportedly filled with macabre artifacts such as slides of Albert Einstein's brain and formaldehyde-filled jars of diseased organs, was not at the top of his to-do list.

"Father took me there once, before my seizures. He's a donor."

"Why am I not surprised?" Brennan reached to open the top file, but Cassie pressed her hand over its smooth manila surface.

"Save it for later. I have to go. I have an appointment with my neurologist at three." She stood and slid the designer tote's straps over her shoulder. "Oh, I almost forget. One more thing." She rooted around the bottom of the roomy tote, eventually extracting a small, shiny object from within its depths.

For the second time in less than twenty-four hours, his daughter's face smiled at him from the glossy surface of a round metal pin. He stared, frozen in place.

Cassie thrust it into his hand. "I found it on the sidewalk outside my front steps this morning. I figured you must've dropped it after the wake."

Brennan, his breathing shallow, struggled to find something—anything—to say. He clenched the round pin in his fist.

Her voice, warm with concern, cut through his jumbled thoughts. "Are you okay?"

"Yes." He shoved the pin in his pocket. "Yes. I wasn't aware I'd lost it. Thanks."

"You're welcome."

He watched her watching him, read the confusion and curiosity on her face as she cataloged his reaction. He forced his shoulders to relax and tucked the file folders under his arm. "I'll read these tonight, right after I meet with the captain." His lips twitched in a wry smile. "Unless she drives me to drink."

"Don't let her." Cassie's phone flashed. The words on the screen faded before Brennan could sneak a peek.

"My appointment reminder." She sighed. "I've gotta run. Call me when you're done with the files. If you'd like, I can introduce you to the others too. I'll even let you read my journal. It's the most interesting of them all." With a casual wave, Cassie glided through the revolving door and hurried out of sight.

The last thing in the world he wanted was to read an eighteen-year-old's journal. A half dozen eighty-year-old cold cases ranked a close second. He tossed the folders onto the table. He had an hour to kill before returning to the precinct. May as well get started.

He slouched in the uncomfortable wooden chair. Something sharp pricked him in the thigh. He jerked, and it jabbed him again. He muttered a curse, pulled the button from his pocket, latched the pin, and shoved it back in place, shifting around until it no longer pressed against his thigh. He hadn't seen one in months. Now, he'd been gifted two in one day. The coincidence felt uncomfortably noncoincidental. It had to be nothing more than a fluke, a freaky roll of the dice. It had to be.

His hand hovered over the top file and he blinked, willing the image of his daughter's pale face to disappear so he could focus. He turned the cover, and a new face, that of the sullen bride from the photo room, stared at him in splotchy black-and-white. The inside of the folder's manila surface contained a single oversized word, carefully penned in cursive using bright red ink. *Ruth.*

CHAPTER

14

Brennan closed the first of Cassie's files and whistled softly, torn between morbid admiration and disgust at what he'd read. Ruth, serial husband killer extraordinaire, was either totally insane or a class-A bitch.

Hell, she was probably both. Had she not herself been murdered, her body count could've easily reached double digits.

He glanced at the clock on the wall and jumped to his feet. Crap. He was gonna be late for his meeting. The captain would be most displeased. He hurried from the library to his car, slammed the door, and revved the engine. His phone rang, and he cursed, answering with a curt "Brennan."

"Dan, you're going to want to see this." Jim Bonino, the CSI who'd processed Erin's dive down the Dolan Mansion stairs, chattered breathlessly in his ear. "Pictures don't do it justice. Trust me on this one."

"Jim, I can't. Captain Mattern is probably signing my termination papers as we speak." He merged into traffic with an angry squeal of his tires.

"I think the victim's related to your case. At least, I hope she is. Otherwise, you're gonna have to explain why she had your card in her purse."

Brennan's fingers turned to ice and his breath caught in his throat.

"You still there? Don't have an accident or anything." As the silence lengthened, so did the worry in Jim's voice. "You'd better be talking hands free, dammit."

"She who, Jim? Young, with curly red hair?"

"She's young all right, but bleach-bottle blonde. Sending you a picture now. You sure you can't swing by for a look-see? I'll be here awhile yet. It's worth it. I haven't seen such a beautifully staged scene in a long time. It's even prettier in black-and-white."

Brennan glanced at the image on his screen. Jim, a forensic photographer who approached slaughter with an artist's eye, was right. The hit was a professional one—stark, simple, efficient.

Hands tied behind the waist. A single bullet to the back of the head. The victim's hair was matted with blood, and the bullet had exited the lower half of her face, taking her jaw with it, but Brennan knew who she was without asking. Ryan McConnell was gonna need a new girlfriend.

"First of all, Jim, you're a morbid, sick bastard." Brennan coaxed his cold fingers into relaxing their death grip on the steering wheel.

"C'mon. Join me."

"I can't. Fishtown's at least a half hour out of my way. The captain may excuse a few minutes, but not the hour it would take me to get there and back. I'm haulin' ass as it is."

"How'd you know I'm in Fishtown?"

"Educated guess. I dropped the victim off there yesterday. Amber Servello's her name. Was she killed in her apartment?"

"Yep. Rough estimate puts the time of death around midnight. I guess I'll just shoot you the file in an email." Jim's disappointment was palpable.

"I owe you one. We're going out for a cold one once this thing wraps."

"Sooner, I hope." Jim chuckled. "I'm holding you to it. And speaking of cold ones, good luck with the captain. Better you than me, buddy. Better you than me."

The precinct—every precinct—reeked of stale coffee and sweat. Brennan ignored the inquisitive glances his coworkers didn't bother to hide and rapped his knuckles against Captain Mattern's door. No response. He turned the tarnished brass knob and stuck his head around the door frame. His boss, pen in hand, sat frowning at a stack of brown folders piled on her desk.

Without looking up, she scribbled something in the topmost folder and shoved it aside. "You're late."

Ten minutes. He was ten lousy minutes late. "I texted you—I got caught in traffic. We can reschedule if you want." Please. Pretty please.

"Don't bother." She waved him toward a chair, removed her dollar-store cheaters, and tossed them onto the cluttered desk. "Have I ever told you how much I hate doing these annual employee evaluations?"

"Only every year for the past decade or so."

She snorted. "It gets worse every year."

Brennan waited in silence, knowing she would get to the point when she was damned well ready. Though he appreciated the captain's political pragmatism, he didn't like his boss, and he didn't need to. He respected her, and that was enough. Captain Shanice Mattern had broken through a glass ceiling everyone liked to pretend didn't exist. The woman was stone-cold fierce. Ten years into their work relationship and Brennan had yet to receive a genuine smile.

As best he could tell, only her mother and the commissioner truly liked her.

She tapped her pen on the desk. "The McConnell case."

"Yes?"

"How goes it?"

"The body count is higher."

"So I've heard."

Stone. Cold. Brennan squelched the urge to fidget under her inscrutable stare. "Amber Servello's murder may or may not be related. I plan to get the particulars from Jim Bonino, the CSI processing the scene, after I finish with you. I also need to question Dr. Ryan McConnell in more detail before I finalize my report."

"Why?"

"The medical examiner found high sedative levels in her bloodstream and marks on her chest possibly consistent with trauma other than the fall." Not a lie, but not exactly the hot hands of death, either. The captain didn't need that level of detail. Not yet. Not until he could explain it.

"You think she was drugged and pushed?"

"It's highly possible. The husband was having an affair, and I'm assuming with his wife gone he stands to inherit a chunk of the Dolan family fortune. He has motive. His own daughter thinks he did it. So does Leland Dolan."

The tapping grew faster. "You're never gonna guess who paid me a visit this morning."

Brennan paused. "Ryan's big brother, Beck McConnell."

The captain's pen hovered mid-tap over the desk. "That's a helluva guess." She leaned back in her chair. "Along with his dick of a lawyer. I assume you realize the delicacy of the situation."

"Maybe you should spell it out for me, just in case."

Her eyes narrowed. Abruptly, she stood and rounded the desk, leaning against it with her arms crossed and her back to the clear glass overlooking the busy precinct's open office. She lowered her voice. "Everyone knows Beck's entire family is dirty—"

"You're on a first-name basis?"

The captain's eyes glittered like polished jasper. Brennan kicked himself in the mental pants. He should not have said that. Not out loud. He was so off his game.

Her voice was tight and low. "Shut up and listen. You want me to spell it out for you or not?"

"Yes, but for the record, I think it's pathetic as hell that Ryan has to send his bully of a big brother to protect him." Brennan snorted. "This isn't high school."

"He didn't kill his wife, Detective."

"How can you say that? You haven't gotten my report yet."

"Beck looked me square in the eye and essentially said if Ryan or the McConnell family wanted Erin dead, we would've never found her. That's as true a statement as any liar can give, especially in the presence of his lawyer."

"Who probably didn't even bat an eyelash."

The captain paced the small room. "Here's the thing. Not one person in the McConnell family has gotten so much as a speeding ticket. No one. They keep their hands clean and let their soldiers take the fall. On paper, Beck McConnell runs a successful import-export business and is a generous donor to local causes, including the annual Mummers Parade. He told me you've been harassing his baby brother, and he wants it to stop. If it doesn't, he's lodging a complaint with the commissioner and every other woo-hoo in the department, with whom he seems intimately familiar. He dropped names like they all share one goddamned giant toothbrush."

"That's a bunch of bullshit, and you know it." Brennan shook his head. "I've crossed paths with Ryan McConnell once—no, twice. I only talked to him once, and that was a week ago at the hospital the day his wife died. I saw him again yesterday at the wake, but we didn't speak. If that counts as harassment—"

"He says you've been calling and leaving multiple messages."

"If he would answer his goddamned phone, I wouldn't have to. He's trying to influence the investigation."

"Obviously." She opened a file on her phone and held the screen in front of his face.

The magnified image included only a square foot or two of a blood-stained carpet, but Brennan recognized it for what it was—a crime-scene photo, probably one of Jim's.

Broken fingernails added lurid dots of color to the beige carpeting. A few strands of matted blonde hair embroidered the edge of the photo's frame.

In the foreground, a designer handbag rested on its side with its contents artificially spilled into an artful display.

He pushed the phone away. "Amber's, I presume."

"Another excellent guess. She was carrying your card."

"I know. I gave it to her yesterday after I questioned her."

The captain clicked off her phone. "Did she tell you she's a mob mole?"

Brennan blinked. "No. I guess it didn't come up. A mole for who?"

"*La Famiglia*—the Italians. And us, on occasion. Whoever writes the fattest check. She's been spying on the Irish competition via Ryan McConnell for years. Apparently, he's not good at keeping secrets."

"Talks in his sleep."

She raised an eyebrow.

"Or so I hear." Brennan massaged his forehead. "But if Beck knew, why kill her now? It makes Ryan, if not the whole McConnell family, look guilty of both murders."

"I think that's the point."

"You're assuming she was killed by her own?"

The captain shrugged. "If *la Famiglia* thinks Amber ratted to you, why not take advantage of a bad situation? Betrayal equals death. They can off a mole and implicate their enemies all in one move. Brilliant. Gotta admire the efficiency."

"No, I don't." Brennan slumped in his chair and pictured Amber laughing at Erin's wake. Dolan's response had been immediate and visceral. "Your theory makes sense, but don't rule out Leland Dolan. He hates Ryan, and he wasn't exactly fond of Amber either. In fact, as far-fetched as it sounds, she implicated Dolan in Erin's murder. Essentially said the old man was batshit crazy. He can certainly afford to hire someone to do his dirty work, like revenge killing his grandson-in-law's mistress."

"He also contributes large amounts of money to the department. You're beginning to see the extent of our dilemma. Deep pockets on both sides desiring opposite outcomes."

"Your dilemma, not mine. I'm a due-process-and-evidence kind of guy. Do I have an opinion? Yes. My gut tells me Erin was murdered, probably by someone in the McConnell family. But we can't prosecute based on opinion. My report will hold the facts, all of them, unfiltered and unbiased. Then it's up to you and the prosecutors as to how you want to proceed."

She stared him full in the face. "That's not gonna work out well for one of those sides, and it might not work for me."

"Really? How interesting." The air between them, thick with insinuation, caught in his throat. "I don't work for either side. Do you?"

Her right hand clenched into a fist. Brennan's biceps tensed as, for one wild moment, he believed she might take a swing. Thank God for glass walls.

Her voice shook with barely restrained fury. "You've been walking a thin line for the last six months, Detective. I suggest you watch your mouth, or you'll be facing early retirement. I want that report by

Friday. You're a smart guy. Figure out a compromise that'll serve Lady Justice while meeting the department's needs."

He bolted to his feet, causing his chair to teeter precariously. "I guess I'm dismissed."

The slamming door triggered a lull in the crowded precinct's chatter. Curious eyes followed his departure. He slowed his gait to a casual pace and unclenched his teeth. No need to add to the rumors, especially since the meeting's only tangible outcome was a titanic shift in his opinion. He no longer respected his boss. The feeling was clearly mutual.

CHAPTER

15

Light snow, the first of the season, cooled Brennan's flushed cheeks as he stalked through the precinct's lot toward his car. Too powdery to be pretty, the snow melted on the dirty streets and sidewalks, coating them in drab gray slush.

He slumped into the driver's seat and watched the tiny flakes burst into tears on his windshield. He cranked up the heat and dialed Jim.

The forensic photographer answered on the first ring. "Are you sufficiently flayed?"

"To a bloody pulp. Are you still at the scene?"

"Unfortunately. Some kind of bottleneck at the local morgue. Business has been brisk today, from what I hear."

Brennan flipped on the wipers. "Okay if I swing by?"

"The more, the merrier. I'll text you the address."

The traffic on I-95 had snarled to a crawl thanks to the unexpected snow. Brennan, his mood darker than the dreary sky, cursed the entire way to Fishtown. He slid his car to the curb and double-checked the address. Amber's apartment building, an unimpressive hunk of concrete in a not-so-trendy corner of town, loomed tall and gray. Outside the entrance's dirty glass doors, an undertaker, apparently awaiting the go-ahead to claim her cargo, loitered against her idling vehicle.

Despite its gloomy outward appearance, the building's art-deco lobby was spacious and clean. The elevator buttons capped at twenty, which made Amber's twentieth-floor apartment the penthouse. He stepped off the elevator and whistled. Whoever was forking over the monthly rent had impressively deep pockets. No way Amber's tutoring salary paid for this, even if she was banging the boss. Judging by the old-world décor, his money was on *la Famiglia*.

The rapid clicking of a camera's shutter guided him to the living room, where the murder had been staged in front of a sumptuous velvet sofa laden with tapestry pillows. Jim, sitting cross-legged on the only blood-free patch of carpet, was snapping photos of Amber's hands.

Brennan squatted nearby, trying to ascertain the reason for Jim's keen interest. Most of Amber's bright orange nails and at least one of her fingers appeared broken. Blood crusted the gold bling gleaming from every other finger. "Looks like she put up a hell of a fight."

"Wouldn't you?" Jim's camera clicked a final time, and he lowered it from his face. "Hopefully, those talons of hers will give us some usable DNA."

"You swab underneath?"

"Already done."

Despite Amber's apparent struggle, her apartment appeared tidy. No signs of forced entry. Nothing knocked over or in disarray. Not a damned thing out of place. "Who found her?"

"Cleaning lady. She has her own key."

Brennan rose to his feet, grimacing as his knee clicked in protest. "Care if I poke around?"

"We already pulled prints and bagged her phone, laptop, and the contents of her purse. Nothing else seems overly interesting."

"Yeah, about that—the captain showed me your photo of my business card lying next to Amber's purse. Not standard protocol. Care to explain?"

"I wish I could. She called me shortly after I hung up with you. Said she wanted everything emailed to her ASAP. I sent her what I had. I assume she heard about it over the scanner when the responding officers called it in. Must be a special case." Jim twisted his camera's lens. "I hated to put you on the spot, but I knew you'd have a good explanation. You always do. Was she nasty to you?"

"You could say that. You owe me a beer." Brennan reached into his rear pocket for a pair of gloves. "I'm gonna look around."

"Knock yourself out."

Brennan turned, and his knee popped again.

Jim grinned. "I didn't mean that literally, old man."

"You're less than ten years behind me, junior. Just wait. Your time will come."

Brennan made a methodical pass through the apartment's spacious, orderly rooms, notable for an interesting lack of personal items. No photos on the wall or dresser. No books or stacks of papers, bills, or receipts. Even her bedroom and bath, the most personal areas of any home, contained utilitarian items only: clothing, makeup, shoes. He saved the medicine cabinet for last. The most obvious places were often the most revealing.

Why anyone opted to hide anything in there he'd never know. Amber's didn't disappoint.

A small medicine bottle, partially obscured behind tubes of toothpaste and mascara, held two tablets out of the prescribed thirty. LORA-ZEPAM, ONE MILLIGRAM DAILY AS NEEDED FOR SLEEP OR ANXIETY. It'd been prescribed ten days ago by a physician from South Philly, which was hell and gone from Fishtown.

He carried it back to the living room. "Got an extra evidence bag?"

"Sure. You find something?" Jim tossed him a baggie.

"A bottle of benzos. May not mean anything—they're commonly prescribed, from what I hear—but the same medication was found in Erin McConnell's tox screen, so it's worth bagging. If they were for Amber's personal use, she was hitting them hard. Then again, if I were Ryan McConnell's girlfriend, I'd want to be sedated too."

A clatter outside the door alerted them to the gurney's arrival. Jim stashed his camera in a duffel. "It's about freakin' time."

They stepped out of the way, watching as Amber was zipped in a body bag, loaded onto the gurney, and wheeled into the elevator. They waited for the next one. By the time they stepped off the elevator and into the lobby, the undertakers had left, their mission completed. Jim and Brennan exited the high-rise to a much smaller crowd than when they'd entered. Jim shoved his hands in his pockets.

"Shit, it's cold out here. When did it start snowing?"

"Hmm? About an hour ago, I think," Brennan murmured, his attention elsewhere. A half block away, a man in a puffer jacket loitered despite the cold. And he looked familiar.

"Keep looking at my face." Brennan smiled at Jim and nodded as if carrying on a casual conversation. "There's a dude down the street scoping the scene. I saw the same guy on patrol the night I drove Amber home from the wake."

"You think he's the killer? They like to watch the investigation, you know. It's a vicarious-thrill thing." Jim's gaze drifted over Brennan's shoulder.

"Eyes on me. You're gonna spook him."

Brennan subtly shifted his weight to block Jim's view. "You've been watching too much TV. He's not our guy. A pro would never return to the scene, and Amber's murder has the hallmarks of a professional mob assassination. More likely, he's a watchman. When I first saw him, I assumed he worked for the local drug lord, but now that

I know Amber's connections . . . he probably has to report the who, what, and when of the police response to Fishtown's capo, mob captain." He paused. "It's the who that bothers me."

Jim's eyes widened. "You mean us."

"I mean me, primarily. Remember, my card was in Amber's wallet. He's holding a cell phone, which means he's likely snapped some pictures."

"Two can play that game. And I have a telephoto lens." Jim reached for his duffel's zipper.

"No, don't. Not yet. He'll run, and he and I need to have a little chat first. You want to play detective?"

Jim's face lit with puppy-like enthusiasm. "Hell ya. I mean, I kind of do that already, but in my line of work, everybody's, like, already dead. Not as dead as Pete's dead, but still—"

"How can you be 'not as dead'? Dead is dead, Jim."

"Pete's are cold and dead. Sometimes mine are still warm."

Brennan stared at Jim's face. "Are you done?"

"Yes."

"Excellent. Here's the plan: give me five minutes to round the rear of the building and position myself at the end of the block. Then you walk toward him. Tell him you'd like to ask him a few questions. That'll flush him in my direction. Oh, and make sure to duck if he pulls a gun."

The enthusiasm drained from Jim's face. He readjusted his thick glasses. "On second thought, I'm more of a scientist than a detective. Maybe—"

"I was joking. He's a lookout, Jim. He won't have a gun." He grinned. "Not usually, anyway."

"I'm not reassured."

"Look, I'll be watching the whole time, and I do have a gun. Talk loudly so I can hear what's going on and send him running my way. Everything'll be fine."

"What if he doesn't run?"

"He will. They always do." With a casual wave, Brennan strolled into the narrow alley between Amber's apartment and the parking deck next door. As soon as he was out of the mobster's line of sight, he dashed to the end, rounded the corner, and waited, flashing Jim a thumbs-up.

The photographer adjusted the duffel on his shoulder, cleared his throat, and approached the young man. "Um, sir, I'd like to ask you a few questions, if you don't mind."

The lookout turned and bolted down the street. Brennan crouched in wait. One, two . . . He timed his action to the slap of sneakers on wet pavement and extended his foot at exactly the right moment. The watchman tripped, shielding his face with the crook of his arm as he pitched forward. Thanks to his puffy coat, he landed with a muted thud and slid another yard on the sidewalk's icy surface before petering out in a flailing heap.

Brennan grabbed the lookout by his collar and hoisted him to his feet. "Oh, hey. Geez. Sorry about that, buddy." He squinted at the man's face in mock surprise. "What a coinkydink. You're just the guy I wanted to talk to."

Panting, the watchman squirmed out of Brennan's grasp. "I've got nothing for you, man. Nothing."

"Keep your hands where I can see them. We don't need this to get ugly over a few lousy questions."

Jim, huffing and puffing under the weight of his heavy equipment, ran down the street to sandwich the young man between them.

Brennan gestured at Jim. "My friend here is a photographer. How'd you like your pretty face circulated around the police department? Guaranteed to end your career in a flash. Worse yet if we took you in for questioning. Might even get you killed, depending on your employers."

The lookout glanced over his shoulder. He swiped his brush-burned palms on his damp jacket. "I'm nobody. Watch the girl. See who comes and goes. That's it. They don't tell me nothing. I didn't know she was dead until youse guys showed up this morning. Someone else has the night shift."

"Who's 'they'?"

The man scuffed his sneakers over the slick pavement.

"Who's 'they'?" Brennan repeated the question, amping up the volume.

His voice echoed down the street.

The watchman flinched. "I work for a guy who works for Mr. McConnell," he mumbled.

"Ryan McConnell?"

The mobster maintained his stoic silence.

"Okay, then—how about his big brother, Beck?"

The lookout shifted his weight.

"Ding, ding, ding!" Brennan shouted. "We have a winner. Because everyone knows Beck looks out for his baby brother, right?"

"I'm not sayin' you're right. I'm not sayin' you're wrong either. I will say the chick was playing them, working for the goddamned dagos. If they killed her—and I'm not sayin' they did, but *if* they did— what else were they supposed to do?"

A shiny black SUV zoomed down the street, slowing as it approached the intersection where they stood. The lookout licked his lips and averted his face. "Can I go now?"

"Let me see your phone first. Nice and easy now."

"You got a warrant?"

"You got a death wish? Seriously, Slick—mind if I call you Slick?— they don't pay you enough for this. Not enough for bail money, anyway. I'm sure if I check, you have an outstanding arrest warrant or two. Or five. And we already talked about what happens to watchmen who pay a visit to the precinct."

Scowling, the watchman unlocked his phone and handed it to Brennan.

Brennan opened the photos and deleted five headshots of himself and Jim. Next, he skimmed through the contacts and checked the sent folder for recent texts or emails. None. His tension ebbed. "You'll notice I didn't ask you your name."

The lookout's forehead furrowed in confusion.

Brennan tossed the phone in the air; the lookout scrambled to catch it. "That's how this works. I forget about you, and you forget about me. I wasn't here; we never spoke. We can play it differently if you'd like, but it's liable to get messy real quick." He stepped aside to offer an unimpeded exit. "We good?"

The mobster bobbed his head. "Yeah, man, we're good." He backed out of arm's reach, turned, and fled.

As soon as he disappeared around the corner, Brennan pulled out his phone and began typing.

Jim exhaled. "Man, that was intense. What are you doing?"

"Writing down his name in case we need to squeeze him again in the future. The owner's name and number are usually at the top of a smartphone's contact list. In his case, so was his address." Brennan flashed a wicked grin. "Intense, you say? No punches. No bullets. No blood. We may as well have been sipping tea at the Bellevue. But, hey—if you say so."

"Some of us lead less-exciting lives. I, for example, take pictures of dead people, and they rarely talk back."

"Rarely?" Brennan raised an eyebrow.

"Rarely." Jim hoisted the heavily laden camera bag onto his shoulder. "That's a story best told over copious amounts of cold beer."

By beer number three, Jim was singing like a second-rate rock star on acid. He strutted the bar's tiny karaoke stage, wailing to a 1980s hair band. Brennan lounged at a corner table, which afforded him an unobstructed view of his colleague's antics. Pete arrived late, and Brennan waved him into an empty seat.

Jim shrieked a window-shattering and exceptionally off-key note. Brennan chuckled at Pete's pained expression. "I didn't know he had it in him."

Pete frowned. "You know the old saying 'Work hard, play hard?' Jim-Bo lives by it. It's a Monday night, for cripes sake. Doesn't he have to work in the morning? I know I do."

"Relax. You'll be snug as a bug in your bed by ten. Besides, your clients can wait." Brennan flagged the waitress and ordered Pete a beer. "On me. Jim's bought the other rounds."

"See what I mean?" His scowl deepened.

"My, aren't we a cranky old fart this evening? Bad day at the office? Or do you have something scandalous to report?" Brennan sipped his winter lager.

The karaoke machine screeched with feedback, and Pete cringed. "Honestly, could there be anything worse than this?"

"I wanted to go to our old standby, but Jim said this is the precinct's hip new hangout." A dude with a mullet and leopard-print tank strolled by their table. Brennan suppressed a grin. "How'd I let him drag me into this?"

The waitress delivered Pete's drink. He stared at the trickle of foam tracing a circuitous path down the glass and onto the table. "I've been asking myself that for almost a year."

The throbbing bass filled their awkward lapse in conversation. Brennan set his pint glass on the table. "What is it, Pete?"

"Does he know you invited me here?"

"No. We drove separately, and I texted you from the car. Figured the more, the merrier. Did you two have a falling out or something? I know between Elle and the divorce, it's been a while since the three of us have gotten together . . ."

"During which time he asked me for money—a lot of money—to cover his gambling debts and overdue child support. It's an ugly story. And that's not the worst of it." Pete shook his head. "We need to talk somewhere privately. 'Ugly' doesn't even begin to describe it. Maybe he's drunk enough to tell you himself."

The song ended to tepid applause from the crowd. Jim, face flushed and forehead beaded with sweat, bounded off the stage and tottered toward the corner table. His gait faltered when he spied Pete by Brennan's side. "Hey, Pete. Long time, no see." He tumbled into a chair and elbowed Brennan. "What do ya think, old man? Pretty good, huh?"

"I'm thinking you weren't even born when that song hit the airwaves."

Jim flashed a lopsided grin. "I was in preschool. I look young for my age. All that clean living."

Pete snorted his beer.

Jim's gaze flicked between the two older men. He crossed and uncrossed his legs, nearly falling off the chair in the process. "Whatcha talking about? Did I miss anything exciting?"

Pete took a swig of his beer. "We were chatting about Dan's case. I examined the corpse, and—"

Jim interrupted. "Which one?"

"Erin McConnell. I noticed some red marks on her skin, and Dan asked me if they might've come from her necklaces twisting around her neck during the fall."

Brennan shoved a handful of bar nuts in his mouth to hide his expression. They'd discussed no such thing. As a matter of fact, he'd been so perplexed by the burns on Erin's chest he'd totally forgotten about her necklaces.

Pete rocked his chair onto its rear legs. His face disappeared in the dimly lit bar's shadowy corner. "The funny thing is, she wasn't wearing any necklaces. I checked with evidence collection to see if the police removed them before transferring her to the morgue. They had no record of any jewelry being logged during intake, not even a wedding ring." He paused. "Maybe you remember. Was she wearing any jewelry when you processed the scene? I guess I could pull your photos . . ."

Jim brushed a lock of damp hair off his forehead. He glanced over his shoulder at the stage, where an Ozzy wannabe gyrated and slurred a drunken version of "Crazy Train." "I . . . I don't remember right now. Too buzzed, I guess. Text me tomorrow. I'll check first thing in the morning, okay?"

He pushed away from the table and stood, swaying on his feet. "I think I've had enough for one night." He fumbled around his pocket for his keys.

"Too much, I'd say." Brennan jumped to his feet and placed a steadying hand on Jim's shoulder. "I'll drive you home."

"No, no. It's too far out of your way. I'm fine."

"Jim, you're not driving." Brennan adopted the same no-nonsense tone he used when he used to walk the beat. "What kind of cop would I be if I let you get behind the wheel? At least let me call you a cab or Uber, or whatever."

Jim scowled. "I've got it." He pulled out his phone and, with a few taps, arranged for a lift.

Brennan threw some bills on the table, and the three men walked outside together. After the heat of the packed bar, the cold air stung. Brennan cupped his hands around his mouth and blew on his fingers.

Jim stared at the sidewalk. "You guys don't have to wait. My driver will be here in"—he glanced at his phone—"less than five minutes."

"We'll wait." Brennan glanced at Pete, who nodded.

"You don't trust me, do you?"

"I never said that."

"You don't have to." Jim, his expression petulant, wiped the steam from his lenses. "I told you I wouldn't drive. I can show you my phone. I called an Uber."

"It's five minutes, Jim. No big deal."

As if on cue, a black sedan pulled to the curb. The driver lowered the passenger window. Jim leaned in, they exchanged words, and he jumped in the backseat.

Brennan grabbed the handle. "Fasten your seat belt." He grinned at Jim's exasperated expression.

"And don't forget to check on those photos," Pete added over Brennan's shoulder.

Brennan slammed the door, and the sedan zoomed away in a cloud of exhaust. Pete shook his head. "Too bad the rear window's tinted. I bet he's giving us the finger right about now."

"Are you gonna tell me what that was all about?"

"Of course." The door behind them opened, disgorging a raucous group of middle-aged men. Pete waited until they'd stumbled down the street. "Somewhere quieter, though. And not crawling with off-duty officers."

"Your place or mine?"

"Mine."

"I was afraid you'd say that. Fine. I'll meet you at the morgue in ten."

Brennan didn't like frequenting the morgue during the day, much less at night. Once the cleaning crew packed up their mops and left, an eerie stillness, unrelieved by the occasional hiss from the HVAC system, reigned. The bright lights made it no less intimidating. If anything, the chilly blue fluorescence and somber sterility added to the unnerving effect.

Pete didn't seem to care. He whistled a random tune as they waited for his ancient desktop to boot up. For some reason, the cursor's interminable spinning made Brennan queasy. He closed his eyes. Maybe Jim wasn't the only one who'd had too much to drink. "Why don't you just tell me what's going on? You don't need to show me too. At this rate, we'll be here all night."

The spinning cursor stopped, and the screen flashed a series of precisely labeled folders. Pete glanced at him between clicks. "You can't guess?"

"Sure, I can guess. You think Jim's stealing bling off dead people and pawning it to fund his gambling habit. Why didn't you tell me this morning when we reviewed Erin McConnell's autopsy?"

"If I had known you planned to bar crawl with Jim, I would have. As you said, it's been a long time since you've painted the town."

"It wasn't planned. Jim and I worked a scene, and he wanted a beer. Guess he doesn't like to drink alone. You're making a serious accusation, Pete. I assume you have proof." Brennan watched as Pete clicked through several subfolders. "You realize you just opened a file of takeout menus?"

"I know." Pete clicked the name of his favorite doughnut shop. Three columns of photos popped onto the screen. The far-left displayed victims at their respective crime scenes. The middle column showed the naked corpses laid out at the morgue. The far-right was a tabletop shot of the evidence collected at the scene.

Pete rolled a second desk chair closer to the screen and motioned for Brennan to sit. "I first noticed an issue about six months ago. Gangbangers missing gold teeth—that sort of thing."

Brennan groaned. "Jesus Christ. Stealing teeth from dead people. I thought that went out with nineteenth-century grave robbing."

"It gets worse. After I'd accumulated a dozen or so discrepancies, I cross-referenced them with the personnel involved, from the first responders all the way to the evidence collection clerks. Only one name appeared in all twelve cases."

"Jim."

Pete nodded. "Shortly thereafter, he hit me up for money. Said he'd lost big on the ponies. The pieces fell into place."

"That's pretty good detective work, Pete. I'm impressed."

"Thanks." He sighed. "I hated to do it, but I took the evidence to his supervisor. Guess what happened? Nothing. I followed up for two months until the supervisor stopped answering my calls. Then, around Halloween, I came to work and found that someone had rooted through my office. The original files were missing—both the hard copies I'd printed and the e-files. Fortunately, I'd thought ahead and saved a second copy in my doughnut file. Sometimes it pays to be paranoid."

"And obsessive-compulsive." Brennan squinted at the array of photos. From the bottom of the first column, Erin McConnell, sans jewelry, stared back. "She had two gold necklaces—a crucifix and a claddagh. I saw them myself."

"I'm guessing Jim edits the valuables from the final prints. But he's not the first one on-scene. A lot of first responders take their own panoramic shots to cover their asses for exactly this reason. They also submit a written list of the victim's personal effects. Jim probably thought no one would notice. Most of the time, those lists and photos aren't cross-referenced unless a loved one complains of something missing."

Brennan pictured the diamond rings adorning Amber's broken fingers. Were they still present when he and Jim packed up and left? He hadn't noticed. "We'll know for sure once Jim files the pictures from tonight's case. She had a fistful of bling. Prime pickin's."

"That's why I brought it up at the bar. Now he knows I'm—we're—onto him. Ms. Servello arrived shortly after you texted me. She's locked up tight behind a refrigerated door. If he stole anything of hers, it's not like he can put it back. It's a test. If he edits the photos, you're going to notice. If he doesn't, there's missing jewelry to explain. His supervisor won't be able to sweep that under the rug."

Brennan frowned. "Why would his boss protect him though? Makes no sense. If word gets out, it makes the whole department look bad, and it's the supers who usually take the fall."

Pete shifted in his seat. "I never planned to involve you in this. My next step was to move it upstairs to Internal Affairs, but when I found out Jim was the CSI assigned to your case, I decided you should know. Plain bad luck on your part, I guess. Feel free to pretend I never told you. I won't think any less of you."

"We're in this together, Pete."

Pete's anxious expression disappeared. He sighed. "In that case, I have a theory that goes beyond Jim stealing bling for gambling money, if you'd care to listen. It's pretty far-fetched, and I have zero proof—"

"Fire away."

Pete dragged the cursor across the screen, highlighting the four most recent cases, including Erin's. "I noticed a trend. The first six months, the thefts appeared opportunistic. As I mentioned, gold teeth from gangbangers, bling from prostitutes—items stolen from people whose next of kin weren't likely to fuss. But the last four cases were different. They seemed handpicked, and the missing evidence wasn't always valuable or easily fenced by the average crook. A cell phone, a set of keys—that sort of thing. I did a deep dive, trying to figure out what they had in common."

Pete lowered his voice. "Turns out, it's the mob. They're all connected, someway, somehow."

The hard drive hummed in the otherwise silent room. When Brennan spoke, his voice sounded artificially loud. "You said you have zero proof."

"Correct. But two of the victims had criminal records and suspected ties to *la Famiglia*. Jim's last name is Bonino. It ain't Scottish."

"That's profiling at its worst, Pete."

"I know, but it fits. It certainly explains how Jim could go from begging money to buying us drinks in six months flat. I'm sure the mob payroll reimburses him well to tamper with evidence."

"Stealing from corpses and tampering with evidence." Brennan's nausea returned. He massaged his forehead. "Who's next in the food chain?"

"Excuse me?"

"Who does Jim's supervisor report to?"

Pete closed the folder and powered down the device. "That would be your buddy, Captain Mattern."

Brennan sighed. "Somehow I knew you were going to say that."

CHAPTER

17

November 7th
4th Journal Entry

"**M**y husband bought me a birthday gift. Awkward. I'd already decided to kill him."

Today was Ruth's birthday and her spirits were high, especially after I managed to painstakingly plunk out "Happy Birthday" on the photo room's baby grand.

She clapped in delight and regaled me with stories of birthdays past. She'd never received a gift of any kind before her first husband surprised her on her eighteenth birthday with a pair of emerald earrings. She briefly considered changing her plans but poisoned him anyway.

"Then I had enough money to buy my own earrings," she explained. Ones she preferred. Diamond, of course. Princess cut, big enough to be noticed but not so big as to imply excess. Extravagance was frowned upon in those days, with the Depression raging and war looming near.

She chafed at being financially dependent on men to survive, as was typical of the times, and envied my freedom, though I was quick to explain I was similarly dependent on my parents.

"I have a glorious surprise planned for today, Cassandra." She clasped her hands in front of her heart. "A gift to myself. Better than earrings and long overdue, I assure you."

"What?"

"It's a secret. If I told you, you'd just blab it to that detective friend of yours. You should never have shown him this room. I told you before—it's our private temple. You're far too trusting, especially with powerful men." She smiled coyly. "Secrets aren't meant to be shared."

"But he can help me figure out who murdered you and the others so you can finally be at peace."

"That's your job, not his. His role begins and ends with your mother." She waltzed around the photo room in her wedding dress, stopping from time to time to play a snippet of a favored tune on the piano. She ignored my pleas to share her surprise and shrewdly changed the subject. "When's YOUR birthday, Cassandra?"

I told her, and her hand flew to her mouth in mock horror. "Oh, dear. I missed it. You should've told me sooner. Oh, well. There's always next year."

A strange sensation prickled my skin, and the room grew dark despite the morning sun streaming through the windows. The phantom odor of a burnt match was my final warning—I was about to seize. I needed to flee the photo room.

"Will you still be here next year?" I asked as I stumbled out the door.

"Of course." Her icy breath licked my neck. "Will you?"

CHAPTER

18

The temperature dropped with nightfall, and snow turned to sleet. Thanks to the slick roads, Brennan's drive home took twice as long as usual. He gripped the wheel until his fingers cramped; his neck muscles pulsed with tension. Between work and the weather, tomorrow was gonna be a helluva a day.

He dreaded it already.

His apartment building appeared even drearier when wet, especially when compared to the gleaming new condos across the street. But what it lacked in charm, it made up for with underground parking. As long as you didn't mind bats. During the winter, at least one colony established its base in the man-made cave.

He eased the car into his designated spot. Devoid of activity given the late hour, the dimly lit and poorly maintained lot acquired a menacing air. He gave his gun an appreciative pat and hurried across the concrete toward the elevator. His footsteps echoed, triggering the bats to stir. Undulating black masses appeared in the garage's four corners. He paused until their shrill chatter faded away. The movement ceased.

Elle would've been delighted. She loved bats almost as much as crows. In retrospect, they weren't that much different, at least in the eyes of a five-year-old. Black like her hair. Black things that fly.

He lightened his tread. A noise echoed from behind a cement support column. Not just any noise. A cough.

Bats don't cough.

The elevator was close, so close. He froze, hand hovering over his gun. A shadowy figure teetered into the dim light. The stench of cheap gin stung worse than the cold.

"Spare a little change?" the man slurred, holding out one hand. The other clutched a brown paper bag.

"How about I call you a cab instead? There's a shelter close by. You'll freeze out here tonight." Brennan eyed the man's tattered coat, two sizes too big. Despite his slurred speech, his eyes were clear, and his chin displayed what looked to be only a day's worth of stubble. And he was wearing a pair of Air Jordans.

"Nah, man. I ain't going to no shelter. Fuggetaboutit." He stumbled toward the exit.

"Who do you work for?" Brennan slid his gun out of its holster and held it by his side. It wasn't against the law to impersonate a drunk, but it sure was suspicious.

The man stopped on the sidewalk outside the garage. "Pig." He flipped Brennan the bird and took off on a dead run. His footsteps, remarkably steady for a drunk, vanished quickly. Hopefully, karma was kind and had sent the jerk skidding across the ice on his ass. Or better yet, his face.

The bat colony pulsed with agitation. "It's okay," Brennan said, unsure if he was talking to the bats or himself. He hustled to the elevator and jabbed the up button. By the time the metal doors closed, the fluttering had stopped.

He sagged against the back wall. He was under surveillance. The question was, by whom? The floors ticked upward and so did his self-doubt. Maybe the bro was just a guy who held his alcohol well. Maybe he'd stolen those expensive sneakers. And maybe tacos were Polish and pizza was health food.

The elevator stopped on the thirteenth floor. Brennan shivered as a frigid gust of air blasted him in the chest. He knew its source without looking. The locks on the double-hung window at the end of the hall were so cheap, the slightest vibration—a large truck idling outside, a car radio's throbbing bass—caused the upper sash to slide down at least four inches.

The landlord didn't care. "Any criminal who scales thirteen floors for a robbery deserves his haul." But the gap gave entry to a wide variety of undesirables, from rain to flies to the occasional bat. Today, it welcomed a crow.

Brennan and the bird considered each other from seven feet away. It sat outside his end-unit apartment, picking at a leather-bound book propped against the door. He sighed. "Did you get stuck in here?"

The crow's yellow-brown eyes stared dolefully.

"You found a way to break in, but you didn't think it through, did ya? No escape plan. I thought you guys were supposed to be smart."

Brennan sidled past the bird to the window. He raised the upper sash and twisted the lock tight. Then he opened the bottom pane as wide as possible. "Here you go. Back outside where you belong, junior."

The bird, more interested in plucking at the journal's decorative metal lock, ignored him.

Another glacial gust ruffled Brennan's hair. "Fine. Stay there. You've got thirty minutes before I close it up for the night." Expecting the crow to fly away in a panic, he strode toward his door—and the bird.

The crow stopped its plucking and skittered to the right as if allowing Brennan clear passage. Eyes warily on the bird, Brennan pulled his keys from his pocket, accidentally flinging a quarter high into the air. It landed faceup on the dirty brown carpet. The bird fluttered its wings, snatched the shiny object off the ground, and soared out the window into the blustery night.

Brennan stared into the darkness until the keys in his hand grew bitter cold and his breath clouded the window with frost. He lowered the sash and twisted the lock with quiet determination. The overhead light at his back cast a shadow on the glass, a black figure with hollow orbs for eyes and no mouth. He raised his hand in a half-hearted wave, and the shadow did the same.

Sleet tapped at the glass like icy fingers on a vintage typewriter. *Go inside. There's nothing to see here.* But the words blurred in streams of melting ice, which slashed away at his shadow until nothing remained except tiny droplets clinging to the pane.

A dull thud interrupted his stupor. He spun around, half expecting to see that the crow had somehow returned. Instead, the hefty journal had slid from its propped position against the door and landed flat on the ground. Brennan scooped it up, unlocked his apartment, and entered a room only marginally warmer than the hall.

The ancient radiators clanged and hissed, their efforts doomed by a cantankerous thermostat that worked only half the time. No matter. A shot of scotch and the cold would disappear in a warm glow.

It took him a while to find the bottle, stashed away in the back of a top kitchen cupboard, far from his curious daughter's grabby hands. Four cut-crystal tumblers, a wedding gift from happier days, sat beside it. He retrieved one and wiped the dust from the tall bottle. The scotch, a gift from his pop, was "for medicinal purposes only." By now, the liquid was aged to amber perfection. His pop would approve.

He plopped into his favorite recliner and sipped at a second shot, savoring its smoky flavor. The journal—Cassie's, he presumed—rested heavy in his lap. The smell of fine leather mingled with that of the scotch. He closed his eyes and inhaled through his nose, waiting for the warm glow in his gut to intensify into a mind-numbing burn. He should go to bed. Big day tomorrow. Confronting a crooked colleague was never easy. Confronting a crooked colleague supported by the mob could be fatal.

The journal shifted with his legs, and he stared at its finely tooled surface embossed with a trio of toga-clad women in classic Greek relief. The Fates, Muses, gods, or ghosts—damned if he knew. He didn't believe in any of them. He flipped it over. The elaborate design repeated on the back. No curlicue hearts. No bold colors. Not the sort of journal one would expect of an eighteen-year-old. Then again, Cassie, with her passion for unsolved murders and vintage photographs, was not your typical teen.

Whether through old-fashioned detective work or bribery, she'd found out where he lived. The thought was vaguely disquieting. Given her macabre obsessions, he doubted her diary contained tales of first dates, young love gone awry, and angst over teenage acne. But what did he know? Elle hadn't made it past age five.

The shimmering amber liquid trembled with his hand. He downed what little remained of his second shot and embraced the burn. Might as well take a peek while he had a decent buzz on. The leather cover creaked at his touch. The parchment-colored pages, thick and fine, whispered as he flipped to the first page bearing ink. Cassie's cursive script—elegant, spare, and so unlike the scribble he'd come to expect from people his age and younger—swam into view.

November 2nd
1st Journal Entry

A single black-and-white photo can damage a man's mind if the image is powerful enough. A thousand can shred it beyond repair. That's what happened to Pap, I suppose—why he simply stopped locking the photo room as if it no longer mattered. The damage to him was done. Mine was about to begin.

He blinked and settled into his chair. Nope. No teenage angst here. The empty glass's crystal facets winked at him from the coffee table. He turned the page and cringed. Thank God for a full bottle of scotch.

The alarm clock jangled, torturing Brennan's hungover brain: 6:00 a.m. Ugh. Eyes shut against the harsh morning light, he groped for his phone. It hit the floor with a thud. The blaring continued. He cursed, opened his eyes, and winced. Poor decisions pay off poorly, his pop used to say, typically after losing an expensive bet. Finishing the scotch had been a piss-poor decision.

Two aspirin and a shower did nothing to improve his mood—or the pounding in his head. He sure as hell hadn't planned to stay up most of the night reading Cassie's journal and case files. And as far as the scotch . . . when he hit the part about Cassie chatting with ghosts of pictures past, finishing the bottle seemed like the thing to do. A dozen more pages and another dawning realization reinforced his decision. It wasn't a diary.

She'd written the journal specifically for him. Started it the day her mother plunged down the stairs. Recorded the last entry yesterday, right before turning over the case files. Then she hand-delivered it to his door.

He stumbled through his morning routine, donning the same crumpled pants he'd worn yesterday and opting to use an electric shaver instead of his razor, thanks to his trembling hands. Too much booze. Too little sleep. A shady colleague. An even shadier boss. And a young girl obsessed with murder who thinks eighty-year-old photos can talk. Just an ordinary day at the office.

He tossed an extra scoop of dark roast into the stainless-steel percolator he'd salvaged from his pop's house before the auction. As a child, the time it took to reach a languorous boil, when the first gentle breath of steam appeared in the plastic cap, was quality time with his pop, usually spent discussing the most recent Phillies game.

As an adult, he'd carried on the tradition—minus the Phillies— with Elle. Now he simply paced the tiny kitchen and waited for the interminable hiss to become a rolling boil, signifying it was time to pour and go.

The heavy percolator shuddered, and a stream of coffee scalded his hand. A flurry of foul language followed. It was a good thing Elle wasn't here to hear that. No. He should never say that. Never.

Coffee in hand, Brennan shrugged his jacket over one arm and headed for the front door, tripping over the open journal he'd tossed on the floor next to the chair. He stopped to retrieve it. The journal was evidence now, evidence of Cassie's state of mind, but it was hers and she'd surely want it back. It weighed heavy in his hand. He hesitated, then quickly snapped photos of her dated entries with his phone. Hopefully, he'd never have to use them.

The morning traffic was stop and go. The giant thermos ran dry somewhere between Vine and Locust. He rushed into the precinct and made a beeline for the bathroom.

As he emerged, a colleague's voice boomed from down the hall. "Hey, Jim-Bo, you're here early. I didn't think you lab rats crawled out of your darkrooms until at least noon."

Jim-Bo. Jim Bonino. Brennan ducked behind the bathroom door. Jim mumbled something about having a meeting with the captain and darkrooms being mostly obsolete, didn't ya know. His footsteps faded into the chatter of the precinct's open workspace. A door slammed, its glass panels vibrating.

Brennan peered around the corner and inched down the hall to the workspace's perimeter. Across the room, Jim, his back to the glass, sat in Captain Mattern's office. His hands gesticulated wildly as he and the captain carried on what appeared to be an animated conversation—at least on Jim's end. The captain had assumed her usual stance:

half sitting on the edge of her desk, arms crossed, face a tight mask of disapproval.

Brennan backed down the hall to the break room and swiped the time clock with his badge. A horde of coworkers milled about, jostling to swipe in on time. He casually acknowledged their pleasantries while considering his next move.

As a rule, CSIs rarely appeared in the precinct. Rarely as in never. And at 8:00 a.m.? He snorted and refilled his thermos from the already half-empty pot. Extraordinary. The situation. Not the coffee.

His cell signaled a text. He sipped the bitter brew and debated whether he should look. He wasn't prepared to talk to Jim or Captain Mattern yet, not without reviewing the photos from Erin's case file. When accusing a colleague, there was no room for error or speculation, and speculation, specifically Pete's wild mob theories, was all Brennan had. Depending on what kind of facts he'd manage to cobble together, he might have to skip over Captain Mattern's head and go directly to Internal Affairs. He cringed at the thought. Right or wrong, the fallout would be nuclear.

His phone buzzed again. He sighed and glanced at the screen.

I need u at the house NOW. Pap fell down the stairs.

Brennan dialed Cassie en route to his car. She answered on the first ring. He slid into the driver's seat and cranked the ignition. "I'm on my way. Did you call 9-1-1?"

"He won't let me. I'm sorry." Her voice quavered. "I didn't know what else to do."

He exhaled with relief. Dolan was alive and barking orders, which counted for something. "How bad is he hurt?"

"I . . . I don't know. He says he's okay, but he doesn't look okay. He's still lying on the stairs. I'm afraid to help him up."

"Don't. Don't move him. I'll be right there." Brennan clicked on his siren and did the Spruce Street slalom, weaving through traffic like a pro. He cut the siren a block from Cassie's house.

During Erin's wake, the tony neighborhood's cobblestone streets had bustled with life. Today, Dolan Mansion stood silent as a sentry, the stillness broken only by the deliberate sweep of the security cameras mounted high above the front door and upper-story windows. Brennan gave a token knock and shook the handle. The heavy oak door creaked on its hinges, its lock not set. He charged through, taking the stairs two at a time.

Like his granddaughter before him, Dolan lay on his back on the second-story landing. Unlike Erin, his skull was intact, and he was anything but still. His rapid, raspy breath filled the staircase. Grimacing, he rolled from side to side, struggling to rise in the awkward, cramped space. Cassie knelt beside him, her hand pressed against his shoulder. She looked at Brennan, her green eyes wild with fear.

Dolan stopped struggling and sagged onto the floor. He turned his head to stare at the detective's worn leather shoes. "Detective Brennan." He coughed, and his face blanched. "What the hell are you doing here?" Despite his obvious distress, his razor-sharp gaze missed nothing.

Brennan crouched beside him. "Just stopped by to check on Cassie. Looks like I picked a good time." The old man's right leg lay twisted outward at an awkward angle. "Cassie, do me a favor and go downstairs to wait for the ambulance so you can let them in."

Cassie, her face taut, nodded and dashed down the stairs.

Dolan closed his eyes. "I don't need a goddamned ambulance. Help me up, and I'll buy you a new pair of shoes."

Brennan ignored his trembling outstretched hand and called dispatch. While giving his report, Brennan did a quick survey of Dolan's condition. In addition to the labored breathing and misshapen right leg, Leland sported a swollen, purple lump below his right eye. His pajama top hung in disarray, with several snaps undone. Brennan frowned and gently tugged one flannel lapel to the side to expose Dolan's chest. Two cherry-red burns, just beginning to blister, covered his rib cage.

"With all due respect, Mr. Dolan, you do need an ambulance. You may have broken your hip." He paused. "What happened?"

The old man opened his milky eyes. "I tripped over my walker and fell down the stairs."

"Is that what you told Cassie?"

"Yes."

"You and I both know that story's not true."

"She didn't believe me either. Smart girl, my little Peach. She didn't say as much, but I saw her look up the stairs for my walker."

"Which I suspect is in your bedroom."

"You suspect right." Dolan coughed again, and his face contorted with pain. "I don't know what you want me to say. I'm old. Old people fall."

"The burns on your chest. I've seen similar marks before."

Dolan's writhing stopped, and his expression stiffened. If it weren't for the rapid rise and fall of his chest, Brennan would've thought the old man had died.

"Where?" The word, soft as a sigh, whistled through Dolan's pursed, blue lips.

"At your granddaughter's autopsy."

Dolan's lower jaw quivered. Outside, a siren wailed, becoming progressively louder. Inside, the foyer's grandfather clock ticked in time with Dolan's harsh breath. Brennan, his feet tingling from crouching too long, shifted his weight. "What happened here, Mr. Dolan? I can't help if you don't tell me the truth."

The old man grabbed Brennan's forearm and, with surprising strength, tugged him off balance. He landed on his hands and knees, his ear inches from Dolan's mouth.

"Watch over Cassie. Get her out of this house." Dolan gasped for breath, his voice a hoarse whisper. "Don't let them hurt her. She already has . . ."

"Has what?" Brennan pried the old man's bony fingers from around his forearm. "Who are you afraid of, Mr. Dolan? Beck McConnell and his clan? *La Famiglia*?"

The old man groaned.

"Who, Leland?"

The siren stopped screeching. A gust of cold air rushed up the staircase. A metal gurney's clatter mingled with muted voices. "Do you hear that?" Dolan's ashen cheeks slackened. "The ambulance is here." Brennan pressed his fingers to the old man's wrist, monitoring his thready pulse. "No. It sounds like music, piano music." Dolan turned his head to gaze up the stairs. His eyelids drifted shut. "It's haunting, don't you think?"

———

Cassie insisted upon riding in the ambulance with her pap. With his siren blaring, Brennan tailed them to Jefferson Hospital and followed behind the gurney as they whisked Dolan through the ER's automatic doors.

Dolan's legend ensured exemplary attention and service. Within two hours he'd been evaluated, diagnosed with a broken right hip, and scheduled for surgery later that day to have the pieces pinned into place. Throughout the ordeal, Cassie stoically held her pap's hand. After the morphine stole his coherence, she signed the surgical consent, functioning as his representative, as Dolan had designated upon admission.

They wheeled him to the OR shortly after noon. By then, Brennan's stomach burned from too much coffee and no food. He looked at Cassie's pale, drawn face and forced a smile. "It's gonna take a while, they said. How about we get some lunch?"

Before she could answer, the room's curtain fluttered aside. Ryan McConnell, his face tense with barely contained rage, charged in. He stopped an arm's length from Cassie. "Do you want to know how I found out about your pap's admission? I saw his name on the OR schedule, that's how. Do you have any idea how embarrassing that was?" He turned his anger on Brennan. "Why wasn't I notified? And what the hell are you doing here?"

The corner of Brennan's mouth twitched. "You're the second person today to ask me that question."

Cassie stood. "You weren't notified because Pap made me his emergency contact. He clearly stated that even though you work here, you're not allowed to access his medical information. He has that right, he says."

Ryan's face flushed. "You're not fit to be his legal representative."

"I'm eighteen. That makes me legal, right Detective Brennan?"

Brennan suppressed a grin. "Correct. I'm afraid, Dr. McConnell, that Leland Dolan, being of sound mind, can make any adult his emergency contact and give them medical power of attorney. As far as being notified, the HIPAA laws state—"

"I'm well versed in the HIPAA laws, Detective." Ryan pointed at Brennan. "You and I need to talk." He turned his back and stalked out the door.

Brennan shot Cassie a reassuring smile. "I'll be right back. Don't go to lunch without me." He followed Ryan down the hall to an empty triage room.

Ryan slammed the door behind them. "What happened?"

"Your grandfather-in-law fell down the steps and broke his hip."

"How?"

"He told me he tripped over his walker."

Ryan, his white lab coat fluttering around his hips, paced the small room. "Do you believe him?"

"Is there a reason I shouldn't?"

"Don't you think it's a little odd that he, too, fell down the stairs so soon after Erin's accident?"

"No odder than your wife and mistress dying within two weeks of each other."

Ryan abruptly stopped pacing. "I hadn't seen Amber since the wake. Our . . . relationship was over."

"Uh-huh. And Mr. Dolan was used to having Erin there to help him get dressed and serve his breakfast. Without her assistance, he was on his—"

"Cassie was home." Ryan's eyes narrowed. "She was home the day Erin died too."

"No, she was not home the day her mother died. I saw her at the library."

"It's walking distance from the house. Maybe you were meant to see her at the library."

"That's ridiculous. I hadn't even been assigned the case yet." Brennan's eyes narrowed. "What are you implying, Dr. McConnell? Are you accusing your own daughter of murder?"

"Every murderer has a father, Detective."

"You don't say? And here I thought they just fell from the sky like acid rain."

"Cassie is mentally unstable. Surely she's told you by now about her imaginary friends. She'll tell anyone who'll listen."

Brennan remained silent.

"She hears voices, Detective. Talks to people who aren't there. Is obsessed with murder. Gets violent when crossed. Suffers blackouts that go beyond her seizure disorder. She probably has schizophrenia or at least a schizoaffective disorder."

Brennan frowned. "She gets violent? In what way?"

Ryan's lips curled in a humorless smile. "Sorry. HIPAA laws, you know. They're even stricter when it comes to a patient's mental-health history."

"And they also don't apply when dealing with law enforcement. Your daughter's mental illness or lack thereof has a direct bearing on my investigation. Who diagnosed her—you? I thought you were a surgeon, not a psychiatrist."

"My medical degree makes me more of a psychiatrist than your badge does. You don't think Erin and I sought help? Cassie has seen the best money can buy—neurologists, neuropsychologists, psychiatrists—you name it. She's run through the entire alphabet of medications. They keep her calm at best."

I needed—still need—to quiet their voices.

Brennan frowned as he recalled a passage from Cassie's journal. "She seems calm to me."

"You're not around her twenty-four-seven. She gets up in the middle of the night and pounds on the piano. The same dozen notes, over and over. Locks herself in the music room for no reason. Stares into space for hours, like she's channeling God, or something. Leland's not much better. The bastard's losing his mind."

Ryan ran a hand through his wavy hair. "Look, my wife fell down the stairs. Your poking around is not going to bring her back. All it's going to do is feed into Cassie's psychosis and Leland's hatred of everything to do with the McConnell name. You seem like a decent man. If you want what's best for Cassie and your career, just let it go."

"Are you threatening me, Dr. McConnell?"

Ryan opened the door. "Come near me again, and my family's lawyer will be asking you that same question."

"One more thing, then, before you go." Brennan rummaged in his pocket and pulled out the photo of the marks on Erin's chest. He handed it to Ryan. "The coroner found these on Erin's chest and back. He says they're burns. I noticed similar marks on Mr. Dolan's chest today. I also found a defibrillator marked as hospital property in your closet. Care to explain?"

"The hospital sold the old AEDs when they updated to new ones. I bought one. Never had to use it, thank God. You can interrogate it if you like. It has a memory card that records every time it's used and stores the details of a resuscitation. I can access my credit-card receipt online too, if you need it."

"Then how do you explain the burns? The coroner says they were deep; they ran all the way through your wife's body. Any theories?"

Ryan held the photo under the bright, sterile light of a gooseneck lamp. He shook his head slowly. "No." His face clouded with confusion. "Burns. No."

He thrust the photo back into Brennan's hands. "I have no idea. It doesn't matter. She's gone. Now let the dead rest in peace."

CHAPTER

20

Brennan watched Ryan McConnell storm down the gleaming corridor and disappear into the room where they'd left Cassie waiting. The father-daughter huddle lasted less than a minute. They exited together. Ryan scowled when he caught sight of Brennan loitering outside the triage room. The surgeon steered Cassie toward the ER's employee exit. After a final pointed look over his shoulder, Ryan huffed away, presumably to finish whatever super-important doctorly work he'd been doing before Dolan's inconvenient injury dared to interrupt. Brennan's phone buzzed. He wasn't surprised.

Meet me outside the main entrance.

He followed the red exit signs to the sliding glass door. Cassie, dressed in a cable-knit sweater and corduroy jeans, stood shivering in the brisk air.

"Coat?" Brennan asked.

"I forgot to grab one. Too much drama."

He shrugged his off and held it out. "You okay?"

She slung it over her slim shoulders. "Yeah, thanks. No matter what my father said, I want to be here when Pap comes out of surgery. I don't want him to wake up alone." Despite the warm jacket, she shivered again. "*If* he wakes up. His breathing is terrible. The orthopedist told me Pap's bad lungs plus his age make him a high-risk surgery."

"The orthopedist clearly doesn't know the legendary Leland Dolan. If anyone can pull through a situation like this, he can." He flashed a wry grin. "C'mon, let's get some lunch before I get hangry."

The city blocks surrounding the hospital hosted dozens of eateries, ranging from tiny falafel shops to chic bistros. They settled on a homey Italian café. Brennan picked a spot in the corner near the emergency exit, bypassing two closer, empty tables. Cassie raised an eyebrow.

"Habit." He shrugged. "Any cop worth his badge would never sit with his back to the front door."

She perched daintily on the wooden seat and sighed. "It's been so long since I've been in a restaurant." She smiled at the rustic old-world décor. "All we need is a strolling accordion player."

"Your parents never took you out to eat?"

"No." She averted her eyes. "They were afraid I'd embarrass them."

"Why? You eat with your feet or something?"

She burst out laughing. "How'd you know?"

"Lucky guess." He studied her while she perused the menu. Dark circles under her eyes marred her porcelain skin, and both hands shook with a fine, barely perceptible tremor. Below her thumb on her left inner wrist, a well-healed scar pulsed with each beat of her heart.

She lowered the menu at the waitress's approach and caught him staring. Cassie tugged her sleeve over her wrist. "I'll have a bowl of the pasta *e fagioli* and a glass of water, please. No straw."

Brennan handed the waitress his menu. "And I'll have a stromboli and an iced tea. No straw for me, either. Save the sea turtles."

The waitress, white hair teased higher than a cloud of meringue, tucked the straws into her apron and strolled away.

Cassie fidgeted in her chair. "Did you read my journal?"

"Yes. It's in my car. Don't let me forget to give it back to you." Brennan bobbed his head toward her scarred wrist. "What happened?"

"Not what you think. I have a collection of scars from my past seizures. I fall and bang into things. Sometimes those things are sharp. You should know. You saw me have one."

"That I did."

The waitress slid their drinks onto the table.

Brennan ripped open a packet of sugar and dumped it in his tea. "You handled today like a champ. I know you're an adult, but will you be okay at home alone? Your pap will probably be in the hospital for a few days, and I imagine your father works long hours—"

Cassie snorted. "My father works just enough to keep up appearances and have some spending money to blow on his man-toys—golf, gadgets, and girlfriends."

"Yeah, about that . . ." He softened his tone. "Amber's dead."

"Father already told me."

"I know she tutored you for years."

"So? What's your point?"

"Okay, then." Brennan hid his surprise by stirring the sugar into his tea, swirling the ice until it tinkled in the tall glass. He'd expected at least a titch of sadness. Clearly, he expected too much.

"As I was saying, Pap's money pays for everything else. My mother's job was to manage the household and budget, although Pap still oversaw everything having to do with his fortune. Says running the numbers keeps his mind sharp. He had a hard time adjusting when he sold his empire in his mid-seventies. He didn't retire until after I was born."

She stopped abruptly. "I'm babbling, aren't I? My father would be furious if he knew I was telling you this."

"Which is why I asked if you were going to be okay at home. You two don't seem to have the best relationship—"

"We hate each other."

Brennan raised an eyebrow. Cassie's emotional response was typical of the sullen teens he frequently encountered in his line of work. But until now, she'd demonstrated composure beyond her years. He set his spoon on the table. "Okay. You hate each other. The way I see it, your pap is the buffer, and he's in the hospital."

Her eyes glinted. "I don't need a buffer."

The waitress returned balancing a tray laden with food. She carefully set Cassie's soup on the table. A loud crash from the kitchen turned everyone's heads. She plopped Brennan's overstuffed stromboli onto the checkered tablecloth and, yelling in Italian, hurried back to the kitchen.

Cassie spoke over the din. "Isolation fosters self-reliance. I've been alone since age twelve, when my parents pulled me out of school. I had my parents, Pap, and Amber—that's it." She stirred her hot soup daintily, releasing a billow of steam. "My 'developmental circle of influence,' as my child psychiatrist called it. I think he found it a bit dysfunctional."

"I bet he did." Brennan carved himself a generous hunk of stromboli. "What about Ruth? You forgot about her. She was there too, according to your journal."

Cassie stopped stirring.

He shoved the chunk of stromboli in his mouth and allowed the silence to linger, gauging her reaction with interest.

She stared at the steaming liquid in front of her. "Ruth would never allow me to forget." She lowered her voice. "Do you believe me?"

"Which part?"

"That the photos talk to me. That their people tell me their stories."

"No."

Cassie closed her eyes.

"Not yet." Brennan paused to wipe a blob of sauce from his chin, and Cassie's eyes flew open. "Here's what I learned from reviewing the case files and your journal: You're a talented, self-taught investigator with meticulous attention to detail who was able to re-create and solve cold cases based on nothing more than faded photographs with dates scribbled on the back. You believe you get intel from the people pictured, primarily a young murderess named Ruth, who sounds like a charming piece of work, by the way."

"Ruth is my friend. She tells me the truth."

"I think you figure out the truth on your own. You don't give yourself enough credit."

Cassie shook her head. "No. It's not just me. I couldn't do it alone. I was hoping . . ." Her voice cracked. "I'd hoped you'd be the one who believed me. It's hard for me to talk about it. That's why I wrote the journal instead. Everyone else I've told thinks I'm crazy."

They finished their meal in silence. Cassie, her expression distant, sipped her soup half-heartedly. Brennan, however, thoroughly enjoyed his stromboli, swirling the last bit of dough around his plate to catch any remaining smears of sauce.

He crumpled his napkin and tossed it next to his empty plate. "You want dessert, or are you done?"

"Are you sure you don't want to lick your plate first?"

Brennan grinned. "I appreciate good food, but I'm no savage. My pop taught me some manners."

She stood. "I'm done, then. I should head back to the hospital to wait for Pap."

Outside the cozy bistro, the cold air burned like a slap in the face. Cassie took a shuddering breath and turned to face Brennan. "What would it take for you to believe me?"

"Cassie—"

"No, really. I've got four unsolved murders I need your help with, remember? I only gave you two of those files."

"And I only read one—Ruth's. That was enough."

"They're important to me. If we're going to work them together, we need to trust each other."

Brennan sighed a plume of frosty breath. A trio of intrepid pigeons pecked the concrete at his feet, seeking a handout. He stomped, and they jittered away. The pin in his pants pocket jabbed his thigh. Elle. He pushed the image of her smiling face out of his mind and shivered. Cassie still had his coat, and the air felt way colder than when they'd left the hospital. He shoved his hands in his pockets, fingered the icy metallic disc, and walked toward the corner.

She matched his pace. The pedestrian walk light disappeared when they reached the intersection. She stopped on the curb. "Well, Detective?"

"I never said I would work with you on those cold cases. I have your mother's investigation to finish, and Captain Mattern is not a patient woman. And since we're on the subject of trust, how'd you find out where I live?"

Cassie looked at the gray sky, the traffic, the storefronts—everywhere but his face. "I'd rather not say."

"Trust is a two-way street."

She hesitated, dragging her toe across the concrete in random lines. "My father sometimes does his charting from home on the computer. I know his password. I logged in, accessed your daughter's medical record, and found your address there." She stared at her sneaker-clad feet. "I'm sorry. I knew it was wrong, but I did it anyway."

"Wrong and illegal." *And clever.* Brennan sighed. "Don't show up at my apartment again. If anyone sees you, I could lose my job."

"I said I was sorry." She lowered her voice. "Ruth was right. She said I shouldn't tell you anything, shouldn't bring an outsider into our business."

"Ah, yes. Good old Ruth. Our favorite serial husband-killer. Who does Ruth say murdered your mother?"

"I told you that in my journal. She says my father did it."

"Yeah, well, Amber told me your Pap did it. Your father says it was you."

Her brittle laugh triggered furtive glances from passersby. "I'm not surprised. I sometimes think he's afraid of me. I know the seizures terrified my mother. And after I told my parents about the voices . . . Did he tell you they had me exorcised? A full-blown Catholic exorcism, for God's sake. As if the Dolans and the McConnells were your typical devout Irish families. Not."

The light changed, and they hurried through the intersection. The crowd thinned when they rounded the corner toward the hospital. Cassie stopped in the middle of the sidewalk, seemingly oblivious to the pedestrians streaming past. "The truth is, it's not God or the devil or my seizures. It's not the meds or mental illness. This is who I am. It's like my super-recognizer ability—a curse or a gift, depending on the day, the need, and my mood. On a good day, those voices are my friends."

"But not every day is a good day," Brennan pointed out, gently pulling her to the side of the walk.

"No." An ambulance screamed by, its desperation reflected in Cassie's bleak eyes. "Sometimes, if I'm lonely and I need to talk, I don't take my medicines. Their voices are clearer then. Otherwise, they sound distant, like they've traveled through a pond of murky water."

The desperation in her voice grew sharper. "Other people hear them too. I'm sure of it. I can't be the only one. Like schizophrenics— what if the things they see and hear are real? I think humans can be tuned to different frequencies, like other animals that can see infrared and ultraviolet light or hear things we can't."

An amber-eyed cat yowled from a side street and darted across their path as if the devil had its tail. A huge crow swooped behind, cawing its displeasure. Cassie jumped. "See? Cats, crows, the schizophrenics, and me."

The cat skirted a garbage bin and dashed across the street. As if aware of their gaze, it stopped and hissed before disappearing into the shadows of a narrow alley. A flock of panicked doves flew to the safety of the nearest roof, leaving the crow as the alley's sole guardian. It perched on a pile of wooden pallets and watched Brennan and Cassie as they resumed their walk down the street.

Something fluttered from behind, and Brennan glanced over his shoulder. The crow was gone. "I don't know about alley cats and crows, but we collared a schizo once, my old partner and I. Dude was running down Broad in nothing but a pair of boots. Thought Tom, my partner, was a vampire. Tried to impale him with a hockey stick. I'm pretty sure whatever frequency he was tuned to wasn't real."

"Yeah? How well did you know your partner?" Cassie's cheek dimpled with a wry grin, and he laughed.

"Well enough to know he didn't drink blood. Now, booze—that's a whole other story."

His car was parked next to the ambulance bay in a spot reserved for law enforcement. He grabbed her journal off the passenger seat and handed it to her. She tucked it silently beneath her arm. They stopped short of the hospital's main entrance to avoid triggering the sliding glass doors. A handful of visitors passed in and out, some carrying flowers, books, and other gifts to make their loved ones' stays marginally more pleasant.

The brief moment of levity drowned in a melancholic wave. His old partner had died here shortly after retirement. So had Elle. In the months before his world collapsed, Brennan had been a happy husband, a doting father, and a detective in his prime. He'd failed to appreciate a single damned day of it. This case was supposed to—how had Pete put it?—give him his mojo back. Instead, he was ass deep in the McConnell family's dirty laundry with no conclusions in sight.

"Detective?" Cassie, her head cocked, was staring at his face.

"Sorry. Zoned out for a minute."

"I know the feeling."

Brennan nodded absently. "Tell your pap I wish him a speedy recovery. Maybe I'll swing by to talk to him sometime during his stay. Text me if you need anything, okay?"

"Okay." Cassie shrugged off his coat and held it out for him. "You might need this. I'll steal my father's from the doctor's lounge."

"You'll borrow it."

"That's what I said." The sliding doors whooshed open, releasing a burst of heat. "I'm not giving up, you know. I solved six cases on my own already. I will solve those last four cases eventually, with or without your help."

"I believe you."

"That's a start."

CHAPTER

21

The evidence-collection clerk, a short, plump lady who cracked her gum with the ferocity of an insolent teenager, was displeased. She hefted herself off the stool and slammed her magazine onto the counter.

"Third time today," she said, as she huffed behind the locked bulletproof partition to retrieve Amber Servello's personal effects. "You know they take pictures of this stuff for the case file, right?"

"Of course I do, Stella," Brennan said in his most conciliatory voice, "but then I wouldn't get to see your smiling face."

"Just sign in, will ya."

Pen in hand, he flipped the logbook open. While Stella donned a pair of nitrile gloves and unbagged the evidence for display, he scanned through the day's previous entries. His lips pursed in a silent whistle.

Stella, her task completed, tapped her foot and stared longingly at the gossip mag splayed on the counter. "You forget your name or what?"

"I bet you didn't ask the captain that question." Brennan added his scrawled signature below Pete's and Captain Mattern's.

"You know I didn't. She's not famous for her sense of humor, am I right?"

"You most certainly are, Stella."

Brennan studied the paltry display. A thin gold toe ring. A scratched, faceted blue-stone ring which even he could tell was fake. And a gold heart necklace with a tiny embedded diamond. "Anything written on the necklace?"

"You mean like an inscription? Nah. Captain asked the same thing. Great minds think alike, I guess."

"I guess."

"I was kind of surprised to see her, to tell ya the truth. She hasn't worked the beat in years. Came in with a big guy in a super-nice suit, complete with a green silk handkerchief—snazzier than any cop I know. Must be onto something special." Stella eagerly leaned over the counter, her eyes begging him to drop even the smallest morsel of gossip.

Beck McConnell. He'd bet his badge on it. Brennan shrugged. "No idea. Maybe she just got tired of sitting behind her glass walls."

Stella's face fell. "Maybe." She gathered the jewelry and tossed each piece into individual evidence bags. "We good here?"

"Yeah, Stella. We're good."

Brennan stared at his ancient monitor and pounded the enter button for what seemed like the thousandth time. If there's a modern life lesson that trumps all the rest, it's that computers freeze when needed the most.

Like when a case report is due in three days and the boss is buzzing around her office like a hornet on meth.

Detective Tan sat at the desk to his right. She rolled her office chair next to Brennan's and shook her head. "The black screen of death. That's bad. Did you try restarting it?"

"Yes, I tried restarting it." Brennan tossed his pen on the desk, and his colleague rolled away. He glared across the room at the captain, cell phone pressed to her ear, pacing her glass-enclosed office. They needed to have a heart-to-heart, but not before he compared what he'd seen in evidence collection to Jim's official photos from the scene. Which, at this rate, might be never.

The black screen flickered, and the hard drive roared to life. Finally. A few keystrokes later, his suspicions were confirmed. Like Erin's neck, Amber's broken fingers were bare, save the fake sapphire ring. The bling was gone, stripped by Jim's expert editing.

Brennan leaned back in his chair and sipped his tepid, hours-old coffee. A spark of anger kindled, souring his stomach. Stealing from the dead. Jesus. Pete was right. He'd seen Amber's rings, several thousand dollars' worth, with his own eyes. Whatever the mob paid, it was apparently not enough.

Not enough for Jim anyway.

His phone rang, the tone signaling a call from Pete. Brennan answered in a low voice. "It's Brennan."

"Did you forget our run at four? Today's the day. We're getting back into shape, remember?"

The only shape Pete, lover of all doughnuts, cared about was round with a hole in the middle. Pete did not run and never would run unless chasing a truck full of Krispy Kremes. Maybe not even then.

Brennan glanced at the clock. 4:05. "Yeah, sorry about that. I got caught up in something. I gotta get changed. Where are we meeting again?"

"Penn's Landing."

"Right. See you in twenty." He gulped the last swig of bitter coffee and grimaced. No time to go home and change. This ought to be good, especially since he was wearing a shirt and tie. He jogged down the stairs to the basement.

The precinct's locker room had been repainted a sunny yellow since the last time Brennan worked out, and the fumes added to the noxious odor. He rubbed his nose. Sweat, chlorine, and now volatile organic compounds, all trapped in a humid, windowless environment utilizing an HVAC system from the 1930s.

A set of swinging double doors, damp with condensation, led to the in-ground pool. He peeked through. The water trembled constantly, agitated by the traffic from the streets above. Original to the building, the pool was considered state of the art in its day. He shuddered to think what life forms lurked in its outdated filtration system.

He blew the dust off the combination lock securing his locker and fumbled with the code. The series of numbers, a combination of Elle's and Julia's birthdays, was his clever way of remembering important dates—daily reinforcement back when he used to swim with Jim, who ragged him about the need to stay fit. He'd missed his wife's birthday once. Big mistake. Never wanted to live through that again. He changed the combination on his lock the day after.

The lock clicked; he tugged on the rusty metal door. It shuddered open, releasing a blast of stale odors. He held his breath and took inventory. Sneakers, crusty socks, a ratty police department tee, and a pair of shorts, all of which should've been laundered long ago. For today, they'd have to do. He changed quickly before he had time to ponder what might be living in his sneakers.

His wife and daughter smiled at him from the photo taped inside the metal door. Below it hung one of Elle's crayon masterpieces, an intersection of black squiggly lines coated with purple-glitter glue stick. Her friend the crow. Most little girls drew ponies and rainbows. Not Elle.

He peeled the drawing off the locker door, folded it into his pants pocket next to the pin, and carried his wadded-up clothing with him to the car. By the time he and Pete finished their "jog," it would be quitting time. Besides, the basement, dimly lit by flickering overhead bulbs and old-fashioned wall sconces, was creepy as hell at night. Especially the pool.

The Delaware riverfront was a short drive down Chestnut. Brennan found Pete sitting on a bench near the twelve-foot-high Irish memorial to *An Gorta Mor*—the Great Hunger. The metal sculpture glowed in the shadowy light of the setting sun. Haunting, hollow-eyed faces cast in stark relief. Desperation etched in bronze.

Gaunt with starvation, these men, women, and children had escaped Ireland's potato famine by making the perilous journey across the Atlantic to the ports of Philadelphia. The statue was more than a memorial. It was a warning. Remember the hunger. Starvation is only ever a blight away.

A little girl clung to her mother, bronze cheek pressed against bronze cheek. Brennan tore his gaze from the sculpture's gleaming surface. "Shouldn't you be stretching?"

He eyed Pete's terry sweatband and too-tight bicycle shorts. "The eighties called. They want their Spandex back."

"Funny. At least I don't reek. You smell worse than my clients."

"Clients? Your 'clients' are dead."

"Exactly. And some of them have been for weeks. Make sure you stay downwind." Pete looked over his shoulder. "Let's walk."

Brennan matched Pete's surprisingly brisk pace. "What's this about, Pete?"

"Someone was kind enough to send me an old-fashioned note today. Found it lying on my keyboard—the computer is totally fried, by the way—when I got back from lunch." He unzipped his teal fanny pack and removed a piece of paper. "I'll unfold it and hold it up for you to read. It already has my prints on it, unfortunately. I picked it up with my bare hands not knowing it would turn out to be so, um, relevant."

The paper was standard white printer stock with eight words typed in a large, bold font.

LET IT GO. REGRET, LIKE DEATH, IS PERMANENT.

Brennan stared at the neatly centered words. "Relevant doesn't begin to cover it, Pete. You've been threatened."

"We've been threatened, I'm afraid." Pete dipped his fingers inside the nylon fanny pack and removed a plastic sandwich bag, which he held to the light. A shiny object winked back. "After reading the letter, I was smart enough to don gloves."

Brennan gasped, and his hand automatically went to his hip. The metal pin, Elle's pin, was identical to the one stuffed in the pocket of his dress pants tossed on the backseat of his car.

Pete, his expression solemn, nodded. "I know. We're in deep, my friend. I'm so sorry I dragged you into this. I should've gone straight to Internal Affairs, then washed my hands of the whole thing."

"Yet you visited evidence collection earlier this morning."

Pete winced. "I know, I know. First time ever. Had no idea you had to sign in. Stupid. But if I would've turned tail and left, I'm sure that nosy desk clerk would've been suspicious."

"Stella does have a nose for gossip. Seriously, Pete, I know I complimented your investigative prowess, but you need to stay in your lane. Leave the detective work to me or you're liable to end up deader than your clients."

"*Deader* is not a word."

"We're not doing this right now. You know what I mean."

"I do, I do." Pete fussed with his sweatband. "I went because I needed validation. I had to see for myself that this wasn't some sort of paranoid conspiracy theory I'd built in my head. That I'm not crazy."

"That little love note is all the validation you need."

Footsteps pounded the pavement behind them. Pete and Brennan jumped aside to allow a solitary runner to sprint past, her hand raised in a friendly wave. Brennan eyed her warily until she disappeared into the horizon.

He took a deep breath. "Okay. Let's back up here. You said you found the letter on your keyboard when you got back from lunch. What about your secretary? What's her name again?"

"Joan. Also at lunch."

"You have to be buzzed into the morgue."

"Unless you have an employee badge with a magnetic stripe on the back to unlock the door. The reader's outside on the wall. You know. You've used it before."

"Your secretary usually beats me to it. How many people have access?"

"More than you'd think. City employees across multiple departments, which include several satellite buildings, use the same badge reader. We're talking hundreds of people. Besides, someone could've easily stolen one. People leave them sitting around all the time. I know I've been guilty of that."

"Badge readers keep a log for at least twenty-four hours, and some have programs that download the data to a server for indefinite storage. I can ask IT to query it." Brennan made a mental note to also check with the human resources department for anyone reporting a lost or stolen badge. "You said your computer was fried. What exactly does that mean?"

"According to the help desk, it means—and I quote—'catastrophic hard-drive failure, files unrecoverable.' They essentially shrugged their shoulders and said it wasn't surprising considering its age. But here's the kicker—all the autopsy reports I filed in the past eight days aren't in the main server's database either. IT said I must've forgotten to back them up, which is a crock of shit. They autopopulate into the cloud at the end of each workday. I know I look like an old fart, but I'm not as techno-dumb as they think."

Brennan's heart sank.

Eight days was just enough time to include both Erin McConnell's and Amber Servello's files.

A long-haired teen on a skateboard weaved by. He grinned and gave Pete a double thumbs-up. "Nice fanny pack, dude."

Pete flipped him the bird and carefully deposited the letter and bag back in the pack. "Will the pin help narrow down the list of suspects? I remember you handing them out a while ago when . . . when . . ."

"When Elle was getting her chemo. Nope. We ordered three hundred of them. The hospital employees and pretty much every cop in the precinct got one. You know—'Team Elle'"—he made air quotes—"for all the good it did."

Pete stared at the ground.

Brennan ran a hand through his hair. "Sorry. That sounded harsh. Julia and I appreciated all the support. We really did. And I know it gave Elle a thrill to see people wearing her pin. I just didn't expect to keep seeing them for months after she died. They're popping up everywhere, it seems."

Laughter floated through the crisp air. A group of chatty teens rounded a bend in the Riverwalk ahead. Brennan spun on his heel. "We should head back."

Pete nodded and picked up the pace. "What comes next?"

"For you, nothing. Go about your business as usual. Exercise common-sense precautions. Lock your doors, maybe get some pepper spray. As for me, I've got some good old-fashioned detective work to do. Color laser printers use embedded metadata—little yellow dots that code the time, date, and often the printer's serial number. I'll follow up on the badge reader and send your note," he held out his hand, "to processing for prints and metadata analysis—"

"No."

They stopped where they'd begun, at a bench in front of the Irish monument.

"It's evidence, Pete."

"I'm out. I know how to heed a warning." He ran a palm over his sweaty forehead. "I have eight days of autopsy reports to redo and file. Erin McConnell's new, finalized report will list her cause of death as traumatic brain injury due to a mechanical fall, accidental, period. No hedging. And Jim can keep stealing all the trinkets his little heart desires. The dead don't care."

"Pete—"

"One of us still has a family, Dan."

Brennan jerked to a stop. The mournful blast from a river barge's horn fractured the long silence.

Pete averted his eyes. "Look, I'm sorry. Sorry for everything. Lord knows I want to see Jim punished. But this can't go any further. And I'd appreciate you not getting us both killed."

He took off in an actual jog, huffing and puffing to his drab beige minivan parked a half-block down the street. The vehicle merged into Front-Street traffic and disappeared.

The chilly breeze off the river ruffled Brennan's hair. He shivered, suddenly cold in his thin tee shirt and crusty shorts. He returned to his car and tried to organize his muddled thoughts using a technique he learned in therapy: Create a mental checklist.

Number one: he couldn't let this go. Hard stop. Number two: he had a report due in a little over forty-eight hours. What he said in that report could impact his and Pete's careers—and their lives. Number three: he couldn't rely on Pete to back him up. He couldn't blame him. They'd both seen what the mob did to Amber.

He started the car, gripped the steering wheel, and stared out the windshield at a sheet of newspaper fluttering down the sidewalk. Driven by the November wind, it swirled around pedestrian legs until a man in a long wool coat stomped it to the ground.

Now that Brennan knew what he couldn't do, he had one hard question yet to answer: Could he live with himself if the outcome turned bad? Was proving Jim's guilt worth Pete's life?

He closed his eyes. Images from crime scenes past, each more graphic than the last, flashed through his mind. Bile burnt the back of his throat. Twenty years of work, most of it spent in Homicide, had hardened his soul, but if there's one thing he learned from losing Elle, it's that death is different when it's one of your own. When you're the one who has to tell the family. Write the eulogy. Attend the funeral.

He sat in the idling car until the windows steamed over and he was forced to turn on the defroster. As the windshield cleared, so did his mind. Erin and Amber's deaths, along with their missing jewelry, were inherently connected in some obscure, convoluted way, but his report didn't have to say so. Amber's case wasn't his. Jim's thievery predated Erin. The mob was the common thread, and they fell under the Organized Crime Unit's jurisdiction or, depending on how high up the food chain the connection went, to Internal Affairs.

A brief, generic report listing Erin's death as suspicious but with inconclusive evidence could buy him time. Captain Mattern would shelve the case for sure, particularly with a normal autopsy. But a cold case can be reopened, and he could amend his report later—after he developed a plan on how to investigate further without endangering Pete. He'd amassed a lot of contacts over the past twenty years; someone would be willing to help. It would have to be on his own dime and time. Off the record. On the q.t. But he'd expose the corruption, the rot within their ranks. The truth would come out eventually. Until then, he'd still have his integrity, if not his reputation.

He drove home on autopilot. His apartment building's underground parking deck only had one elevator, and it moved slower than Leland Dolan. Tonight, it wasn't moving at all. Brennan pressed the button repeatedly but to no avail. No light. No sound of gears and cables lurching into motion. No nothing.

With a heavy sigh, he tucked the bundle of dress clothes under his arm and tugged on the stairwell door. It creaked open, releasing a swirl of dust. The peeling green paint, flickering lights, and crumbling cement steps spoke of a building in decline, left to decay in favor of its younger and flashier counterpart across the street. But the rent was cheap, and he had no one left to impress.

Thirteen flights. He chugged ten, walked three, and cursed them all. Sweaty and gasping for breath, he exited the stairwell and fumbled for his keys. He used to run those stairs. He had to get back into shape. Tomorrow. He'd start tomorrow.

At the far end of the hallway, the elevator dinged.

He stared over his right shoulder. The door slid open. No one got out. To his left, the window's upper sash dropped open with a bang. A gust of frigid air blasted through the narrow corridor. A glossy black feather floated to the floor.

His keys swayed in the lock, their delicate jingle overpowered by the sound of Brennan's ragged breath. The elevator door slid shut, and the numbers dropped one by one as it trundled back to the ground level. He opened the door to his apartment and tossed his clothes inside. Then, he strode to the end of the hall and closed the window, securing the faulty latch as he'd done yesterday.

Or so he thought.

The feather, black with a faint purple iridescence, shimmered against the dull brown carpet. He stooped to retrieve the quill, twirling and brushing its downy fluff with his callused fingers. It was perfect, the sort of treasure that would've made Elle squeal with delight. Another gift from her friend the crow.

Maybe the bird didn't realize she was gone. Or perhaps it knew and felt sorry for him. He scowled and shook his head. He drank too much and slept too little last night, and today—well, today had been a cluster from the get-go. But, Jesus, he was losing his damned mind. Pitied by a stupid bird. How pathetic can one man get?

He locked the door behind him and peeled off his crusty clothes. A hot shower washed the filth away. Clad in a clean pair of sweatpants and a Flyers tee, he emerged from his bedroom refreshed and hungry for a good meal. He glanced in his barren fridge. Frozen potpie and beer. Maybe he should order Chinese instead. His stomach grumbled at the thought of waiting for delivery. Potpie it was, then.

While the microwave worked its magic, he dialed the precinct's IT hotline. After a four-minute hold, his call was answered by a bored tech with a North Jersey accent and an attitude to match.

The tech yawned. "You know we're half staffed after five o'clock. Nightshift only handles urgent requests."

Brennan, phone tucked under his ear, reached into the fridge for the last, lonely bottle of beer. "This is an urgent request."

"Yeah, that's what they all say. Did you place an electronic work order?"

"No, I did not place a work order."

"You need to place a work order."

The cap flew off the bottle and bounced into the sink and down the drain. Brennan cursed under his breath. "I don't think that would be in either of our best interests."

"Say again?"

"Due to the sensitive nature of the inquiry. You can either give the info to me now real quiet-like or I can have Internal Affairs pay a much louder visit."

The microwave dinged. The tech cleared his throat. "What do you need?"

"The badge reader outside the morgue. I need it interrogated."

"What time frame?"

"Today, between late morning and mid-afternoon."

"Oh." The relief in the tech's voice was audible. The keyboard clacked a staccato rhythm. "Got it right here. Quick and easy. Three names—"

"Skip Peter and Joan. Who's the third?" Brennan removed the steaming-hot potpie from the microwave and sniffed appreciatively.

"Tom. Tom Marvin. Do you know him?"

Brennan dropped the dish onto the table. The potpie's fragile center crust deflated, sinking into a pool of peas and gravy. "That has to be a mistake. Check again."

"I don't need to check again. The scanners don't make mistakes."

"Yeah? Well, I know Tom Marvin. He was my partner, and he's been stone-cold dead for over a year."

CHAPTER

22

November 9th
5th Journal Entry

R uth and Paul had an argument today, which was shocking. Why? I shouldn't be able to hear Paul. I haven't heard Paul's voice since I was twelve. Ruth has always drowned him out, him and the others. Either her control is slipping or they're getting stronger. Both possibilities are equally terrifying. He's an evil, monstrous man.

Ruth's voice was clear, but Paul's was like an old-time radio, distant and distorted by static. I only heard about every third word he said. Sounds funny, doesn't it? It's not. Today, I heard my name. And then I heard yours.

Underneath Ruth and Paul, other voices rumbled, an unwelcome resurgence of unknown cause. Could it be my meds? My neurologist tweaked them after my last seizure. They've caused many side effects throughout the years: brain fog, irritability, even formication—the feeling of bugs crawling across my skin. But not hallucinations.

Never voices.

I clapped my hands over my ears to drown out their angry words. I want them all to leave, even Ruth. I know I shouldn't. I haven't kept my promise of finding her killer. Not yet. Besides, she's my friend. Friends don't want friends to go away. But six years is enough. I don't remember what quiet sounds like.

Paul is the only one strong enough to attack Ruth's dominance, and he seems to be growing stronger every day. Even so, I never see him, like I do Ruth. I feel him, though, and it scares me. His presence is malevolent, like a thundercloud on the horizon, spreading insidiously until it blacks out the sky. Ruth has always held him back, kept him in check. What if she doesn't or can't? What will he do to me? To you?

While they argued, the air in the photo room grew frigid, the lights flickered on and off, and the chandelier swung so wildly on its brass chain I was afraid it would come crashing to the floor. At one point, Ruth slammed the piano lid shut, releasing a burst of random notes. She loves drama. Thrives on it. Me, not so much. I awoke on the floor in the middle of the room with my head pounding and a bloody nose.

Ruth stood over me, staring at the blood dripping from my nose with disgust and horror. "It's all right now, Cassandra. He's gone. I won't let him hurt you."

"But what about everyone else?" I asked. "What about Pap and Detective Brennan and everyone who walks into this room?"

She strolled to the piano and delicately perched on its bench, clasping her hands in her lap like a schoolmarm. Her smile was colder than the room. "I can only do so much."

CHAPTER

23

As Brennan found out, badges are easy to clone—easy, that is, for someone younger and more tech-savvy than himself. He kept the poor IT guy on the line for almost an hour, interrogating him as to how a dead cop could've swiped himself into the morgue.

IT guy guessed someone cloned the strip before shredding Tom's relinquished badge. No, he wasn't aware of other similar instances. At Brennan's insistence, the tech ran a search for Tom's identification code and got one other hit, also for the morgue, the previous month, when Pete's office had been sacked. Someone had saved that clone for a year, awaiting the time when they'd need it most.

That thought clamored around Brennan's brain as he brushed his teeth and climbed into bed. A patient criminal was an elusive one, the hardest kind to catch. The kind to haunt a detective's dreams. The kind who could turn a simple case into a nightmare. Like a fall down the stairs. Insomnia, on the other hand, was a common thief, pocketing hours and leaving nothing but emptiness in its wake. A long, empty night. An empty soul. With an impatient toss of the covers, Brennan abandoned his bedroom. He paced the apartment aimlessly until a gentle tapping at Elle's window dispelled his inner turmoil with a single, simple command. Feed the crow. The bird refused to leave until he provided a midnight snack of fruit and crackers.

Truth be told, he welcomed the company. He ruminated out loud, sharing his anxiety while the crow ate, occasionally bobbing its glossy head as if in agreement. At some point, he fell asleep on Elle's bed. When he awoke stiff and sore in the wee hours, the bird was gone, the window still open, and the bedroom was colder than Pete's morgue.

He stumbled to the kitchen and lurched to a stop in front of the fridge. Hanging at eye level, secured by a magnet, was Elle's purple-and-black drawing of her friend the crow.

He stared at its glittery lines until his eyes watered. It had been in his pants pocket. That much he remembered. He must've hung it during his sleep. Sleepwalking. Jesus. He really was losing his mind.

He filled the old-fashioned percolator to the brim and brooded over his morning coffee until sunrise. A damned bird was not going to help him solve this case. Pete wanted no further involvement. He'd made that abundantly clear. And the captain was at the top of Brennan's short list of suspects. Even the IT guy could be on the take. Which left Internal Affairs.

The mere thought made his dark roast taste twice as bitter. While they would be the appropriate people to investigate a cloned badge, one that allowed a mysterious criminal carte blanche access to the entire station, they wouldn't give a crap about the potentially lethal repercussions for Pete and his family. Or Brennan. He and his entire inner circle, small as it was, could at best land in witness protection or at worst at the bottom of the Schuylkill River.

His options sucked.

Last night's empty beer bottle sat atop a stack of manila folders. He grabbed it by its sticky neck, inhaled the residual hoppy aroma, and threw it in recycling. The glass shattered on impact. A round stain marked the bottle's prior position. He flipped the folder open to see if the moisture had bled through the pages. A black-and-white photo of a burly man scowled at him from inside the front cover. Above the photo, penned in the same elegant cursive that graced Cassie's journal, was a name. *Paul Krueg, 1936.*

That stare. Ice-pick sharp, maniacal in its intensity. Face fleshy with jowls so prominent his thin lips seemed to disappear. He wore a long leather apron and stood in front of a shop with a sign reading KRUEG'S: GRAND OPENING. Strings of sausage and thick hunks of ham decorated the windows. A butcher. Somehow, Brennan wasn't surprised. He'd reviewed the six cold cases Cassie claimed to have solved, but not this one. This must be the second of the four murders she hadn't been able to crack. He'd stopped reading after Ruth.

He scanned Cassie's painstakingly detailed notes. She'd organized and cross-referenced the evidence, which included scraps of newspaper articles, interviews, and police reports, into a one-page summary. Never married. No family of record. A solitary man, based on the newspaper obituary. Shot through the face at point-blank range with a pistol in July of 1945. One casing, one bullet. The community mourned the closing of his shop, but not his death. They'd found carefully preserved body parts in his freezer. Tiny ones. Human.

Holy shit. Brennan stopped scanning and dove in, reviewing the entire file. Located a few city blocks from Dolan Mansion, Krueg's had been Society Hill's only butcher shop. Finances were in order. Paul had no prior arrests. Described by neighbors as polite but distant. The community was shocked—shocked—by his murder and even more surprised by the grisly find afterward.

But someone knew what Paul Krueg was doing. And that someone took the law into their own hands.

Brennan frowned and rifled through the stack of folders until he found Ruth's. As with the butcher's file, the first page contained what was in essence an executive summary. God, he loved Cassie's methodical style. He refreshed himself on the details.

Shot through the heart at close range with a pistol in June 1945. One casing, one bullet. Originally from Camden, she moved to Philadelphia when she wed her third husband, who owned a thriving Center City print shop. Though she'd never been caught by the police, Cassie described her as a serial killer. Two dead husbands in Jersey, two in Philly. According to Cassie's journal, that juicy tidbit of information came directly from Ruth's mouth. And that's where the crazy train careened off the tracks.

Cassie's childhood friend and confidante, the woman who prodded the lonely teen into investigating four mysterious unsolved murders, was a serial killer named Ruth who died in 1945. He sagged in his chair. He was gonna need more beer.

He had to admit the parallels between Paul's and Ruth's cases were compelling and implied a single perp, a killer of serial killers, with the murders all clustered in the heart of Philadelphia near the historic and creepy old mansion Cassie called home. The location made sense. The original pictures—Ruth's wedding, Krueg's grand opening—were acquired for the local newspapers by Leland Dolan, back in his days as a teenaged amateur photographer cum photo thief. A teenager in the 1930s, especially a poor one, didn't have the means to travel far.

Cassie had two more cold cases she'd yet to share. Brennan's newfound curiosity triggered a shiver of anticipation, the thrill of the hunt. Would they fit the same pattern—a single bullet fired by someone close enough to stare their victim in the eyes? Were they killed by the same gun?

The bullets themselves might still be buried in the precinct's basement. The long-term evidence storage unit occupied half of the cellar opposite the pool and locker rooms. Affectionately called the Stacks, the area housed the original cellblocks, now stuffed with a jumble of boxes and metal shelves stacked from floor to ceiling behind each cell's thick iron bars.

He'd only been there once, as a rookie. The jackass senior detective accompanying him slammed the cell door behind his back, locking him in. Then they discovered there was no key. Not anymore, anyway. A locksmith tried his best and failed. Too old, too rusty. It took a welder three hours to cut through the bars and locking mechanism with an oxyacetylene torch to set him free. He'd endured months of not-so-gentle ribbing afterward.

He'd rather rip out his nose hair than revisit the Stacks. But when subjected to modern forensic methodology, those old bullets might yield interesting new leads. The potential payoff was enough to stiffen his resolve.

Come Friday, Erin McConnell's investigation would be closed, and he'd have some time on his hands. First, he'd turn his report over to his boss. Afterward, he'd drag himself back to the Stacks. Then, with evidence hopefully in hand, he'd ask Cassie for her remaining two unsolved cases. It'd be nice to work with a skilled partner again, even if she was eighteen and believed her intel came from dead people. Call it atonement for failing to prove her mother's murder.

With a plan firmly in place, he poured the rest of his coffee into a thermos and slogged to the office. The precinct was buzzing when he arrived. Every blaring radio, each bleating phone made him wince. He needed a nap, and it was only nine.

He caught up on garbage emails and those memos flagged as important, which never were, and struggled to stay awake through the mandatory midweek huddle, where the unit's detectives gathered to discuss their cases. The huddles were Captain Mattern's brainchild from when she was promoted, her contribution to modernizing the unit's workflow. Designed to identify potential overlap between cases, it usually degenerated into a bitch-and-razz session, sometimes good-natured, sometimes not, depending on whether the captain was in attendance.

When his turn arrived, Brennan kept his update as succinct and surly as possible. "Death by reverse swan dive. Nothing exciting. On to the next."

Aside from a few snide remarks about his haggard appearance, he escaped substantial blowback. The captain pointed to the next in line, but her gaze, inscrutable as always, flicked back to his throughout the session. Or maybe it was his imagination.

He decided to skip the usual post-huddle chat fest and hurried back to his desk, intent on completing at least the skeleton of his report before lunch. He was staring at the blank form when Detective Tan wheeled her chair from her workstation to whisper in his ear.

"Don't look now, but the boss is heading your way. You might want to straighten your tie." She smirked and rolled away.

Brennan kept his gaze fixed on his computer screen and pretended to be immersed in work.

Captain Mattern was not deterred. She stopped in front of his desk. "Not much of a briefing today, Detective."

"I'm saving the good stuff for my report." He tapped random letters on the keyboard and imagined her thick eyebrows arching at his response.

"Which is due Friday."

"Friday. Yes, I know. You'll have it by noon."

"I'd like it by ten."

His jaw clenched. "Okay, you'll have it by ten."

She lingered as if expecting a more robust verbal battle. When he remained silent, she strode to her office and slammed the door. Its glass panels rattled from across the room. Brennan relaxed his jaw and slowly exhaled.

Detective Tan shook her head. "Whatever you did to earn a spot on the captain's shit list must've been epic."

"Epic. I like the sound of that." Brennan smiled grimly. "Keep watching. I'm just getting started. The best is yet to come."

By noon, Brennan had discovered that writing an open-ended yet factual report chock-full of nuance and innuendo was harder than churning out a standard case file. The hot hands of death were a particular challenge.

But the skeleton was done. Fill in a few details, attach Jim's crime-scene photos, include Pete's new autopsy narrative, and by Friday at ten the captain would have her report. Brennan logged off for lunch, walked toward the main exit, and dialed Pete's cell. The call went straight to voice mail.

Brennan frowned. Pete never worked through lunch.

Never.

He tried Pete's desk and gave up after the tenth ring. A spark of anxiety kindled in his empty stomach. On a hunch, he stopped at the information desk inside the precinct's front door. "Mind if I use your phone?" He waved his cell in the air. "Battery's dead."

The bored secretary gestured toward the desk. Brennan dialed Pete's direct extension again.

He answered on the first ring. "Coroner's Office."

"Are you screening my calls?" Brennan's anxiety fizzled, replaced by a spurt of anger.

"What? Of course not."

"You're the world's worst liar, Pete. You know that? I need your updated autopsy report."

"I'll email it to you."

"And the final results of the tox screen."

"Yeah. About that . . ." Pete's voice trailed off. "Where are you?"

"At the front desk."

"We're not having this discussion with you standing in the most public place of the building."

"Suits me. I'll be there in ten." Brennan hung up before Pete could stammer a protest.

While officially within the precinct, the morgue was located in a modern annex attached to the historic main building via a maze of corridors and a tunnel that ran under the busy city street above. Except at rush hour, when frenzied commuters hurrying to the nearest SEPTA station clogged the sidewalks, Brennan found it quicker to walk around the outside of the building. He zipped his jacket, ducked his head, and headed into the crisp November air.

He stopped short at the sight of a man in a Department of Public Works bucket truck installing sparkly holiday decorations on the streetlights.

The worker caught him staring and shrugged. "Save it, pal. I know what you're gonna say. Heard it six times already."

"It's only—what—the ninth? Tenth, maybe?"

"We won't light 'em up until after Thanksgiving, if it makes you feel any better." He went back to securing the decoration's wire frame.

Brennan did not feel better. It took him the rest of the walk to the morgue to figure out why. His crankiness had nothing to do with silver bells and giant wreaths. Elle would be bouncing out of her snow pants at the sight of holiday decorations, and his best friend, despite his protestations otherwise, was avoiding him. At least Pete had finally answered the phone. If he hadn't and wasn't puttering around the morgue, Brennan would've gone straight to his house and done a safety check. A knock on the door would've really gotten Pete's tinsel in a tangle.

He slid his badge through the reader mounted outside the morgue's double doors. The indicator light flashed but remained red. He repeated the action but slower. Same result. He frowned. It had worked this morning on the time clock. He struggled to recall the last time he'd swiped into the morgue. Usually, he was with Pete. When he came alone, Pete's secretary, Joan, buzzed him in.

To the right of the doors, a small, square window offered a view of Joan's desk while thoughtfully shielding the autopsy areas on the left. Pete's acrylic-partitioned office sat directly behind. Brennan peered through the window's hazy glass. Joan was not at her desk.

He glanced at his phone. 12:30. She was likely at lunch. But where was Pete? Brennan tapped on the glass. The morgue remained as still as its dead occupants. He pounded on the door with his fist. Pete's head popped out from under his desk like a Whac-A-Mole. He hurried out of his office to press the unlock button on Joan's desk.

The buzzer sounded; the lock clicked. Brennan braced himself for a blast of cold air. He sauntered in, smiling to cover his relief. "Hiding under your desk? Am I that unwelcome, Pete?"

"I was NOT hiding."

Brennan grinned at Pete's indignant expression. "Okay, then. Lemme guess. You dropped your doughnut?"

The corners of Pete's mouth twitched. "That would be a crime. If you must know, I was crawling around on the floor for you."

Pete opened his right hand. A tiny flash drive rested in his palm. "My new computer tower is under my desk. I emailed you the autopsy and tox screen reports as usual. But given what happened to my last computer, I thought an external backup was in order. I know you have a report due on Friday. I'd hate for you to miss your deadline because of me."

He tossed the flash drive at Brennan, who caught it midair. He tucked the device into his pocket.

Pete shuffled a stack of papers on his desk. "I also printed out the tox screen for you just in case." He handed Brennan a single sheet labeled with a yellow sticky note.

I THINK MY OFFICE IS BUGGED. ACT NORMAL.

Brennan stared at the bright yellow note, blinked, and folded the paper into his pocket with the flash drive. "You know the real reason I'm here, right?"

Pete's expression froze, and his fingers stopped their nervous shuffling.

Brennan forced a slow smile, grateful that decades of experience had equipped him with a poker face equal to any professional gambler's. "We always do lunch after successfully closing a case. I hate to break it to you, pal, but it's your turn to buy. And I'm hungrier than a pregnant rhino, so bring your wallet."

Pete laughed and snatched his jacket off the back of his office chair. "When are you not hungry?"

"I'll answer that over lunch."

———

Outside, Brennan made small talk about the premature Christmas decorations until Pete reminded him he was Jewish and truly couldn't give a shit. They chose the noisiest diner on the block. Once safely ensconced in a coveted corner booth, Brennan pulled the tox report from his pocket and slapped it on the table.

"What the hell, Pete?" He pointed to the neon sticky note. "Are you sure?"

"No, I'm not sure. But I'm noticing things, little things. Like, I think someone followed me home last night." The bell on the diner's door tinkled, and he glanced over his shoulder.

"I wouldn't call that a little thing." Brennan paused. "Have you told your wife?"

"No, of course not. The less Elaine knows, the better. I never take my work home with me."

Brennan imagined Pete lugging a backpack of organs and other body parts home and unsuccessfully fought to smother a grin. "That's definitely a good thing." The grin faded. "If I'd learned that lesson earlier, Julia and I might still be together."

"Maybe, maybe not. You were both under a lot of stress with Elle." Pete cleared his throat. "Did you read the report?"

"Not yet." Brennan crumpled the yellow sticky note into a ball and scanned Erin's tox screen. He shook his head. "Not sure what you're getting at, Pete. Unless I'm missing something, it looks consistent with what you told me previously from the prelim: positive for benzos, barbs, and not much else."

"But read the amounts." Pete pointed to the first labeled substance, lorazepam. In the righthand column, a number written in micrograms per liter was flagged with a red *H*.

Brennan shrugged. "Context, please."

"That's enough lorazepam to drop an elephant. Overdose level, for sure. A person would have to take at least a handful of pills to reach that level, yet I didn't find any undigested pills in Erin's stomach. By comparison, there's barely any of the barbiturate, identified as primidone, in her system. She probably took one pill the night before to help her sleep."

"Primidone? Sounds familiar. Where have I heard that before?" Brennan mentally flipped through his notes, trying to place the name.

"One of Elle's treatments, maybe? Primidone's typically used for seizures and tremors. Did her brain tumor cause seizures?"

"No." Brennan pressed his lips into a tight line. "We put her on hospice before it went that far. But Erin's daughter, Cassie, has seizures." He pictured the afternoon of Erin's wake when, with Leland Dolan's blessing, he'd searched the mansion's bedrooms and found Cassie's pill bottles: Keppra. Primidone.

And lorazepam.

Pen in hand, a waitress sauntered to their table. Brennan shoved the tox report into his pocket. They ordered, though his appetite had evaporated.

Once she was out of earshot, Pete leaned across the table. "I know what you're thinking. But it's common for kids to take their parents' meds and vice versa. It's especially common with kids on amphetamines for ADHD. Parents love those stimulants. They divert the hell out of them. Just because Erin had a tiny amount of her daughter's primidone in her system means nothing more than she took one. Period. The lorazepam is the problem. Do you know how much Cassie was prescribed?"

"I don't, but I took pictures of the labels. It wasn't just Cassie. I also found a bottle of lorazepam in Amber Servello's apartment." He scrolled through his phone. "Here they are: Amber was on one milligram as needed for sleep and anxiety. Cassie takes one milligram daily for seizure prevention."

Pete folded and unfolded his napkin into origami-like squares. "Those dosages are far too low to account for Erin's blood level."

"Amber's bottle was missing twenty-eight out of the original thirty pills."

"But I still should've found undigested tablets, pill casings, residue—something."

"Injected?"

"No needle marks. Trust me, after I found those weird burns on her chest and back, I performed a comprehensive skin exam under magnification. If she had a puncture somewhere, it was extremely well hidden."

"Her husband is a surgeon."

"I know." Pete dropped his napkin on the table. "There is another way. I researched it. Lorazepam comes in a concentrated liquid. Just one milliliter—a quarter of a teaspoon—has eight times the amount of medication contained in a single one of Cassie's pills. Put a full teaspoon in someone's morning coffee, and you've got a lethal dosage that's rapidly absorbed with no puncture marks and no pill residue. She would've died even if she hadn't fallen down the stairs. The fall was just a cover."

"And I'm sure that's exactly what you said in your revised report."

"No." Pete stared at the table. "I told you. I'm out."

"Yet you made me a flash drive of the files for safekeeping. You looked up everything there is to know about lorazepam. You're not acting like someone who's out, Pete. You don't WANT to be out. You're better than that, and you know it. You just want to protect your family and maybe save your hide in the process. I get it. But if anyone asks, you're going to have a tough time reconciling a bland autopsy report with a smoking gun of a tox screen."

"Not really. I do it all the time. In this case, the primary cause of death remains traumatic brain injury due to a mechanical fall. I just added a comorbid condition—accidental overdose."

The waitress returned with their food. Pete flashed a strained smile. "Can I get mine packaged to go, please? Gotta get back to the office."

The waitress muttered something under her breath and stalked back to the kitchen, returning a minute later with a Styrofoam container. Pete tipped his plate into the box, cursing when a greasy chunk of pastrami splattered on the table.

Brennan tapped the top of the Styrofoam container. "You know those things are bad for the environment."

Pete scowled, wiped his napkin over the mess, and tossed some bills on the table.

Brennan shook his head. "We're supposed to be acting normal. The Pete Ecker I know does not eat and run. Or in this case, order and run. He enjoys his food in a leisurely fashion."

"Yeah, well, I'm gonna be off for a while, and I have a lot of loose ends to tie up before the wife and I skip town."

Brennan raised an eyebrow. "In a normal world, Pete Ecker never takes vacation."

"I booked a two-week trip to Hawaii. Second honeymoon, long overdue. I've been promising Elaine for years. Now seems as good a time as any. As we've been recently told, regret, like death, is permanent." He slid from the booth. "I'll call when we get back."

Pete grabbed his to-go container and left. He paused at the door, his expression a muddled mix of emotions. "Take care of yourself, will ya?"

Brennan nodded and raised fork-to-mouth in the habitual act of eating. Despite the diner's ambient chatter, Pete's departure left Brennan alone in his corner booth, enveloped in a gloomy bubble of solitude. His cell chirped a reminder. He didn't look at the calendar. He already knew what it said.

The phone hummed a different alert, this time indicating a text. He glanced at the screen, swallowed too fast, and choked on meat loaf with a side of guilt.

Pap did great. Discharged tomorrow, maybe. Thought you might want to know.

Shit. He should've checked on them. Or at least on her. He tapped out a quick response.

Fantastic.

He paused.

I read Paul Krueg's case file last night. Interesting stuff.

Ready for the rest?

Yes.

Meet me in Reading Terminal at the doughnut stand tomorrow at 10?

His fingers hovered over the screen. Months ago, at his counselor's advice, he'd scheduled the day off. A "mental health day," she'd called it. He was fairly certain reading through gruesome cold cases was not what she had in mind.

Perfect. See you then.

He set the phone on the table, only to be interrupted by yet another chirp. The neglected calendar reminder popped onto the screen.

Flowers.

He swiped it away. He'd deal with that tomorrow.

CHAPTER

24

T he Reading Terminal Market was a magical place, a vibrant reflection of an eclectic city that cherished its past. The byzantine
maze of restaurants, shops, and grocery stalls offered "good eats,"
as Brennan's pop would say: Italian meats, a kosher deli, fresh produce, traditional Philly cheesesteaks, exotic spices, and everything in
between. Brennan did most of his shopping there—except maybe the
spices. His spice rack started with salt and ended with pepper.

Every Sunday, he'd follow his nose or let the throngs carry him
along while he imagined what the market must've been like back in
the 1800s, when the Reading Railroad operated the train station above.
It saddened him how much Elle hated the market. Frightened by the
clamor, the glassy-eyed fish, and hunks of freshly butchered meat,
she'd bury her face in his shoulder, only chancing a peek when tempted by one of the three stalls she found sufficiently enticing: the candy
shop, the Amish bakery, and the flower stand. He'd hoped that one

day when she was older, she'd learn to love the market, in all its chaotic glory, as much as he. That day never came.

His right temple pounded with the abrupt onset of a headache. His own fault, for sure. Last night was another late one. He'd stayed up, determined to finish his report so he wouldn't have to think about it again until tomorrow. He'd just logged off his computer when his wife called. Ex-wife. He still got that wrong. His counselor would be disappointed.

Julia was a transplanted Floridian, having moved to Philly for her doctorate studies. She never learned to love the city. She especially hated the market. What he called charm, she labeled grime. She missed the sun, the vibrancy of her Latina community, her mother's *ropa vieja*. He wasn't surprised when she chose to move back to the beach after Elle died.

She'd tried to take Elle before, arguing the medical care would be better at the Mayo Clinic near her parents' home in Jacksonville. Brennan balked, touting CHOP's—Children's Hospital of Philadelphia's—stellar reputation. Truthfully, the thought of not holding his baby's hand, being her strength during her treatments, terrified him.

And that was the beginning of the end of their marriage. She blamed him for Elle's death; he blamed himself more. The what-ifs tormented him day and night and ate away their marital bonds like a corrosive acid. What if they had taken Elle to Mayo instead of CHOP? What if they'd been more aggressive instead of placing her on hospice when the suffering seemed too much to bear? At the time, they thought they were making the best decision for Elle. Maybe they should've done more. He should've done more.

Julia claimed to be "just checking in." He knew better. She hadn't checked on him since the day the ink dried on the divorce papers. She was looking for a shoulder to cry on, even though she had her parents and the Florida sunshine and probably a boyfriend by now. And what did he have? Pete. He had wish-you-were-here Honolulu

Pete. The conversation soured quickly and ended with profanity and tears. Then, once again, Brennan couldn't sleep. He'd thought ahead and bought more beer, hence the hangover.

He winced with another sharp jab of pain. Despite the hour, the market seemed unusually frenetic. Cassie had wisely chosen a meeting time after breakfast and before the lunchtime rush, yet the jostling crowd buzzed with energy, and the fishmonger's strident calls hung in the dank air. Even the market's usual odor, a heady mix of spice and grease, held strange undertones. For the first time, Brennan detected decay, the cheerless smell of a one-hundred-and-fifty-year-old building infused with rotting meat and the filth of a thousand footprints per day. Maybe Elle, in her five-year-old wisdom, had sensed what he just now perceived.

The flower stall occupied the terminal's north corner. He stared vacantly at the wicker baskets overflowing with freshly cut blooms.

"Can I help you?" A middle-aged woman with lilac hair and tortoiseshell glasses smiled over a vase of fragrant white lilies.

Funeral flowers, his mother called them. Brennan rubbed his nose. "I need a bouquet. Thirty dollars' worth, please."

"An arrangement or loose? It'll be tough to do something in a vase for that price."

"Loose is fine. Can you throw in some purple ones? It's her favorite color. And black, if you have any."

The woman peered over the rim of her gaudy frames. "Mother Nature does not birth black flowers."

Brennan stared at her pastel hair and bit back a retort. "Fine. Mix them up, then. Maybe something pink instead. Surprise me."

The woman fussed over selecting an assortment of blooms, gathering them in green tissue paper and binding the bunch with a shiny pink ribbon. "She'll love these." She winked. "Whatever you did will be forgiven."

Brennan clenched his jaw. "I can only hope."

The tissue paper crinkled in his fist. He paid in cash and, flowers held high to avoid the crush of humanity, stalked to the Amish bakery. The sweet aroma of fried dough dusted with sugar always drew a crowd.

Cassie, cruller in hand, loitered at the counter. "Would you like a doughnut?" She pointed over her shoulder at the enticing array behind her.

"No, I'm good. Let's grab a seat. I'm looking forward to reading those last two cases of yours."

Reading Terminal Market boasted a central plaza, which held a jumbled assortment of mismatched tables and chairs suitable for a quick dine-and-dash and nothing more. Lunchtime was standing room only. The perpetual din and angry stares from those coveting a seat precluded leisurely conversation.

Brennan laid the bouquet on a tiny table tucked awkwardly between a rusty support post and a garbage can. His folding metal chair wobbled with every fidget.

Cassie wiped her sticky fingers and pulled two manila folders from her bag. She placed them next to the flowers, taking care not to bruise the delicate blooms. Her gaze lingered on the vibrant mix of carnations, mums, and baby's breath. "For Elle?"

He straightened in his seat. "Yes."

She nodded, her expression downcast. "It's her birthday."

The market's pandemonium receded. A rush of adrenaline cleared the melancholy that had clouded his mind since sunrise. "How did you know?"

"I told you before. I accessed Elle's medical record using my father's credentials. That's how I found your address. And her birthday." Cassie stroked a pink carnation, its pale petals as soft and dewy as a baby's lips. "My pap started as an investigative reporter, remember? He always researches his inner circle. Now that he's older, more often than not, I'm the one conducting that research."

"I wasn't aware I was part of his inner circle."

"You should be flattered. Pap is quite discriminating."

Brennan shuffled the pair of files. "How's his hip doing?"

"Great. Still hoping to come home either later this afternoon or early tomorrow. His pain is controlled, he's out of the wheelchair, and he's already taken a few steps with a walker. He refused to go to a rehab hospital, but his doctor said as long as we can arrange for home nursing to start in the morning, he should be good to go." She paused. "He's looking forward to your visit."

"My visit?" Brennan frowned. "You mean at the hospital? I never said anything about a visit."

"Oh. Are you sure? He said you were supposed to visit him today. I thought that meant you'd made arrangements . . ." She trailed off, fluttering her hands in confusion.

"No, we did not." Brennan silently seethed. He was being summoned, and old King Dolan was using his great-granddaughter as the unwitting page. He pulled out his phone to mask his annoyance. "While we're on the subject of visiting strangers—"

"Pap's hardly a stranger to you at this point."

"—I've been meaning to test that super-recognizer ability of yours. Have you ever seen any of these people?" He held up a photo of Jim, taken during his birthday bar crawl a year ago.

"No. Never."

"How about him?" He did the same with Pete.

Cassie pursed her lips. "Yes. He gave a talk about autopsies a few years ago at the library. 'Voices from Beyond the Grave: How a Corpse Can Speak.' I attended, of course."

"Of course."

"It was really good, as I recall."

He pulled up the precinct's website. Captain Mattern, sporting a rare smile, graced the home page.

"What about her?"

Cassie nodded. "She visited the house over the summer. Early July, I think." She frowned and leaned closer to the small screen. "But she wasn't wearing a uniform or a badge. I answered the door. She said she was the director of some charity my parents support and that she had a meeting with my mother. They spent over an hour talking in the library."

"Did you overhear anything?"

"No. The pocket doors were shut. I wouldn't have paid attention anyhow. Their charity work bores me. It's all for show. Gotta keep up appearances, you know."

"Was your father home?"

"No, he was working."

Brennan, mind racing, clicked off his phone. Showing her the pictures had been a long shot. He hadn't really expected her to recognize any of them, but if she did, he would've placed his bet on Jim, not the captain. "You're sure it's the same person?"

"I told you before—I never forget a face. I couldn't if I tried. It's a blessing and a curse."

"You could get a mighty fine job at one of the lettered agencies— FBI, CIA, NSA—with that curse."

Her face brightened. "Really? I hadn't thought of that." The happy glow faded. "But with my seizures . . ."

"Lots of people with seizures hold full-time jobs. Who told you you can't? Your father? Amber? I mean, I wouldn't want you flying me around in an airplane, but picking out perps from a crowd, that's a whole different skill set. Between your research abilities and the super-recognizer-thing, they'd be lucky to have you."

He flipped open the top file. A photo of a smiling man in black robes and a stiff white collar adorned the inside cover. "Who do we have here?"

"Father Salvatore Pignotti. A priest, obviously, and my third unsolved case. He baptized my pap."

"When was that?"

"Nineteen twenty."

"Back in the Dark Ages, eh?"

"More or less."

"What does Ruth have to say about our friendly friar?"

"She told me Father Pignotti married her to her fourth and final husband. She said she knew even then there was something off about him."

Brennan furrowed his forehead. "Huh. Weird how everything intersects."

"The Philadelphia neighborhoods were smaller then. According to Pap, everyone knew everyone—and their business." Cassie shifted in the uncomfortable seat. "You should probably read that somewhere else, somewhere more private. The pictures are nasty."

"Nastier than the butcher's?"

"Yes."

Brennan raised an eyebrow. If this case followed suit, the priest was no saint, and someone offed him for a reason. He heeded Cassie's warning and closed the file. "Leisure reading for tonight, then, after . . . after . . ."

"After you visit Elle."

"Right." Brennan pushed away from the table and winced as the metal chair screeched across the concrete floor. "And maybe your pap too."

Cassie threw her purse over her shoulder. "Take him a bag of Jordan almonds."

"A bag of what?"

"Candy-coated almonds. He adores them. You'll be on his good side forever. Candy shop's around the corner, right behind the bakery."

"I'm familiar."

"Call me once you've read the cases, and we can get together to brainstorm ideas. I can't wait to hear your theories."

She waved and disappeared into the crowd.

"Sure," he mumbled. "Why not?"

Somewhere to his right, a griddle sizzled with grease. The unmistakable aroma of steak, onions, and melting cheese wafted his direction. Was it too early for lunch? His stomach rumbled a reply. *Never.* First, a cheesesteak. The Jordan almonds could wait.

CHAPTER

25

Brennan, holding a damp cloth in one hand and the tissue-wrapped flowers in the other, stood outside the cemetery's arched iron gate. He always carried a wet rag when visiting. His little girl's headstone was invariably sullied with something—bird shit, mud, dried tree pollen—you name it. Once he'd even found crayon. What kind of parent lets their child scribble on a gravestone? His face flushed at the memory.

Society Hill's historic cemeteries were closed to funerals unless you belonged to an old and obscenely rich family with an existing plot or a crypt, like the Dolans. Elle, therefore, was buried on the city's northern outskirts. Despite being just seven miles from his apartment, it took a half hour by car and most of his good humor to get there. He'd tried taking the train once. He ended up whacking a pickpocket with his flowers.

It was gentler than punching him in the mouth.

The tiny cemetery, a green oasis in an asphalt desert of strip malls and busy streets, was anything but peaceful, thanks to the ever-present roar of traffic. But rows of willows stood gentle guard, their weeping branches murmuring condolences into the wind. The iron gate was locked at night to cut down on vandalism, and as an added bonus, the humble little graveyard was rarely crowded.

Brennan had seen a handful of people over the past six months. After mere weeks of tearful pilgrimages, most drifted away from their public displays of sorrow and returned to the normal ebb and flow of their lives. A few, like him, persisted. He noticed patterns. The elderly visited more often and usually brought those God-awful plastic bouquets designed to survive anything except the melting heat of a nuclear holocaust or an asteroid strike. Young women formed the other cohort of frequent flyers. They visited graves bearing tiny headstones, like Elle's. He'd taken to placing morbid bets with himself on how long the others would last. He'd been wrong only once, having misjudged a woman about his age who haunted a plot with an adult-sized memorial. A widow, he assumed. He saw her at least once per week.

At first, her eyes, puffy and red, avoided his. Gradually, they began nodding acknowledgments from across the swathe of stone-studded grass, replete with plastic flowers and wreaths. They'd never spoken, preoccupied as they were with their grief. Today, of all days, she seemed determined to break that comfortable pattern.

He watched the conflict play across her face as he approached his daughter's grave. She stared at his daughter's tiny stone, took a step in his direction, and hesitated. She squared her shoulders and tried again, striding across the grass to where he stood clutching the tissue-wrapper bouquet.

She stuck out her hand. "Breonna."

"Dan."

"I'm sorry for your loss." She winced as if realizing the banality of her words.

"Thank you."

She fixed her gaze on the flowers. "I see her sometimes."

His grip on the fragile stems tightened. "Who?"

"Your daughter." She winced again. "Your other daughter. She was here yesterday. I watched her stand here and talk for the better part of a half hour. She left the bear." She pointed toward Elle's grave.

Brennan stared at the usually empty space in front of the stone. On the left, a collection of shiny objects—bottle caps, gum wrappers, even an earring—formed a neat pile. On the right, a ratty stuffed bear with glassy eyes rested with its back against the cold granite. Between them, a single black feather fluttered in the breeze.

"No." He shook his head and blinked. The bizarre diorama did not change. "This girl, does she have curly red hair?"

"Yes. Sometimes she brings her cat with her, a tabby with amber eyes. Or it follows her in, at least. I see it skulking in the bushes." She paused. "She's not your daughter? I assumed from the date on the stone, I mean, I assumed this was her younger sister. Why else would she visit so often?"

Brennan stooped, hiding his face while he struggled to produce a plausible explanation that didn't involve a murder investigation, talking photos, or the notorious McConnell family. He placed the bouquet next to the bear and stood up too soon, based on her reaction to his expression.

She took a step back, her face stricken with remorse. "You know what? This is none of my business. I'm sorry for bothering you. Forgive me. I just thought it was sweet that she visits on her own and spends so much time talking to her sis . . . friend. I wasn't sure you knew, and I thought it might make you happy."

"It does. She's . . . she was Elle's babysitter. They loved each other." The lie rolled off his tongue with surprising ease. "Thank you."

The woman nodded and flashed a tentative smile. She walked across the grass to her car and waved as she drove through the gate.

The willows whispered good-bye. Brennan exhaled between his teeth. He picked up the bear, damp with frost. It was old and well-loved, with a button in its left ear. He'd seen it before during his investigation of Dolan Mansion. It'd sat on a shelf in Cassie's bedroom.

He swiped his forearm over his eyes. Yes, Elle and Cassie had frequented the same library, overlapping visits several times a month. Yes, his daughter often babbled about—and to—the red-haired princess in the corner, sometimes loudly enough for him to see the corners of Cassie's mouth twitch into a smile despite her grim reading material. Was that little bit of a connection enough? While Cassie stood talking to Elle, could his daughter possibly, somehow be talking back? He struggled to suppress the unrealistic surge of hope, pushing it to the deep recesses of his mind, where it was sure to fester.

"Happy birthday, baby," he whispered, placing the bear back where he'd found it. With the damp cloth, he polished the granite headstone until the reflecting light made his eyes tear. Time to go home. Head bowed against the low sun, he trudged back to his car for the long ride home.

His counselor had warned him to expect this. She even gave it a label—the trauma of firsts. The first anniversary. The first major holiday, like the rapidly approaching Thanksgiving. And today's trauma, the first missed birthday. The firsts, she claimed, were the hardest. It got easier with time. His aching heart hoped she was right.

ather Salvatore Pignotti was one sick bastard. Brennan blinked
and rubbed his dry eyes. He'd started reviewing the priest's file
as a distraction after his aggravating commute home from the
cemetery. Four hours later, he'd finished both case reports.

The pair of open files lay empty, their contents scattered across his
kitchen table. Gruesome black-and-white photos rubbed corners with
dry police reports, witness testimonies, and miscellaneous ephemera.
He shook his head, stunned by what he'd read. Stunned for feeling
stunned. He'd been a homicide detective for going on twenty years
now; not much was supposed to shock him. Yet here he was, unsettled
over a pair of eighty-year-old cold cases.

He'd read Father Pignotti's first. The priest had a thing for nuns,
the older and more pious the better. According to a written statement he'd provided upon arrest—he stopped short of calling it a confession—he believed strongly in the cleansing power of pain. Pain

revealed those souls who weren't worthy or not ready for admission to heaven. It was his duty to torture. And torture he did. After a nun staggered to safety and his crimes were made public, he'd disappeared into the custody of the Catholic archdiocese. Nine years later, someone found him and brought him back.

Father Pignotti, each bloodied hand bound by butcher's twine to a silver crucifix, was found on the altar of the Cathedral Basilica of Saints Peter and Paul in August 1945 with a bullet through his heart. His wide eyes stared at the vaulted ceiling in eternal horror, as if he'd seen the devil himself. And maybe he had.

Artie Taylor's case was tame by comparison. Photos revealed a dapper man with slicked-back hair and the smarmy smile of a sociopath. He owned a speakeasy turned club, the members-only kind that fed society's elite over the dinner hour but offered more carnal fare late at night. Boys, girls, gay, and straight—he provided something for everyone and was handsomely compensated for it. When the club was shuttered for prostitution in 1936, Artie got off easy, thanks to his influential acquaintances.

His business moved underground, and when the Philadelphia Naval Shipyard quadrupled in size during the war, he added a new specialty—catering to Marines and sailors on shore leave. Most left happy. The gay ones left dead, strangled by their dog tags and dumped in the street like garbage. Which is where, in the fall of 1945, they found Artie.

The blood-encrusted dog tags cinched around his neck belonged to a dead Marine, but not any of Artie's victims. The nineteen-year-old from Mississippi was one of the twelve thousand who had died or gone missing in the Battle of Okinawa. His remains were never returned. But somehow, his dog tags had made it home.

The case was quickly closed due to its "delicate" nature. The coroner labeled Artie's death, as well as the others, as accidental erotic asphyxiation, which Brennan doubted. Homosexuality was a crime in those days, and after pouring over the details and character profiles, he suspected Artie was simply a bastard who liked to kill gay servicemen for sport. And whoever killed Artie took exception.

Brennan gathered the photos one by one, giving them another long look in case he'd missed any details before stuffing them in their appropriate folder. By now, the late-afternoon sun had begun to wane. If he was going to visit Dolan in the hospital and ply him with Jordan almonds, he'd better get a move on. He had a new and burning desire to chat with Leland Dolan.

A theory festered, one that had developed insidiously as Brennan read, then metastasized like a cancer the longer he stared into Father Pignotti's glassy eyes. Like the husband-killing Ruth and butcher Paul, Artie and Father Pignotti were serial killers, but the latter cases varied in one key detail. Artie had been strangled, not shot, and Father Pignotti had been "lightly" tortured, as the police report so dryly stated. Their deaths were slower, more painful—strong evidence that for the killer, their murders were personal.

Close-up photographs of the priest's bloodied hands revealed fragments of bamboo jammed under the fingernails, a technique made familiar in the States by servicemen returning from the South Pacific after World War II. Like Battle of Okinawa hero and prisoner of war Leland Dolan.

Dolan had been baptized by those hands. Those same hands blessed Ruth's fourth marriage. When Ruth's high-society wedding and the priest's crimes became sensational news in 1936, it was a sixteen-year-old photo thief named Leland Dolan who provided the papers with pictures. Nine years and one world war later, the villainous pair was killed by bullets through their black hearts. A pattern was emerging. Dolan was the common thread.

Brennan weaved through downtown traffic, his mind spinning as fast as his wheels. Prodded by Ruth, her imaginary best friend, Cassie had solved a wall full of crimes, yet she claimed she couldn't crack these cases—a quartet of brutal murders possibly committed by her beloved pap. One of those cases was Ruth's. That seemed awfully coincidental. Premeditated, even.

He screeched to a late stop at a red light and glanced guiltily in his rearview mirror at the squeal of tires behind him. The black sedan's tinted windshield precluded eye contact, which was a good thing. Dude was probably flipping him the bird. Most Philadelphians would've run that light.

While his car idled, Brennan thumbed through the pictures of Cassie's journal on his phone, searching for entry number three and a line he only vaguely recalled: *None of us can see our own killer's face. A quirk of the afterlife, I guess.* But Ruth had been shot through the heart at close range. She had to have seen who killed her. Whether Ruth's "ghost" remembered was anybody's guess. Cassie's elaborate rules of the afterlife and its populace of spirits seemed arbitrary at best.

A truck rumbled past, hitting a pothole deep enough to drown a giraffe. The loud clang jolted his attention from the screen. Shit. The light turned from green to yellow. He floored it. The sedan did the same.

They didn't honk. He adjusted the angle of his rearview mirror as he rounded the next corner. They almost sat through a green light and the bastards didn't honk. A couple of unnecessary lefts and one hard right later and his suspicions were confirmed. He was being followed.

Finding a place to pull over in downtown during rush hour was nigh to impossible. The hospital's well-lit and trafficked parking deck was as safe a place as any to let the scene play out. He lucked into a spot near the exit, with its security gate and cameras, and waited with the engine on, gear in reverse, and foot hovering over the accelerator. *Your move, asshole.*

The black sedan cruised to a stop lengthwise behind his bumper, blocking his car in place. Shit again. His pop's voice echoed through his memory. *Poor decisions pay off poorly.* He pulled his gun from the holster tucked under his jacket and placed it in his coat pocket. At the end of the row of parked cars, an elevator dinged. A group of women wearing scrubs strolled out of the elevator and headed toward the exit. Now, with a bevy of witnesses, was as good a time as any to make a move of his own.

He dialed dispatch. "This is Detective Daniel Brennan, District Six, badge number 50432. I've been followed by a black sedan into the ground level of the hospital parking garage at Tenth and Walnut. Contact pending. Please stand by." He put the call on speaker and the camera on video.

"Standing by." The female voice at the other end was crisp and professional.

With one hand in his pocket and the other on his cell, Brennan slid from his car and quickly rounded the hood, relying on the car's partial protection should he be met with a spray of bullets. At his back, a waist-high cement wall separated him from an alley. He glanced over his shoulder and got a whiff of rot. Didn't matter. If things went south, he was fully prepared to roll over the wall and land in a heap of garbage.

The sedan's doors opened. Two large men in expensive suits with green pocket handkerchiefs exited to stand side by side. Heavy-lidded and impassive, they stared him down with their burly arms folded across their chests. Which was all right by him. Crossed arms meant visible hands. They weren't holding guns.

He raised his phone in the air, camera lens pointed at their faces. "Smile pretty, boys. Care to tell the police department who you are and why you're following me?"

The larger of the two smiled.

Brennan smirked back. "At least one of you can follow directions."

The smile vanished. The man took a step forward. Brennan tightened his grip on the gun.

A level above, a door slammed, triggering a car alarm. The horn echoed through the cement garage. Wings fluttered behind him as a flock of startled birds took flight. A crow swooped by Brennan's ear and landed on the roof of the black sedan. Its brown eyes stared at the back of the mobster's thick neck.

Dispatch spoke through the speaker. The disembodied voice held a tinge of concern. "Status, please, Detective Brennan."

"Stable. Continue to stand by."

The man stared Brennan in the eye. "Regret, like death, is permanent. Your coroner friend made the right decision. Now it's your turn. You know what to do." He cocked his head at his partner, and they returned to their vehicle. The crow took flight, leaving a large chalky mess on the sedan's windshield and hood.

The exit gate opened and closed, and the sedan disappeared into city traffic. Brennan exhaled. "All clear, dispatch. Thank you for your support."

"Any time, Detective." The relief in her voice was audible. "You'll be filing a report?"

"Of course. Video included at no extra charge."

She chuckled, and he disconnected the call. The car alarm abruptly stopped. In the relative quiet, his pulse—too fast and too loud—pounded in his neck. He closed his eyes and took a slow, steadying breath. That could've gone bad, very bad. The green silk hankies . . . Those were Beck McConnell's men. They wanted him to know. That was the point.

Point taken. He would not be filing an incident report, not until he turned in his investigation files to Captain Mattern tomorrow. The video was his bargaining chip, hard proof he was being targeted. Proof that Ryan McConnell, via his big brother Beck, was trying to influence the investigation. And depending on the captain's response to his briefing, proof that she didn't care.

Brennan grabbed the case files from his car. He kept the gun in his pocket for safekeeping; he might need it after his visit with Dolan was complete. He hurried through the garage toward the hospital's main entrance, aware from prior experience that only the emergency-room doors boasted metal detectors.

The hospital's gleaming lobby teemed with visitors, and he slowed his pace to a casual stroll, foregoing the elevator to run the stairs. Six flights later, he regretted his decision. He arrived at Dolan's floor sweaty and out of breath but alive—at least for the moment.

As one of Philly's elite, Dolan was afforded a spacious and private corner room at the end of a long corridor. Brennan raised his fist to knock. The door flew open before his knuckles met wood. A young nurse, tears flowing down her cheeks, rushed out of the room and ran down the hall. Chest tight with anxiety, Brennan peered around the doorjamb.

Dolan sat gripping the edge of his bed. "For God's sake, come in and shut the damned door before they send in another one. Lock it if you can."

Brennan glanced over his shoulder at the nurses' station, where the young nurse, dabbing her eyes and gesticulating wildly, was talking to an unseen person behind the desk. He entered and shut the door behind him.

The room had two walls of windows with decent city views. A third wall held a large-screen TV. Private bathroom. WiFi. A hobnailed chair in the corner. The only thing missing was a minibar. He bobbed his head. "Nice."

The IV pump beeped, reminding him he was in a hospital. Dolan scowled. "Turn that thing off, will ya? I told them I'm leaving in the morning come hell or high water. I don't need it anymore. Pulled the needle out of my arm an hour ago. Missy was determined to put it back in. Needs the practice, I think."

Brennan stared at the electronic array. "I have no idea how to operate this machine. But I can quiet it down for a while." He jabbed at the "silent alarm" button, and the beeping stopped. He'd learned that trick with Elle.

"Good enough." Dolan gestured for Brennan to sit.

Without a word, Brennan pulled the bag of Jordan almonds from his pocket and offered them to Dolan.

He accepted with an appreciative nod. "An odd number, I hope."

"Excuse me?"

The old man held the cellophane bag to the light as if counting the candies. "Tradition. In the Old World, every party and wedding reception has these in dishes or as favors. And always an odd number. Strong. Indivisible, like a marriage." He glanced at Brennan's bare ring finger. "Or like marriage should be."

The heat rose in Brennan's face. "What do you want, Mr. Dolan? You called this meeting."

The old man's eyes narrowed. "To the point. I like that." He untwisted the metal tie cinching the cellophane bag. "What have you discovered about my Erin?"

A firm rap on the door offered Brennan a reprieve. A male nurse entered the room. Dolan raised a staying hand. "Don't even bother. Just take that damned thing away. I'm allowed to refuse. I'm still in my right mind, you know."

The nurse muttered something under his breath, unplugged the pump, and wheeled it from the room. The door slammed behind him.

Dolan chuckled. "They'll be happy when I'm gone. A lot of folks will."

Brennan's gaze followed the sagging neckline of Dolan's thin hospital gown. The faint burns on his chest had become redder and more obvious with time. A few had blistered. And damn if they didn't look exactly like handprints. "Living and dead, it seems." He opened the case files to Father Pignotti and Artie's photos and placed them on the bedside table next to a folded newspaper. "Look familiar?"

Dolan squinted his milky eyes. "Can't say that they do." He slid the newspaper out from under the corner of one of the files and dropped the open bag of almonds in its place. The candies spilled across the table, dotting the macabre photos with pastel splashes of color. Grimacing, he carefully lifted his legs onto the mattress and reclined against the raised head of his hospital bed.

With a flick of his finger, Brennan scrolled through the photos on his phone until he landed on those he'd taken of the other two files. "How about her?"

He held the phone to Dolan's face so Ruth, replete in her vintage wedding gown, could stare the old man in the eye.

The hiss of oxygen flowing through the cannula in Dolan's nose filled the silence. Dolan nodded almost imperceptibly. "I took that photo back in the day. Marriage didn't last long, if I recall. Ended badly—real badly for him, the poor sap. He picked the wrong girl."

Gotcha. The right side of Dolan's face chronically drooped, which Brennan assumed was due to residual weakness from the old man's prior stroke. When Dolan smiled, his face twisted into a lopsided grin which, in other circumstances, might appear endearing. Today it gave Brennan chills.

He swiped his finger across the screen. The next picture—a crime-scene photo of Ruth with a gaping hole over her heart—appeared. "Didn't end well for her either. Someone made sure of it. Cassie has been studying four cold cases based on your old photos. The police reports identified three out of the four victims as being serial killers themselves. Ruth here was not, yet she murdered four husbands."

The old man's hand shook as he picked one of the blue candy-coated almonds off the table and tossed it in his mouth. The hard shell clacked against his teeth. "So Cassie says."

"So Ruth says. Crazy, right? For eighty years, no one knew Ruth was a killer until she told Cassie herself, in explicit detail. Then Cassie proved it with her research. So how did you know, I wonder? Does 'photo whispering' run in the family?"

"You're talking gibberish, boy. Cassie's ghost stories have gone to your head."

"Her research is sound."

"That's how she ropes you in, with reams and reams of research. Trust an old newsman: everything looks good on paper." He lowered his gravelly voice so Brennan was forced to lean in close. "I know what you're thinking, Detective. Do me a favor and keep your crazy theories to yourself. I never claimed to be a saint, but I love my Peach, and she loves me. I don't give a shit what the world thinks of me, but I won't go to the grave knowing Cassie thinks I'm a monster. Do you know what happened to the last person who called me a monster?"

Brennan shook his head.

"Neither do your peers."

"Are you threatening me, Mr. Dolan?"

"No, son. I'm encouraging you. Encouraging you to do the right thing."

Brennan snorted. "Encouraging me to continue your charade. Cassie worships the ground you walk on. She thinks you're a hero. And you were. What happened?"

"War. War is what happened. Every hero is another man's enemy. I learned that on the battlefield. What they call you afterward depends on whether you were on the winning side."

Dolan picked up the folded newspaper and twisted it like a rope. "I was ass deep in an island trench when I got a Dear John letter from my best girl. Like most of us, I drank too much when I came home. One day after I'd had a few too many, I decided to pay her a visit. Thought maybe I could change her mind. Turns out she was already hitched to another guy." He shook out the twisted paper with a snap. "I took it poorly."

"How poorly?"

Dolan's voice hardened. "Let's just say I shocked myself, which is hard to do. I've made a lot of mistakes in my life, but never twice. She didn't deserve what I did. After that, I poured my rage into worthier pursuits. Sobered up when I met my wife. Life was good until my boy was killed in 'Nam. Had a relapse. But then my grandbaby Erin was born, and things were good again."

Worthier pursuits. Brennan's stomach tightened. "You murdered those four people. I know it, and I think Cassie knows it too, on a subconscious level. It's just too painful for her to accept, so she's using her 'best friend' Ruth to tell the tale. Ruth can't see her killer's face anymore. None of them can. But 'Ruth' remembers. You looked her in the eye and shot her at point-blank range. She figured it out from there. She can't see your face or the face of the person who killed the other three; therefore, the murderer must be one and the same. He must be you."

"Now you are talking crazy. Got any evidence to support those wild claims?"

Brennan looked away. "Didn't think so." Dolan's crooked grin widened. "If you're expecting a confession, you're about to be sorely disappointed. Maybe on my deathbed. Not before. You're supposed to be proving my shit pile of a grandson-in-law killed Erin. I knew Ryan was worthless from the moment I shook his hand on their first date. Smooth as a baby's bottom. He'd never put in a hard day's work in his life. Still hasn't. I warned Erin, but she told me I was being too protective. You had a daughter once, didn't you, Detective Brennan?"

Brennan nodded. Cassie's investigative skills had a downside. Dolan obviously knew everything about him. No point in lying. "You're changing the subject."

"Cassie told me what happened to your baby. You know there's no such thing as being too protective. You would've moved heaven and earth for her, I've no doubt. I feel the same about Cassie. I won't let her money-grubbing leech of a father ruin her life. I'm old news. Start focusing your attention where it should be—on Ryan McConnell and his mobster brother."

"The case closes tomorrow. I've got my boss and Beck McConnell's goons breathing down my neck, and I can't prove shit. I've got some sedatives in her system and burns on her chest and that's it. It's not enough for an arrest, much less a conviction."

Dolan's smirk disappeared, and he grew quiet. "Do you think Ryan killed her?"

"Yes. But I think he had help." Brennan hooked the tip of his finger in the collar of Dolan's gown, fully exposing the burns on his chest. "I was hoping you could help me with that."

"I can't. You wouldn't believe me anyway."

"Try me. I'm getting used to the Dolan brand of reality."

"No. No one would believe you either. A good cop is hard to find. No sense ruining your career this late in the game." Dolan leaned back in his bed and nested his head into a pile of fluffy white pillows. Their stiffly starched covers crackled with each subtle twitch. He closed his eyes. "It's over, then. He'll commit her or have her killed."

"I won't let that happen."

Dolan opened his eyes. "How, exactly?" He carefully plucked another almond out of the bag and studied it as if it were a rare gem. "You have no idea what you're dealing with."

"Then tell me."

Dolan coughed, a deep phlegmy spasm that shook the metal bed until it rattled. "It's not your job to protect my family, Detective. It's mine. I've done a piss-poor job of it over the last twenty years. Got lazy. Grew old. I aim to fix all that. Go back to your life. You tried. I appreciate your efforts." He crushed the candy between his yellowed teeth and sighed. "Tastes like marzipan. Thanks for the almonds. You're a good man. It takes a bad one to know."

CHAPTER

27

November 11th
6th Journal Entry

Father Pignotti prayed for me today. How disgusting is that? He told me I'm surrounded by sinners and their sins—dirty by proxy. I need to be cleansed.

"Let me save you, my dear. I wasn't always a bad man. A life can be made right."

"You're already dead." I pointed out the obvious with a hint of snark.

"I live on in your mind, Cassandra. With photographs and memories, is anyone ever really dead?"

I asked why he would pray for me now after six years of torment and epilepsy, after six years of him silently judging me from his prominent place on the photo room's walls.

"Because the lions are circling, my little lamb, and soon they will pounce. You could use my kind of divine intervention right about now."

He whispered a prayer in garbled Latin, afraid, perhaps, that Ruth might overhear and intervene.

She did. She told him to go to hell.

I think he's already there.

CHAPTER

28

Brennan was pleasantly surprised to arrive home alive. No car bomb. No goons trailing his bumper. No killer bats in the building's dark and creepy parking garage. The window at the end of the hallway was ajar as usual, but aside from the wind's eerie whistle, all was quiet. Not a creature was stirring—not even a crow.

He was mildly disappointed. He expected Elle's avian friend to make an appearance. Crazy. As if the bird would know it was her birthday. As if it would know how badly he needed that connection. The crow, his personal liaison. But perhaps he had another. He could think of only one way to find out.

The apartment was as silent as the hallway. Usually, he clicked on the TV for background noise, but not tonight. Tonight, he was a man on a mission. He yanked five printed photo books—one for each year of Elle's life—off the bookshelf and spread them across the table. Julia was a photo freak. She took hundreds, if not thousands, of pictures and turned them into calendars, books, pins—you name it. Their family Christmas photo card, with a different theme each year and color-coordinated outfits to match—was the stuff of legend. With Elle's birthday being in late November, the Christmas card marked the first page of each photo book. Brennan flipped hurriedly through years one through four, pausing over any image that triggered a particularly happy memory. The fifth and final book was the thickest, as if Julia believed Elle's cancer "journey"—God, how he hated that word—would someday represent nothing more than an unforeseen side trip worth documenting for posterity. His hand hovered over the thick volume. He wanted a specific photo, which he recalled being near the end of the collection. But he didn't want to look through the rest to find it.

Time for a beer. He paced the room and finished half the bottle in a few gulps. Now he was ready. He strummed his fingers across the book, and the cover swished open. Elle appeared healthy at first, and their Christmas photo, in which he wore the world's ugliest sweater, was as epic as the rest. But with each turn of the page, his baby got thinner, her skin paler. Julia's smile grew forced and brittle, and a hint of panic lurked within her wide brown eyes. He knew the feeling well.

His chest tightened with the same anxiety he'd experienced every damned day for six months and then some. He pursed his lips, exhaled slowly, and kept flipping, ignoring the thickening in the back of his throat that spoke of impending tears. Two-thirds of the way through, he stopped and smoothed the page flat. This. This was it. The perfect one.

He'd swooped her into a big ol' hug. Julia had caught the exact moment Elle, her bald head hidden by a tiara and veil, squealed with delight. The joy on their faces was indelible. They'd gotten a good report from her MRI after finishing a brutal round of chemo. He'd bought her ice cream. For a split second, everything seemed right in the world. It was going to be okay. Until it wasn't.

He stared at the photo, his breath hard and fast. With a quick flick of the wrist, he ripped the page from the photo book, slammed it shut, and threw it across the table. It slid off the edge and hit the floor with a slap. If Julia knew what he'd done, that he'd mutilated one of her precious books, she'd stick another pin in that voodoo doll of hers. His right temple spasmed as his morning headache flared back to life. He rubbed his temple and groaned. Maybe she already had.

CHAPTER

29

Brennan shaved and dressed carefully for the day ahead. The meeting with the captain was bound to be cantankerous. No need to give her any unnecessary ammunition. He knotted his nicest tie, which meant the one without the stain, and cinched it tight. This was it. Game on. Time to decide whether to lay it all on the line or live to fight another day. Today's boxing match with his boss would help him choose.

The rarely worn blazer draped stiffly around his shoulders, and its wool collar made his neck itch. But he looked good, or decent, at least—as long as he didn't try to button it. He stowed Erin McConnell's case report, Cassie's files, and Elle's picture in an equally pristine leather attaché, a first-anniversary gift from Julia, and drove to the office. Coffee in hand, he strolled through the precinct and was met by raised eyebrows and a high-pitched wolf whistle from across the room. Sexual harassment. They should know better.

He slung the attaché onto his desk and booted up his computer. Detective Tan eyed his attire with open curiosity. "What gives?"

"Nothing." Brennan sipped from his steaming mug. "Why?"

"You haven't worn a blazer since the last inspection. Got a date after work?"

"A date with the captain is more like it. She wants my report by ten, but I was hoping to get it done and over with so I can move on with my day. Have you seen her yet?" He glanced across the room at the glass-enclosed office, which sat dark and empty.

"Nope."

Brennan frowned. Captain Mattern had her faults, but laziness wasn't one of them. She was routinely the first to arrive and the last to leave. "She's usually here by now. Did she call off?"

His coworker shrugged. "How would I know? Maybe she's just running late. The radio said there was a big pileup on I-95 this morning." Her cell phone rang, and she turned her attention back to her desk.

Figures. His shoulders tightened. How was he going to kill two hours? He finished his coffee while leisurely scrolling through yesterday's email, which took all of twenty minutes. With a click, he emailed the captain Erin McConnell's case report, then double-checked that the hard copy remained safely stowed in his attaché. He'd carry it into the meeting and hand it to her in full view of anyone who cared to watch through her glass office. Old school? Yes. But at least it wouldn't conveniently disappear into the electronic ether, like Pete's original autopsy report.

The folder smelled faintly of fine leather. He slid it back into the attaché next to Father Pignotti's and closed the flap. The priest's gaping chest wound flashed through his mind. The Stacks. He'd planned to search the precinct's long-term storage area for physical evidence. A bullet or casing would be nice—anything he could subject to modern forensics. On Monday, if he wasn't dead or fired, he'd be assigned a new investigation. He may not get another chance. Now was as good a time as any.

He hung his blazer over the back of his chair, slung the attaché over his shoulder, and jogged the stairs to the basement. To his right, stragglers running late after their morning workouts rushed down the yellow hall from the locker room, which would now sit largely silent until the lunch hour or change of shift. With every whoosh of the locker-room door, an acrid gust of body odor and chlorine wafted toward the stairwell, where it mingled with the faint mustiness from the hallway to his left. No one except the occasional historian or ghost hunter visited the Stacks.

Within its iron-barred cells, filing cabinets and a jumble of boxes sorted more or less by date acquired a thick layer of dust. Spiders, undisturbed for months at a time, spun elaborate webs in the corners. The stone walls, slick with mold, retained a tinge of their original industrial green paint, and the low ceiling added to the overall sense of claustrophobia.

Brennan flipped a switch. The overhead lights, retrofitted in the 1950s, flickered on one by one, illuminating the long corridor with their sickly yellow glow.

He shuddered. Twenty years had passed since he'd last visited the Stacks. He'd forgotten how bad it was. Even after half a century of disuse, a vein of misery marbled the crumbling stone and despair still filled the dank air. He ran his finger over the first cell's rusty lock and peered inside.

The cells were more like tiny cages, designed at a time when Americans were shorter and thinner and prisoners were treated worse than circus animals. They lined both sides of a narrow passage barely wide enough for a single guard to patrol down the middle without being grabbed through the bars by desperate hands. In front of each cell door, a number stenciled on the floor in red paint marked the year. The countdown started at 1980.

In the distance, the cages seemed to merge into one, and the light tapered like a tunnel. The optical illusion dampened what little enthusiasm he'd managed to muster. He had almost forty years of cells to pass. He glanced at his phone, hoping that time had magically passed and he had to bail for his meeting. Not even close. He sighed, squared his shoulders, and trudged into the Stacks.

Layers of grit and plaster from the deteriorating ceiling crunched underfoot. The subterranean air grew damp and cold—cold enough for him to see he was breathing far too fast. 1975. Bruce Springsteen's "Born to Run." Nobody beats the Boss. 1971. Led Zeppelin's "Stairway to Heaven." He could use one of those right about now. 1968 . . .

Bang! He spun, crouched, and drew his gun. A shower of sparks and shattered glass rained from above. He pressed his ribs against the closest cell's icy bars and shielded his eyes with his forearm. The noise fizzled to a slow hiss; the sparks vanished. One of the feeble overhead lights faded to black.

Brennan exhaled a cloud of breath and holstered his gun. He grabbed at the bars and pulled himself to his feet. Something soft brushed his fingers. He jerked his hand away. The cell door rattled and creaked. He stumbled out of reach. A spiderweb fanned in the draft.

"Jesus Christ, Dan. Get ahold of yourself." His voice echoed down the hall. Hands on his hips, he stared at the ceiling until his pulse returned to normal, grateful that the only cameras in the Stacks were at its beginning and end. He'd put on quite a show.

He resumed his slow passage to 1945. A subtle twinge in his shins implied the floor was sloping downward, penetrating deeper into the Stacks. With each passing year, the bright light from the stairwell dimmed, and the shadows grew bolder and more menacing: 1946 . . . He stopped in front of what should've been cell number 1945, its red paint obscured by layers of grime. He scraped the sole of his shoe over the pockmarked cement, revealing the badly faded numbers.

Finally.

The cell door was slightly ajar and its keyhole lock filled with epoxy—a precaution put into place by administration after his unfortunate incident decades prior. He grabbed the heavy iron bars with both hands and pulled. The door shrieked, its rusty bearings forced into halting motion after years of lazing in the dark. It slid a few inches, jerked, and shuddered to a stop.

A cloud of dust made his eyes water. Panting, he covered his nose and mouth with the crook of his elbow. After the air cleared, he squared his shoulders and yanked until his fingers ached, forcing a gap barely wide enough for him to slip through. Good enough. He peered through the bars and wondered if it had been worth the effort.

The cell's back wall was lined floor to ceiling with six columns of stacked file boxes in various stages of decay. Those on the bottom had collapsed, the evidence contained within forever lost to history. The rest were coated with a thick layer of slime—a foul mixture of mold, rotting cardboard, and heaven knows what else. But at least they were labeled with a range of file numbers.

He scrolled through the pictures he'd taken of Cassie's cold-case files. The murders occurred in sequential months—June, July, August, and September—so the spread of file numbers wasn't obnoxiously broad. Should be easy enough. He rolled up his sleeves, tucked in his tie, and slid on a pair of nitrile gloves. He'd learned early and hard to always carry a pair in his back pocket in case of noxious slime and assorted bodily fluids. The glamorous life of a detective.

A cursory inspection of the columns revealed his quest would not be so easy after all. Serial killers aside, the summer of '45 must've been otherwise light on crime. According to the numbers scrawled on the box fronts, three of the case files—Ruth's, Father Pignotti's, and the butcher's—rested in the collapsed, decomposing cartons at the bottom of column four. Retrieval would require an extra pair of hands, a hazmat suit, and a respirator. He doubted he'd find anything worth saving anyway. What a waste of time and anxiety.

Only Artie's file remained. Brennan stretched onto his toes to pull two boxes off the top of column five. As he turned to set them on the ground, the lower box's cardboard bottom disintegrated, showering musty old papers and bits of evidence across the cell floor. A giant plume of dust and mold sprayed into the air. Coughing and with eyes streaming, he stumbled out the cell door, tripping over the scattered folders. A clump of three skidded under the bars and came to a rest next to the tip of his dust-coated shoe.

He picked up the top two and skimmed the pictures, hoping by some miracle one of them was Artie's. No such luck. The third slim file lay splayed open on the ground. Brennan swiped his sleeve across his gritty eyes and blinked. That face. He'd recognize that mug shot anywhere, even in black-and-white. He crouched for a closer look.

The young man sported a swollen cheek, bloodied nose, and a familiar scowl. Three-quarters of a century earlier, Leland Dolan's smooth face lacked its rugged handsomeness, but one thing remained unchanged—his fierce stare, capable of penetrating time and space to raise gooseflesh on Brennan's forearms. He held the file to the dim light and turned the yellowed pages.

Per witnesses, the barroom brawl had been epic, with two intoxicated Irishmen beating each other senseless for reasons neither could later recall. But only one was left a bloody pulp, and it sure as hell wasn't Leland Dolan. Fortunately, his opponent, a young lad with the surname McConnell, survived. Both declined to press charges. Dolan spent the night in a cell sobering up and was released the next day on probation. The file was dated just one week before Artie's strangulation.

Brennan shook his head. So the bad blood between Dolan and the McConnell mob family went back generations. Dolan must've been absolutely apoplectic when Erin married into the clan. The McConnells likely considered it a win, much like when princesses were married off by their fathers to diplomatic rivals, uniting their kingdoms by blood. It worked for almost nineteen years. But now that Erin was dead, Leland Dolan had no reason to play nice.

His phone blared an alarm, the noise bouncing off the Stacks' low ceiling. Twenty minutes until his meeting. He snapped photos of Dolan's file and waded through the pile of papers and miscellaneous evidence strewn around the cell floor, hoping something would catch his eye. Artie's case file, or what was left of it, was buried in there somewhere. It would take hours to sort through the mess, plus a new box to stash everything in. A job for another day. Something to look forward to—a third trip to the Stacks.

A loud clang, followed by the sound of a cell door rattling as it closed, reverberated through the windowless passage. Brennan, heart racing, dropped Dolan's file and squeezed through the narrow gap in the bars to the safety of the hall. Yes, the lock was filled with glue, rendering it inoperable. Did he trust that? Not for one sweet minute.

Fists clenched, he stood in the hall and waited. Nothing. The Stacks were as silent as Pete's morgue. He started the slow march back to the stairwell.

The lights went out at 1950. The sudden darkness seized Brennan in its icy, malevolent embrace. He froze in place, his raspy breath echoing in the silence, and waited for his vision to adjust.

A dim light glowed at the far end of the tunnel. Ghostly laughter drowned out the pounding of his heart. A tall, black shadow partially blocked the light. The light flickered again, and the nebulous shadow disappeared, taking the laughter with it.

"Asshole!" Brennan screamed. He took off in a full sprint but soon screeched to a halt, overcome by vertigo. Damned funhouse effect. Uneven floor, low ceiling, darkness . . . He swayed and grabbed the nearest cell door for support. He'd have to feel his way, door by door, back to the stairwell.

A faint clink sounded from within the cell. He yanked his hand off the bars. Plaster falling from the walls, that's all. Or maybe the ceiling.

He stared into the darkness of the bleak cell. The darkness stared back. Perhaps the guards of old were onto something when they opted to walk in the middle of the passage, safely out of reach.

He stepped away from the bars and fumbled to find his phone's flashlight app. The meager beam of light did little to pierce the suffocating darkness, but it did manage to illuminate the ground in front of his feet. He aimed it at the floor and resumed his slow trek toward the stairwell.

At 1965, his phone blared, sending his pulse through the stratosphere. He jerked; the phone flew out of his grip and skidded into the shadows. It pinged off one of the iron bars before falling dark and silent. Shit, shit, shit. He dropped to his hands and knees and patted the ground in widening circles.

"C'mon, baby, give me a sign. Proof of life. Something. Anything."

Dear God, he was pleading with a cell phone.

The phone vibrated, signaling the missed text. He followed the sound to the cell to his left. Nothing in front of the door. He gingerly slipped his hands between the bars and swept his fingers side to side. His pinkie bumped against the phone's hard case.

The screen was cracked, but the phone still worked. He tapped the icon, and the flashlight app clicked back on. The thin beam of light landed on a pair of glowing red eyes. Shit, shit, shit again. Brennan scrambled off his knees and backed away. With a scurry and a squeak, the eyes disappeared.

He exhaled, glanced at his phone, and gasped. Seven minutes. He had seven minutes until his meeting. He covered the next fifteen years in record time and headed straight into the locker room. The mirror confirmed his suspicion; the situation was not good. Sweat stains marred his white button-down shirt. His dress shoes were caked with dirt, and he'd somehow managed to rip a hole in one pant leg. His tie, tucked into his shirt, had survived unscathed. He grabbed a bar of soap and went to work.

Five minutes later, his shoes gleamed, and his face, forearms, and hands were clean and dry. His jacket would cover the sweat marks. There wasn't much he could do about his filthy knees and pants. He'd emptied his locker the day he and Pete went for their walk by the river, but he checked anyway, hoping for a miracle. Nada. Of course not. He slammed the door. The locker next to his rattled, its door slightly ajar. Jim's.

They used to swim together almost every day before Elle's cancer. Jim liked to look and smell good and always kept spare clothes and a complete line of hygiene products at the ready. They often joked about his expensive taste in cologne.

Jim was about his height and weight. Maybe he'd have a pair of clean pants he could borrow. Brennan peeked around the row of metal lockers. The room was empty. Who was he kidding? He just wanted to know what was inside. Amber's missing jewelry would be a pleasant if unlikely surprise.

He crooked his finger around the door's edge and gave a gentle tug. It creaked louder than a haunted mansion's gate. He winced and glanced over his shoulder. The room remained quiet and still. He wrenched the door wide; his face fell. Nothing. Jim's locker was empty. A faint musky odor was all that remained.

He didn't have time to think about it. Brennan dashed up the stairs to his desk and shrugged his jacket over his shoulders. He pulled Erin McConnell's file from his attaché and straightened his tie. He was ready with thirty seconds to spare. He squared his shoulders and turned toward the captain's office. It was dark and vacant.

Detective Tan stared at his dirty, torn trousers with morbid amusement. "You lose a fight with a Chihuahua?"

"Funny. You're very funny, Tan. Where's the captain?"

"She hasn't come in yet. Not that I've seen, anyhow."

"We were supposed to have a meeting at ten."

She shrugged. "Maybe she canceled it. Did you check your texts?"

"Of course I checked my texts." Brennan scowled and walked toward the captain's glass-enclosed office. Shit. He forgot to check his texts. He turned his back and casually pulled his phone from his pocket. The missed text he'd received while sprawled on all fours in the Stacks remained unread. He tapped the cracked screen.

Swim before lunch? We need to talk.

Jim. Brennan furrowed his forehead and tried to glean the implication behind the words glowing on the screen. They hadn't swum together in months. Given the current state of their friendship, an olive branch, if that's indeed what this invitation represented, was unexpected—suspicious, even.

His fingers hesitated above the screen. The door to the precinct flew open. Captain Mattern, flushed and flustered, hurried in.

Brennan quickly tapped a response.

Meeting with the captain now. See you at 11.

Captain Mattern's eyes met his; her gaze flicked over his disheveled appearance. Her harried expression faded to an aloof mask. "I'll be with you in five, Detective. I have more important things to finish first." She brushed by him and strode into her office. "I'll let you know when I'm ready."

The door slammed. Brennan gritted his teeth and shoved his phone in his pocket. "Yes, ma'am." He stomped back to his desk. This meeting was going to hell and it hadn't even started yet. *Five minutes my ass.* He plopped in his chair. May as well get comfy. Somehow he knew he was in for a wait.

Five minutes turned into thirty and included three trips to the break room for bad coffee, two potty runs, and one argument with the mail clerk. Brennan fumed as he watched Captain Mattern, her face once again drawn and tense, pace her office and yell into her cell. Finally, she slammed her phone on the desk, collapsed into her chair, and waved him in.

He entered without knocking.

They considered each other from opposite sides of her expansive desk. She sipped her coffee from a metal thermos heavy enough to use as a weapon. It trembled ever so slightly in her grip.

His eyes narrowed. "Everything okay?"

She positioned the thermos carefully on a fancy glass coaster etched with the Philadelphia Police Department's official seal. "No, but thank you for asking."

"Do you want to talk about it?"

"No." Her gaze dropped to his torn pant leg. "Do you?"

"No."

"Excellent. We're on the same page, then. Do you have the McConnell report?"

"I emailed it to you first thing this morning."

"I haven't had a chance to check."

"I brought a printed copy, if you'd prefer." He dropped the attaché strap from his shoulder.

"That might be best. I'll be in and out of the office today."

So polite. The calm before the storm. Or maybe this was the storm. He pulled the file from the leather case and held it across the desk. Two manila folders, both stamped CONFIDENTIAL in bold red letters, occupied the space between her keyboard and conference phone. The names typed on the tabs gave them away. Personnel files. His and Pete's.

He opened his mouth.

She snatched the folder from his hand and flipped through the pages, giving them a perfunctory look. "I need time to review this. Come back in an hour. In the meantime, consider yourself relieved from this case." She tossed the file on top of the others. "Ryan McConnell filed a restraining order against you."

"What? Why?"

"You were at his hospital yesterday."

"It's not his hospital. It's Jefferson Hospital. He doesn't own the place. But, yes, I was there. Didn't see him."

"He saw you. Says you threatened him."

"Bullshit. His goons paid me a visit, though. Did he mention that part? They delivered a nice pep talk in the parking deck."

"Several witnesses corroborate his story." The captain leaned back in her chair.

"Paid witnesses, I'm sure. Dispatch can back mine, as can hospital security cameras. I walked from the parking deck to Leland Dolan's room and back out again. Period."

"It's his word against yours." Her civil tone never changed. They could've been discussing the weather.

He flung the attaché over his shoulder. "Yeah, the word of a police detective with a clean record versus that of a mob-connected asshole surgeon with a dead wife and mistress."

"A monstrously wealthy, high-society, mob-connected asshole surgeon." She sighed as if suddenly weary of the whole thing.

"This is bigger than me, isn't it?"

"This is bigger than both of us." She reached for Erin McConnell's file. "Go put on a clean pair of pants. You're embarrassing the department and me. Be back in an hour. We need to close this case for good. Trust me—you'll feel better when it's over. I know I will."

Brennan texted Pete from the break room.

We need to talk.

He loitered, poured himself another cup of rancid coffee, changed his mind, and dumped it down the sink. He was already jittery. He didn't need an ulcer to boot. After ten minutes of silence, he gave up. No surprise, really. It was, what, about seven in the evening in Hawaii? Pete was probably shimmying his hips at a luau.

Jim was next.

On my way.

Sure, Brennan lacked the one thing necessary to swim in the precinct's pool—namely a pair of trunks. Shit, he didn't even have a clean pair of pants handy, which was embarrassing, as the captain had so graciously pointed out. But that didn't mean he and Jim couldn't have a heart-to-heart. He sincerely doubted Jim's invitation had anything to do with exercise.

Brennan trudged down the steps to the basement locker room, expecting to see a Speedo-clad Jim primping by his locker. The room was empty. The air, heavy with chlorine, grew warmer and thicker the closer he got to the heated pool. As he approached the swinging double doors to the pool area, his foot hit a slick spot.

With a jolt, he skidded out of control, arms and legs flailing in the air. He hit the tile floor with a thud and a splash. His left hip bore the brunt of the fall.

Groaning, he rolled onto his back and thought of Leland Dolan. The old man had broken a hip with his fall. Here's hoping youth and a few extra pounds spared him the same fate. He gingerly flexed his left knee and hip. No pain. He rolled onto his hands and knees. His palms slid on a thin layer of water, and he scowled.

The number-one rule for using the department's pool was to clean up any tracked water. Okay—the true number-one rule was not to pee in the pool, but that was a given. Either way, the janitors always left a mop propped inside the swinging doors to prevent this exact situation. The asshole responsible, whether too lazy or too rushed, was lucky Brennan hadn't broken his neck.

Mumbling under his breath, he struggled to his feet, pushed the swinging doors open, and hobbled inside. The hum of the ancient filtration system mixed with the warm haze of chlorine made his head spin.

The doors clapped shut behind him. A body floated facedown in the pool.

"Jim!" He limped to the edge and jumped in, releasing wisps of steam that curled languorously into the humid air. The water pushed against his thighs as he splashed and waded toward the middle of the pool. Jim bobbed in the turbulence, each ripple pushing him tantalizingly out of Brennan's reach.

With a final lunge, he latched onto one arm, threw it over his shoulder, and hauled Jim to the shallow end. Grunting under Jim's weight, he heaved him over the pool's edge onto the hard tile, where he landed with the slap of a water-logged towel.

Overheated and exhausted, Brennan hoisted himself to kneel next to Jim. He flipped him onto his back and gasped. Jim's eyes and mouth were open, but he was still. Deathly still.

He pressed his fingers against Jim's neck. No pulse. He grabbed his cell from his pocket. Water pooled under the cracked screen. It flickered and died. A black rotary phone hung on the far wall. Circa World War II, the relic likely hadn't worked since the 1950s. It was worth a try. His bruised hip screamed as he hustled across the tile. His sopping clothes dripped a trail of chlorinated puddles behind him.

The heavy Bakelite receiver felt foreign in his hand. He held it to his ear. No dial tone. He stuck his finger in the rotary dial and spun it clockwise, hoping to connect to the precinct's switchboard. Nothing. He slammed the receiver back in its cradle and rushed back to Jim, slipping and sliding on the water bombs he'd left in his wake. They were on their own. Jim was so screwed.

Frantically debating his options, he pushed hard and fast on Jim's chest. With each forceful blow, water spurted from Jim's mouth and ran down his gray face to join the puddle forming beneath his limp body. *This is useless.* Brennan pushed anyway.

Squish, slurp. Jim's bare skin made obscene sucking noises as it contacted, then released, the wet tile. Beads of sweat formed on Brennan's forehead and trickled into his chemically irritated eyes. The salt added to the burn. His vision clouded, and his arms quivered with fatigue.

Squish, slurp. Laughter. Brennan's racing heart skipped a beat. There it was again. Two voices in the hallway. Friend or foe? Only one way to find out.

"Hey! Man down. I need help in here."

The laughter stopped. *Squish, slurp.* The swinging door burst open, and Brennan braced for whatever came next.

Detective Tan, trailed by a female uniformed officer he didn't recognize, rushed through. Tan turned to her friend. "Go get help." She hurried to Jim's side and dropped to her knees. "Who is he, and what the hell happened?"

"Jim Bonino, and I have no idea. I found him facedown in the pool." A bead of sweat dripped off his forehead onto Jim's chest. "Can you take over? My arms are fried."

"How long have you been working on him?" Tan nudged Brennan out of the way and began chest compressions.

"I dunno. Five, ten minutes. But who knows how long he was floating before I found him."

It couldn't have been that long. What time had he gotten that text? Brennan flashed back to the Stacks. Some asshole had pranked him by turning off the lights. The text came through a few seconds later. He shook his head. It's a short trip from asshole to murderer. The text was now evidence. He shook his wet phone, hoping for a miracle.

Nothing.

Tan looked up from her compressions. "Put it in a bag of rice. And next time, don't drown it in a pool."

"I'm not planning on doing this again, I assure you."

The black rotary phone rang. And rang. And rang.

Tan gave Brennan a strange look. "Were you expecting a call?"

"No. I thought the damn thing was broken. I tried to call for help a few minutes ago, and it didn't work then. Didn't even get a dial tone."

The insistent ringing continued. Brennan limped across the slick tile and raised the receiver. "Hello?"

Static crackled in his ear.

"Hello? Is anyone there?" He strained to hear over the loud hum of the pool's filter. A pause in the static revealed a second sound—someone's slow and steady breath. Brennan whispered into the receiver. "Listen, you bastard—whoever you are, I will find you. You hear me?"

Tan's officer friend ran back into the room carrying a hard-shelled case. "Help is on the way. I brought the automatic defibrillator from the locker room."

Tan eyed Jim's wet torso and the expanding puddle beneath him. "What do you think? Should we risk shocking him?"

Her friend shrugged.

Brennan slammed the receiver onto the wall and hobbled back to Jim's side. He smiled grimly. "Your call. I've already had one shock for today. I'm not sure my old heart can handle another."

CHAPTER

31

The eerie basement pool hosted an unprecedented crowd, including a dozen first responders and an assortment of gawkers spouting quasi-legitimate reasons to leave their workstations and visit the locker room. They filled the hall and crammed themselves into the area around the rectangular pool's near end, their combined body heat turning the space into a giant wet sauna.

Brennan stripped off his sopping tie and socks and wrung them into the pool. Drenched and miserable, he separated himself from the crowd to linger at the far end and observe the scene from a distance.

The paramedics moved beyond his and Tan's basic attempt at resuscitation by placing an IV and inserting a breathing tube into Jim's lungs. Twenty minutes later, they radioed hospital command, and their efforts ceased. One of the rescuers stood, stretched her back, and chatted briefly with Tan, who nodded.

Tan duck walked the slick tile surface to give him an update. "They called it." She eyed the tie and socks piled in a soggy mess at his feet. "Said there was nothing more they could do. They tried their best. So did we."

Brennan nodded and stared at the dilapidated pool's shimmering water, always in motion as if agitated by an invisible hand. A different motion, a strange undulation deep beneath the surface, caught his eye.

He squinted. "Do you see that?" He pointed to an area near the bottom of the deep end, where tiny bubbles continuously rose to the surface and a gentle *bloop, bloop* hinted at the presence of a filter along the far wall.

They walked closer and crouched for a better look. A metal screen, similar to the strainer in an average kitchen sink, covered the filter. The pump's forceful suction had attracted a green piece of cloth, which now partially clogged the screen. Its free hem undulated like kelp in the tide.

Tan frowned. "It looks like a handkerchief."

"It *is* a handkerchief." Brennan's throat tightened, and he jumped to his feet. "A silk handkerchief, to be exact. And it doesn't belong to Jim."

Four hours crawled by in spits and sputters of activity separated by long stretches of tedium, the "hurry up and wait" pace of childbirth and police investigations. Since the usual coroner was unavailable— thank you, Honolulu Pete—they first had to wait for his coverage to arrive and decide if Jim's death was accidental or suspicious. The coroner chose the latter. Then, since assigning a detective to investigate a death within their own precinct would be a conflict of interest, Captain Mattern was forced to call in the state troopers—and Internal Affairs.

Brennan recited the facts until his voice grew hoarse, first to a brusque pair of troopers and next to a more genteel inspector wearing expensive suede shoes he clearly didn't want to get wet. The troopers retrieved the handkerchief and confiscated Brennan's phone.

He told them everything. Almost everything. Jim's open locker. The strange incident in the Stacks. Jim's text. The water outside the pool's swinging double-doors. The green handkerchief. He left out the details of their estranged friendship and only paused once, when the troopers asked if he knew any reason why someone would want to kill Jim. He finally stuttered something about Jim's propensity to drink hard and bet big on the ponies. The troopers seemed satisfied with that. The inspector did not.

He wanted to tell them Jim stole from the dead and tampered with evidence for the mob, but something held him back, an inner voice warning him the time wasn't right. The inspector, an experienced detective in his own right, knew he was holding back. Brennan knew he knew. He saw it in the arch of the inspector's gray brows, heard it in the gentle persuasion of his voice when he asked, "Are you sure there's nothing more you'd like to share, Detective?" Brennan shook his head, not trusting himself to speak.

It didn't help that Tan, during her own interrogation, kept pointing at Brennan's torn clothing, undoubtedly regaling them with details of his dirty and disheveled appearance after his mishap in the Stacks.

And then there was the captain. She hovered in the background near the swinging double doors, now propped open to release the oppressive heat. She exchanged a few words with the inspector as he was leaving and watched as Jim's body was loaded onto a stretcher and wheeled from the room. She turned on her heel and left with the coroner.

The locker room was abuzz, which helped Brennan secure a borrowed pair of sweatpants and a clean sweatshirt. He parried questions while changing and slogged up the stairs to his desk. His blazer, dry and in pristine condition, hung over his chair, taunting him. He was tempted to throw it over his sweats and call it a day. Keep it classy on the drive home. At least it would hide his gun holster. Captain Mattern thwarted his plans.

"Any day now, Detective." She turned her back and strode to her office without waiting to see if he would follow.

Because of course he would. Brennan clenched his jaw and stalked through the open door. Ass whipping, part deux. Except now he was sore, exhausted, and not in the mood. Oh, and thanks to Detective Tan, a murder suspect too. Nice.

She sat in her chair and steepled her fingers. "Your report's too vague. You labeled Erin McConnell's death as suspicious but inconclusive, yet you gave no clear evidence to support a homicide versus an accident. I'm not stupid, Detective. I see what you're trying to do. Your report is one giant hedge, designed to keep the case open and in limbo. I told you before—this case needs to close."

"I'm fine, thank you for asking. No craziness at all. Just business as usual here in the precinct."

She stared coolly at his face.

His weariness dissolved in a surge of anger. "You asked me to wrap this up in a pretty little bow. But Erin McConnell deserves better, and so does her daughter. I wrote the truth without speculation."

"All I asked was for you to finish it by Friday, which is today. I didn't think I needed to be more specific."

"You want specifics? How's this: Ryan McConnell drugged his wealthy wife, and a mob accomplice pushed her down the stairs. Now they've set their sights on Leland Dolan, who also conveniently fell down the stairs, except the tough old bird survived."

"You talked to him yesterday at the hospital. Don't you think he would've told you if someone pushed him down the stairs?"

"I asked him point-blank. He denied it, but he's hiding something. I could feel it. He thinks he's sheltering Cassie. Said he'd deal with it his way, whatever that means. Meanwhile, mobster Beck is covering his baby brother's tracks by having Jim tamper with the evidence and using his goons to intimidate me and Pete into playing nice. Pete folded. I'm trying to preserve my life while not compromising what's left of my integrity. But there's still one piece of this puzzle I can't figure out. You. Why did you visit Dolan Mansion in July?"

Her face flashed with emotion, and her eyes widened. The instinctive response was there and gone before Brennan could accurately assess its source. It may have been fear.

The captain's voice was calm and steady. "I've never been to Dolan Mansion."

"Cassie McConnell says otherwise. Did you know she's a super-recognizer? Probably not, or you wouldn't have gone. She never forgets a face."

"I have never been to Dolan Mansion." Captain Mattern echoed her prior words. "Dr. McConnell's told me about his daughter. Apparently, she's heavily medicated and mentally ill. And in this case, totally wrong."

She rose from her chair and brushed by him to stand with her back to the glass wall. "Choose your next words carefully, Detective. I don't know where you're going with this, but I assure you, it's a game you will not win and can't afford to lose." Her gaze traveled deliberately from his face to the wall behind her desk.

Brennan followed her line of sight. A clock ticked high on the wall.

The captain folded her arms across her chest. "I met with Jim Bonino earlier this morning. That's why I was late. He said you'd try to set him up. Said you acquired a lot of debt, unpaid hospital bills from your daughter's illness and that your friend the coroner, Pete Ecker, has been stealing jewelry and watches from the dead. You've been fencing the items and splitting the profits. Interesting that he could afford a long, expensive trip to Hawaii on a public servant's salary. Also interesting that Jim is now dead, and you were the one to find him."

"You've got to be kidding me." The end game was unfolding. He knew this was coming, but it was chilling nonetheless. "If anyone's getting set up here, it's me. You know as well as I do by the time a corpse lands in Pete's morgue, it's already been stripped of its personal effects. Besides, there's got to be security-camera footage of Jim somewhere in this building. Detective Tan knows I was at my desk—"

"Detective Tan reported there was an hour's gap during which you left your desk and returned from the basement a sweaty, dirty mess like you'd been involved in a fight."

"I was crawling around in the Stacks." Hadn't he told Tan that? The entire day was a blur of mishap and mayhem. "I told Internal Affairs. I'm sure of it."

He hadn't told them enough. The voice in his head advising discretion with the inspector had been wrong, dead wrong. Now, if he revised his statement to include Jim's connection to the mob, it would look like Brennan was covering his tracks. And he was.

Captain Mattern stepped around Brennan and turned so they were facing each other and both visible through the glass. "I spoke with the inspector. He felt you weren't completely . . . forthcoming." She took a deep breath. "You've left me no choice. You're hereby placed on an administrative leave of absence pending the investigation of Jim Bonino's death. You're not to set foot inside this building until I say so. Is that clear, Detective Brennan?"

Shocked into silence, he stared at her face, hoping to see a flicker or glimmer of something besides grim determination. "Crystal, ma'am."

"Excellent. Badge, ID, and gun, please." She held out her hand.

He looked down at his borrowed sweats. "They're in my jacket pocket. And the gun is my own, not the department's. It's registered, and I'm qualified to use it. You can check my personnel file, which I see is conveniently sitting on your desk."

"Then turn in your badge and ID to security on your way out the door. You're dismissed."

CHAPTER

32

S hopping for a new cell phone added another layer of misery to
an already wretched day. But he needed one ASAP. Pete might
be trying to call.

Brennan fidgeted in front of the counter. All he wanted was to get
in, get out, and get home. But transferring the phone number, contacts, and photos, which fortunately he'd saved to the cloud, took what
seemed like forever, considering he was starving, upset, and wearing
someone else's pants.

The lost texts were an even bigger headache. Since he was no longer in possession of his phone, he'd have to retrieve them from the
mobile company's server. But the companies didn't want to be bothered every time some asshat drowned his phone in a pool, so the request often required an incentive—like a subpoena.

The long-haired dude behind the counter fed him the hard sell
while programming Brennan's new phone, offering everything from a

family plan to a 5G upgrade. If Brennan still had his badge, he'd have shoved it in the guy's face and arrested him for being boring. The blabber would stop—guaranteed.

By the time the torturous encounter ended, darkness blanketed the city. Mumbling like a madman in his sweats and fancy wool blazer, he swung by the closest Wawa for a meatball hoagie and some beer. When he finally arrived at his apartment building, he pulled into his designated spot in the parking garage, cut the engine, and just sat.

He and Elle used to do this sometimes. She'd sit on his lap and stare out the windshield into the darkness, patiently waiting for the bat colony to awaken from slumber and take flight. The first bat earned a squeal of delight, her chubby hands clapping as it swooped through the air to sample the hapless moths drawn to the overhead lights.

Tonight, the air was still—too cold, perhaps, for insects tasty enough to entice the bats from their warm lair near the ceiling. Brennan crammed his tattered dress shirt and pants into the plastic grocery bag with his hoagie. Six-pack in one hand and bag in the other, he tucked his chin against the bitter cold and trudged toward the elevator.

A tire squealed. The noise echoed around the concrete box of a garage, masking its origin. The bats stirred. Brennan froze in the middle of the underground lot. The quiet returned, broken only by the low rumble of an idling engine. He took a step. Headlights rounded the corner at an ungodly speed. An engine roared.

Acutely aware of his vulnerable position, he dashed toward the closest parked car and crouched behind the hood. If this was one of his neighbors, he was gonna look like an idiot. But if not . . . better safe than sorry. Bullet holes would be a lousy end to a lousy day.

The station wagon shuddered to a halt exactly where he'd been standing. He peeked around his makeshift shield. No wonder the tires squealed. They were balder than Mr. Clean. Based on the Datsun's rust, dents, and scratches, the poor thing had been abused since the seventies.

The driver's window rolled down. Brennan quietly set the six-pack on the ground and drew his gun from its holster.

A baseball cap appeared first. Then the head, chin tucked to obscure the face. Next, a black quilted jacket with the collar rolled high. Finally, a voice, husky and low, but unmistakably female—and familiar. "Do the security cameras work in this dump?"

He had no idea. "They sure do."

"Then get in before somebody sees me." The driver lifted her chin, allowing the overhead light to chase the shadows from her face.

"No, ma'am. Besides, security-camera footage can be altered. You know that better than I. In fact, I believe you're counting on it."

"We need to talk without prying eyes or ears."

"You come to me."

Captain Mattern grumbled something he assumed was a profanity and threw the Datsun in reverse, expertly backing it into the nearest open spot.

Her window closed; the door opened. She pulled the baseball cap low on her forehead, hunched her shoulders, and got out, leaving the door ajar.

Brennan clicked his gun's safety to the off position with his thumb. She stopped in her tracks. "For God's sake, Brennan."

"Anyone else in the car with you?"

"Do you really think Beck's men would be caught dead in a junker like that?"

She had a point. "Where'd you get it?"

"I borrowed it from impound."

"Glad to hear it's not yours. Open the back door."

She cussed aloud this time and flung the door wide. The Datsun was empty. "Satisfied? Now will you get in?"

"Only if you toss me the keys."

She flung the keys directly at his chest. They bounced off and hit the concrete with a clink.

He stooped to retrieve them and cocked his head toward the open door. "Ladies first."

She climbed into the driver's side and slammed the door. The car shuddered and groaned.

Keeping his eyes—and gun—trained on her face, he rounded the vehicle and slid into the passenger seat. "You wanted to talk. Go ahead. Shoot."

She cringed at his choice of words. He couldn't blame her. Bad puns at bad times—one of his worst faults. He never acted anxious; years of on-the-job training and a smidge of therapy had taught him how to hide his nerves. The puns were his tell. Tom, his old partner, expected them. Hell, he looked forward to them. Said he found them "endearing." Brennan wasn't sure Tom actually knew what that word meant.

Captain Mattern twisted in her seat to stare him in the eyes. "I understand your distrust. But as your senior officer, I'm ordering you to stand down. This conversation will go a hell of a lot better if you get your gun out of my face."

The shadowy light of the garage accented the hollows of her face. Dressed in ratty jeans and a puffy jacket too large for her petite frame, she looked scruffy and haggard. If it weren't for her contentious attitude, he'd barely recognize the incisive, polished professional he knew her to be. He warily lowered his gun.

"Thank you." She sighed. "My office is bugged. So is the coroner's. I'm sure you figured that out already."

He didn't respond, intentionally allowing the silence to drag. The "borrowed" vehicle, her disguise—she went to a lot of trouble for this little tête-à-tête. Like a felon seeking redemption, Captain Mattern had something she had to say. He was gonna let her talk as long as her wicked heart desired.

She slumped in her seat and stared out the chipped windshield. "Last spring, Erin Dolan McConnell opened the door for us to launch an investigation into Philly's entire Irish mob operation. All we had to do was walk through, which we did. Big time. Erin knew Ryan was cheating, and between his expensive tastes and a pricey mistress, she got sick of him hemorrhaging money—her money. She cut him off, so he turned to his big brother Beck and fell deeper and deeper into debt. She was concerned where that might lead."

"How heroic." Brennan kept a firm grip on the gun resting in his lap.

"I wouldn't go that far. She wanted to protect the Dolan family's name and fortune. And, as we all know, hell hath no fury . . . She let us install a tracker in his car, helped us clone his phone, and gave us access to the security system and cameras. We were in. The head of the Organized Crime Unit assigned several of us to earn Beck's trust—"

"You went undercover as a mob mole?"

"I guess you could say that. Jim, myself—we let ourselves be bought by Beck and reported back to the OCU. Unfortunately, Jim launched a side gig, stealing and fencing evidence. He got greedy and careless. Beck noticed, and so did the OCU. I think Jim assumed one of us would protect him. But I couldn't. Not without blowing my cover. When others outside the operation took notice"—she lowered her gaze to the steering wheel—"something had to be done."

"By 'others' you mean Pete." Brennan rubbed his palm over his mouth and chin. "Jesus Christ. I can fill in the blanks from there."

"I figured you could."

"Beck's goons, probably the same ones who threatened me at the hospital, killed Jim. I heard them laughing while I was in the Stacks. They also left their calling card, a green handkerchief, in the pool. But who ordered the hit—us or them?"

The captain remained stone-faced and silent.

"Did. You. Kill. Jim?"

Her voice carried no emotion. "Everyone will soon learn that Jim had a drinking problem. Employee records will document that he showed up at the precinct visibly intoxicated on more than one occasion. His tox screen will show a mix of alcohol and downers, similar to those noted in the nearly empty bottle at Amber Servello's apartment. The official autopsy report will document he drowned while under the influence—an unfortunate accident. I doubt there will be any questions."

"I've got one for ya." Despite his best efforts, his voice trembled with anger. "Why me? You could've assigned any detective to Erin's case. Why choose me?"

"You were fresh off your daughter's death, and Tom's before that. You were off your game. Also, you carry a lot of respect in the lower ranks and—"

Brennan snorted. "Save it. Your first few words said it all. You thought I'd screw up."

"I was hoping if you declared Erin's death a clear-cut accident, no one would question it."

"You forgot about Pete. He questions everything. It's his job."

She shook her head slightly. "I didn't forget about Pete. I just didn't plan on any . . . unusual physical autopsy evidence, like those burns. Without them, I doubt he would've worried so much about the benzos in her bloodstream. Socialites pop pills and fall. It's a common, tragic story."

The hot hands of death.

She'd paid attention to Pete's original autopsy report—the one that evaporated with his computer. They fell silent, their combined breath frosting the windshield and windows, cocooning them with their morbid thoughts.

A huge black mass swooped out of the darkness. It swept in front of the windshield, blocking the overhead light, then disappeared.

The captain jumped in her seat. "What the hell was that?"

"A bat, probably." Brennan tilted his head sideways to better peer through the window. The space near the ceiling was clear.

"That was too big to be a fucking bat."

"A crow, then. Whatever it was, it's gone now." Brennan's knuckles ached, and his fingertips grew numb. He relaxed his grip on his gun. "Can you see the irony here? The old man was right from day one. I called it on day two. Ryan killed Erin for money. My report was dead-on." He winced at his own bad pun. "Not that it makes me feel any better. She sounds like she was the only semi-noble soul in this whole soulless mess."

Captain Mattern nodded. "For what it's worth, I liked Erin. I was . . . I was sorry to hear what happened. It wasn't part of the plan. Not mine, anyway. My plan and that of the OCU haven't always meshed." She gripped the steering wheel. Its cheap vinyl cover crackled in the cold. "Ryan's mechanic discovered the tracker when the car was in for routine service. At first, he and Beck assumed it was Amber's doing—"

"So they blew her brains out."

"This is the Irish mob we're talking about. They don't mess around with moles—or disloyal wives. According to Ryan's tapped phone records, he and Erin had one of their frequent fights, and she let slip some information only she could have known from the tracker. Beck told Ryan if he didn't do something about her, his men would, and it would be a lot less pleasant. So he drugged her, and she either fell down the stairs on her own or someone helped. Your report says no one else was home except Leland Dolan. The security system corroborates it, but as you said, footage can be easily faked. We may never know the whole truth. Fortunately, Beck never traced the trail back to us; otherwise, this whole elaborate scheme would've been for nothing."

"From where I'm sitting, it has been for nothing. Three people dead, my career teetering on destruction, and zero arrests. I'm set up to be a fall guy, like Jim."

"No, because you get to live."

"Gee, that's mighty swell of ya."

Headlights flashed around the corner. An SUV zoomed past and parked in a spot five or six vehicles down. A car door slammed. Captain Mattern reached toward her hip.

Brennan pushed her gun back in its holster. "Steady."

Rapid footsteps clacked across the concrete. Shrill laughter pierced the air. Cell phone to her multi-pierced ear, a thin woman in a fur jacket and rhinestone-crusted ball cap strode toward the elevator. Her animated conversation faltered when she skirted past the Datsun and spied the captain's brown face and ratty clothing through the windshield. She picked up her pace, skipped the elevator, and ran into the stairwell.

The captain scowled. "Do you recognize her?"

"Relax. She lives here. I've seen her a few times. Name is Karen, I think."

"Figures." She clenched her jaw. "Back to you and your career—you'll both be fine if you allow things to play out according to my plan. I know you think I'm a terrible person. Frankly, I don't care. But we're days, maybe weeks, away from having enough evidence to bust Beck McConnell and his cronies. A clean sweep and the entire Irish mob organization will fall."

"And then they'll reorganize. There's always someone willing to fill that power void."

"True. But by that time, it won't be my problem anymore."

"Are you talking about a promotion?" The blood rushed to his head. The surge of red-hot anger chased the winter chill away. "Are you kidding me? Jim and Erin died so you can get a fucking promotion?"

"Of course not. They died so the Philadelphia police department can take down a brutal organized crime network that's been terrorizing our great city for over a decade."

"You're so full of shit. How can you expect me to believe a word you just said after spouting garbage like that?" He reached for the door.

She grabbed his forearm. "Listen to me. Do your part and stand down. I know you don't want to. I can see you don't plan to either. Your attitude tells me that for some reason, you can't let this one go. But you have to—"

"You want attitude? I'll give you—"

"Once we do our sweep and Beck's in custody, you'll have your due. I promise. I'll call off the troopers and Internal Affairs. Everyone will know you were right. Do it for your brothers in blue and all their hard work on this case. Do it for the city."

"And do it for myself because if I don't, I'm goin' down for Jim's death. Is that right?"

The captain flashed a cheerless smile. "I'm glad you understand."

CHAPTER

33

His beer was warm and his meatballs were cold. Brennan threw the six-pack in the fridge and sat with his elbows on the kitchen table and his head in his hands. It was his move. The captain made that clear. But his options were limited, and each held a downside. Like death.

He unwrapped his soggy hoagie, popped it in the microwave, and watched marinara bubble onto the plate. Usually, the comforting aroma of too much garlic melted the day's stress like mozzarella on a meatball. Not today. The decisions he'd make over dinner would impact the rest of his life—especially how much of it remained.

He couldn't stay in the department. His career was over, no matter what the captain said. Sure, she could clear him of wrongdoing in Jim's death. The rumors would stop circulating eventually. But the whispers, the sidelong glances—those would never fade. He imagined facing Tan every day at the office, her desk an arm's length from his.

The thought made his stomach churn.

The microwave dinged. He ignored it, his appetite gone. He opened the fridge, closed it again, and paced. He never planned a second act, always assumed he'd retire in his fifties with a wife and a daughter in college and maybe even a grandbaby on the horizon. He wasn't qualified to do anything but law enforcement. With Julia and Elle out of the picture, the precinct was his world. He had no hobbies, few friends . . .

Shit. Panic bubbled in his chest, constricting his breath. He stopped pacing, closed his eyes, and inhaled through his nose. *Breathe in, breathe out, like the therapist taught you. Go to your happy place.* And if all else fails, warm beer is better than none.

An overwhelming urge to run aborted his relaxation attempts. He stripped off his borrowed clothes and hopped in the shower, scrubbing his skin to a rosy glow. The bathroom filled with steam, but he lingered, hot water streaming down his face, and tried to imagine what his daughter, with her simple wisdom of childhood, would advise him to do. A glimmer of suppressed hope rose to the surface. *Maybe there's a way to find out . . .*

He closed his eyes, but her tiny voice failed to penetrate the chaos of his churning thoughts, and the urge to escape remained. When the water ran cold, he toweled himself dry and dressed in street clothes, not sure where he was going but certain he couldn't stay there.

He could start over somewhere, become a private investigator like Philip Marlowe from those pulp noir books his pop adored. He'd have to drink more booze. Shouldn't be hard. No way in hell he was moving to Hollywood, though. Vegas held some attraction. His sister lived there. But then who would put flowers on Elle's grave?

No, Philly was his home. Like her friend and frequent visitor the crow, the city was his connection to Elle. The places they'd gone together, like the library. The hospital. The cemetery. Every city block held a memory. Combined, they whispered to him day and night, reminding him of the purest love he'd ever known. Without them, what would he have? Just a bunch of photos. And photos can't talk. Not for him.

He grabbed the leather attaché from where he'd dropped it on the kitchen floor, ran out the door, and jogged down the thirteen flights to the garage. The urgent cadence of his footsteps echoed throughout the subterranean chamber. The bats stirred. Shoulders hunched, he warily eyed the dark corners and shifting shadows. The bats. Fallen leaves. Tornadoes of paper and garbage. Every twitch was a potential predator, and as he crossed the wide expanse of concrete to get to his car, he was easy prey.

He slammed the door tight and clicked the lock. While the engine warmed, he texted Cassie.

Call me if you can.

His phone rang within seconds. "Don't you know we young people hate talking on the phone? That's what text messages are for."

"I know, but this is important."

"Everything okay?"

How should he answer that? No, your mother was a mob mole and I've been framed for killing a coworker and I'm about to lose everything including my mind?

"Yeah. Sure. But I need every last bit of evidence you have on those six cold cases you solved on your own. You asked me to work with the department to bring their killers to justice. I have to do it tomorrow."

"You have to, or you want to?"

"I have to. If I don't do it then, it won't happen at all."

"Okay." She sounded puzzled.

He couldn't blame her. "You still there?"

"Yeah, just thinking. You, um, you still have the folders, I think. All of them—the six cases I solved and the four I didn't. I just have the original photos from the wall and a few other notes if you want to swing by and pick them up."

"Is your father home?"

"Yes."

"He filed a restraining order against me."

"Oh. Figures. He sucks. Okay, how about this: Meet me in the backyard. I'll unlock the iron gate. Follow the gravel path to the patio. There's a bench under the pergola near the armillary. I'll bring my notes and wait for you there."

"Are you able to deactivate the security cameras?"

"Of course." She paused. "What's going on, Detective?"

"I'll tell you when I get there. Give me a good half hour. Friday-night traffic stinks." He disconnected the call and threw the car into gear. He wasn't sure he'd recognize an armillary if he tripped over one. Or a pergola, for that matter. He'd figure it out when he got there.

Brennan parked several blocks away and approached Dolan Mansion from the rear. The neighborhood's rewired gas lamps were stately but dim; unfortunately, the moon shone full, and last night's storm clouds had dissipated just when he could've used their cover the most.

A choppy layer of ice and snow remained. It glistened like shards of glass in the moonlight and rendered the worn cobblestone streets slicker than a bloody blade.

Feeling more like a cat thief than a cop, he stepped carefully, hugging the redbrick houses' shadowy corners. When he thought he'd reached the proper location, he cocked his head and pulled out his phone to confirm the address. Yep, this was it. The moonlight must be hampering his sense of direction.

Dolan Mansion loomed behind an eight-foot-tall wrought-iron fence topped with jagged spikes that would make Vlad the Impaler swoon in fear. Perhaps it was Brennan's mood or the darkness, but the building looked different from the rear. Instead of the street-facing entrance's gracious façade, odd angles and sharp corners jutted threateningly, and a service entrance offered bland passage.

Lead-glass windows on three different stories glowed from within, casting pale yellow and red light onto the brick patio below. The yard was small but immaculate, every inch manicured into a three-foot-tall boxwood maze that began at the semicircular patio and ended at the iron gate. Brennan shook his head. Cassie left out the maze part. He'd have to find his way through in the dark. Guess the Dolans didn't want to bother mowing a lawn.

The iron gate swung silently open with the slightest touch of his palm. He sighed with relief. She'd remembered to unlock the gate. Maybe she'd left a trail of bread crumbs too. Worst case scenario, he'd have to jump the rows. At least they were low enough, though probably prickly.

Left, left, right. That wasn't so hard, even without using his flashlight app. He made it to the center of the maze, where a trio of shrub roses, their thorny branches bereft of petals, shivered in the stiff breeze. He scanned the second half of the low maze and planned his passage.

Right, left, left. A neighbor's dog howled at the moon—or something else. The hedge rustled and parted; a furry creature scurried across the gravel path in front of his foot. He jerked backward and tripped over a stone. Off balance, he succumbed to gravity and dropped to one knee. His hand automatically went to his holster.

With another frantic disturbance of branches, the creature broke free of the hedge and disappeared under the iron fence into the alley. Amber eyes stared unblinkingly at him from behind a stack of wooden pallets. Brennan exhaled and slowly rose to his feet. He'd damned near pulled his gun on a cat. He waited for his heart to stop racing, then resumed tracing a path toward the house. Two false turns and multiple expletives later, he exited the maze onto the patio.

A latticework grid heavily intertwined with tangled grapevine covered the brick courtyard. In the center, a hollow bronze sphere surrounded by multiple rings rested on a stone pedestal. The armillary, no doubt. Fancy. He'd ask Siri about it during his drive home. As promised, a bench with ironwork similar to the gate sat a few feet away. But Cassie was nowhere to be found.

He brushed the light layer of snow off its hard surface, sat, and jumped back to his feet. Shit. That sucker was cold.

"Now you know why I changed my mind." A hushed voice floated out of the shadows. "About waiting for you on the bench, I mean."

Cassie, bundled in a traditional Irish cape and scarf, stepped from beneath the eaves. Her moonlit face glowed translucent against the deep green of her scarf, which fluttered around her chin in the stiff breeze.

If not for the soft click of her boots against the patio's frozen brick, Brennan could've easily believed she had no substance at all—just an ethereal, armless shroud strolling daintily under a full moon.

An arm poked from beneath the cape's heavy folds. "This should have everything you need." Her gloved hand held out a folder for him to claim. "There's not much. Just a few extra bits of information I managed to gather together from older files."

He accepted the file with both hands and stared silently at its plain manila surface.

Her arm disappeared under the cape. "Were you expecting something else?" She looked over her shoulder, no doubt eager to return to the warmth of one of the mansion's many fireplaces.

He opened the attaché, shoved the folder inside, and pulled out the four cold-case files—the ones she claimed she couldn't solve. "I keep forgetting to return these to you."

"Thanks." Another pause ensued. "And?" she prodded.

He took a deep breath. "Your mother's murder had nothing to do with your dad's affair. She was a spy, feeding the police evidence about your Uncle Beck's mob operation. It was a dangerous mission, and they killed her for it."

Her eyes widened. "My mother was working for the police?"

"Not working. She volunteered. Like you solving these cold cases, she did it because it was the right thing to do. And because she was worried about you." That might've been a stretch. Erin did it because Ryan was a lying, cheating, spendthrift son-of-a-bitch, but what the hell. Erin Dolan deserved something for her sacrifice. If he could deliver her daughter's respect, that had to count for something.

A solitary tear landed on the weathered brick, melting its skim of snow. Cassie took a shuddering breath. "I had no clue. Zero. And I'm supposed to be super-observant. I should've realized what was happening."

"And done what? I'm sure your mother took every precaution, shielding you from what was happening as best she could. There was nothing you could do."

"I could've told Pap." She shivered. "He'll be furious when he finds out. He already hates my father's family and has for a long time, since before I was born. This will mean war."

"Which is presumably why your mother didn't tell him herself, and why I'm debating whether we should either. Wars are ugly, and the risk of collateral damage is too high." He handed her a crumpled but clean hankie from his pocket. "And by collateral damage, I mean you. She loved you, Cassie. The evidence stands for itself." He waited until the sniffling stopped and she'd wiped her damp cheeks. "Why don't you ask her yourself?"

She froze with the hankie wadded tightly in her hand. "What do you mean?"

"I'm sure you have dozens of family photos."

"It doesn't work that way." She stared at her brown leather boots.

"Then tell me. How does it work?"

"I . . . I don't know. What I do . . . it's unnatural. Some photos never speak. Some chatter constantly, or did before I learned to control them. Their voices were always yammering in my head, asking for help. They're loudest here in the mansion, especially in the photo room. Sometimes Ruth drowns them out. Some talk for a while and then suddenly stop, as if they've said what they needed to say and are finally at peace. I like to think they've gone somewhere better than this, better than here."

Brennan chewed on his lower lip and scraped his shoe over the moss-covered brick. Slowly, he reached into the attaché and withdrew the page he'd torn from Julia's carefully curated photo book. His breath caught at the sight of his daughter, chocolate ice cream smeared on her thin cheeks and tiara teetering precariously, wrapped in his arms on a perfect day.

The photo trembled as he held it in front of Cassie's pale face. "I want to talk to Elle."

Cassie gently removed the page from his grip. Her fingers skimmed across its glossy surface as if she were stroking Elle's cheeks. A sad smile flitted across her face. "I knew you'd ask eventually."

Brennan shifted his weight. "You met her at the library. You've visited her grave. You've talked to her already in some way or form. I need to know what she said, what she's told you." He looked at the ground. "About me."

She opened her mouth to speak.

He held up his hand. "Don't try to deny it. I know you were at the cemetery—you, the crow, and that damned yellow cat. It's bizarre. I don't understand it, the strange connection, but can you at least tell me . . ." He cleared his throat. "Can you at least tell me if she's still here? I think she's trying to tell me something, but I don't know what it could be."

She turned her face to stare at the bronze armillary, its surface aglow with moonlit frost glittering like turbinado sugar on a red velvet cake.

He looked up at the clear night sky and shook his head. "This is crazy. I'm crazy."

The pergola's grapevine roof rustled. A bird took flight, its wings a dark silhouette against the brightness of the moon. It cawed, triggering another howl from the neighbor's dog. Brennan jumped. Cassie did not.

The voluminous folds of her cape masked any movement beyond the slight tremble of her gloved hand. If not for the sound of her shallow, rapid breaths, she could've been a marble statue, a lawn ornament like the armillary, meant for prestige, not purpose.

He touched her shoulder. "Are you okay?"

She didn't respond.

"Maybe you should go inside." He reached for Elle's photo. "Forget it. We're done here anyway. It's too cold to be standing around—"

"She says her hair grew back. It's long now and black like her crow's. She's pretty again and nothing hurts anymore, so you shouldn't worry."

"What?" he whispered. His chest tightened.

Cassie's voice rose an octave higher. Her pupils, already wide from the dim light, dilated into shimmering pools of the deepest black, their glassy surface concealing mysteries only she could see. "She's always with you, watching, because she knows you're not ready to let go. She wants you to be happy again. She says you look sad, and you need to stop it."

The photo slipped from her fingers and fluttered to the ground. He snatched it off the brick before the dampness could soak through.

"How? Ask her how. How do I stop it?" Brennan crumpled onto the iron bench and buried his face in his hands. "Tell her I'm sorry. I'm so sorry. I gave up too soon. I let her die. I should've done more . . ."

The squeezing in his chest intensified, and he gasped for air, struggling to keep his heart from breaking into a million tiny pieces. When he looked up, Cassie's entire body was shaking.

Her face glowed in the moonlight. She smiled at him, but the smile wasn't hers. She touched his cheek. "You did everything, Daddy.

Everything." The smile vanished, replaced by confusion. Arms outstretched, she stumbled into the darkness, swaying on her feet.

He pictured her on the day they'd first met, her head slamming rhythmically against the cobblestone street as the paramedics stowed her mother's body into the ambulance. "Cassie! Cassie, sit down." He guided her to the bench by the shoulders. "Look at me. Focus on my voice."

Through a film of tears, he watched her try. Her eyes struggled to find his, and her mouth strained to form words. "I can't," she whispered. "I can only hear hers."

For the next twenty minutes, Brennan sat next to Cassie and cried, holding her hand as she alternated between lucidity and catatonia. She whispered and rocked on the cold bench, the rhythmic motion seeming to soothe her agitation.

Twice, when the shaking intensified, he wiped his eyes and pulled out his phone, intent on dialing 9-1-1. He'd have one helluva time explaining his presence in Dolan's backyard, but that was a problem for another day.

He'd think of something.

She'd batted his hand down and reached into a hidden pocket in the lining of her cape to produce a small pill box, dry swallowing its contents in a single gulp. The shaking subsided. By the time her seizure—or whatever the hell this was—broke, his emotions were as numb as his frozen ass.

She stood abruptly and held out her hand. "Could I have that picture back, please? I'd like to hang it on the wall in the photo room. Sometimes . . . sometimes it works better there. Ruth helps. She makes me stronger, I think."

He blinked at the rapid transformation. "What just happened?"

"I talked to Elle. That's what you wanted, right?" With an impatient wave, she brushed a stray lock of hair off her forehead. "Did you expect it to be prim and pretty like we were sitting down to tea?" He shook his head more out of bewilderment than as an answer to her question. Although Elle did love tea parties—the fancier the better.

She rubbed her forehead. "Sorry. Sometimes I don't feel well afterward. Bitchy, a little confused . . . postictal. I think I explained that word to you before. The extra meds don't help my mood either." She glanced over her shoulder at the firelight flickering behind the third-story windows. "I should probably go inside."

"I agree. Before you freeze to death or someone misses you."

"Not super likely. But a warm bed would feel nice." She grasped the corner of Elle's picture and waited for him to let her go.

He forced his fingers to relax and slowly lowered his arm. "You said you could 'only hear hers.' Did you mean Ruth's voice—or Elle's?"

Cassie silently tucked the photo inside her cape.

He thrust his hands into his pockets and then took them out again. "I can't believe what I'm about to say." He blurted the rest in one long breath. "Whether she's real or make-believe, I don't want Ruth talking to my baby."

Cassie raised her brows. "You and I have no control over anything that happens outside this realm, Detective. You can't protect her there."

"I know." Anxiety thawed his numb emotions, and the hollowness in his heart filled with tension. "That's why I'm worried. Ruth was a horrible human being. As a matter of fact, she and I should have a conversation. Tell her she's next."

"Ruth was not a horrible person. She had a tough life, and marriage was the only way out. The world was different for women then. She did what she had to do."

"Are you justifying four counts of premeditated murder?"

"No. I'm pointing out that most people are not all bad. Everyone has at least one redeeming virtue. Except maybe Paul. He's a monster through and through." She paused. "If it helps, Ruth can't hurt her. Not anymore. And Ruth won't talk to anyone but me."

"Are you one-hundred-percent sure about that?"

"Yes."

"Fine." He thrust his cold hands back into his pockets. "Keep the photo for now. I want it back tomorrow. I plan to spend tonight typing your research into police reports. I'll turn them and your case files over to my boss first thing in the morning. Afterward, I thought we could tell your pap that your mother's case is officially closed together. Will your father be home?"

"He usually golfs Saturday mornings if the weather's warm enough. If not, he goes to the gym."

"Perfect. Either will work. As long as he's not home when we arrive. You wanna meet at the library at ten?"

"Sure. When will you be arresting my father and Uncle Beck?"

"I won't." *And I can't tell you why.* "I don't have enough evidence." Cassie couldn't know about the upcoming sting operation. He prayed he hadn't told her too much already.

One little slip of the tongue and she'd end up buried alongside her mother.

Cassie balled her fists by her sides. "But you said my mother collected the evidence for you. She did your job and died for it. You're letting them get away with murder." She stepped closer. "Now I get it. I know why you want to turn in those six cold cases I solved. They're my consolation prize—a pat on the back for a job well-done."

Her shrill voice carried in the cold, dry air. The neighbor's dog howled in response.

Brennan glanced at the shifting shadows beyond the gate. The amber-eyed cat was gone, spooked, perhaps, by the dog's barking— or Cassie's anger. "It's not over yet. It only looks that way. I said I couldn't arrest them. I, singular. *I* can't. In your journal, you said your pap trusts me, and so do you. Now more than ever, I need you to hold that thought close. Justice will be served in the end. I promise." He inwardly cringed.

He sounded like the captain.

She glared at him with an expression eerily similar to one he'd seen somewhere before. It hit him like a lead slug. Her pap's old black-and-white mugshot. The resemblance was chilling.

The fury faded into icy composure. She shrugged and turned away. "I can tell you exactly what my pap will say to that, Detective."

"What?"

"You can do better, son. That's simply not going to do."

CHAPTER

34

P ete finally called, and his timing couldn't have been better. Brennan had circled the block twice, inspecting the entrance to his apartment's garage for suspicious activity and struggling to quiet his anxiety long enough to enter.

Parking garages had not been kind to him lately.

When his phone blared Pete's ringtone—a Grateful Dead song, naturally—Brennan whipped the car through the entrance, parked, and vowed to keep Pete on the line until he reached the safety of his apartment.

"It's about freakin' time." Brennan eyed the expanse of crumbling concrete between him and the elevator.

"Yeah, well, I'm on vacation, you know, and I'm trying to lay low. Besides, Elaine will get cranky if I introduce work into our island paradise. She's taking a dip in the pool before dinner, so talk fast."

Brennan, phone to his ear and hand on his gun, hurried to the elevator. He jabbed the up button, glanced over his shoulder, and lowered his voice. "Jim's dead."

Pete fell silent. The elevator dinged.

"Pete, I'm getting into the elevator to my apartment. I'll probably lose you." He stepped inside. "Call me back in a minute, okay?" The door whooshed shut, and the line went dead.

No music. In the bleary-eyed haze of a typical morning, he appreciated the lack of sugary pop or even worse, a bastardization of his favorite classic rock. Tonight, as he stared at his phone's blank screen and prayed for an empty hallway, the silence was smothering.

The cables groaned. The elevator, as cold as a meat freezer, shuddered into motion. The floors passed slowly, the burned-out display flickering partial numbers in a shade too faded to qualify as red but not yet pink. The lift stopped on the seventh floor. Brennan lived on floor thirteen.

The display lights sputtered. The red disappeared. He hugged the inside corner and held his breath, waiting for the doors to move. They opened to an empty hall and paused. And paused. And paused. They finally slid shut, and he sagged against the cold steel wall. The display sparked to life.

The elevator lurched upward. Eight, nine . . . By the time it reached floor thirteen, his head was ready to explode.

He peeked into the hall. Empty. The window at the far end gaped open, easy passage for the bone-chilling wind. Screw it. Let somebody else close it for a change. Clutching his phone, he dashed into his apartment and slammed the door. His phone rang, and he nearly stabbed his finger through the screen to answer it.

"Pete, you have no idea how happy I am to hear your voice. It's been a rough week."

"Not as rough as Jim's, from the sound of it. What happened?"

"He drowned in the precinct pool."

"Oy vey." Pete paused, and Brennan imagined the gears in his coroner friend's brain beginning to turn. "Accidentally or on purpose?"

"Depends on who you ask."

When he'd first texted Pete, Brennan intended to tell him everything—the investigation by Internal Affairs, how they were being set up—everything. But that was before his little heart-to-heart with Captain Mattern in the parking lot. Now, what did it matter? Pete had already bowed out. The captain made it explicitly clear that what happened next depended entirely on how Brennan handled the next few days. Pete was counting on him to do the right thing. Brennan couldn't let him down.

Pete's voice was low, solemn. "I never meant for this to happen. Jim had issues, but he didn't deserve to die. I should never have reported my suspicions, minded my own business—"

"Processing the dead is your business, Pete. You did the right thing. Trust me, none of this is your fault. I just thought you'd want to know. Plus, it's good to hear your voice—"

"You have had a tough week. You're getting sappy."

"You don't know the half of it."

"Look, Dan: Elaine and I talked this morning about how much we love it here. We debated buying a condo or a small cottage and renting it out until we're able to comfortably retire. But this . . . this . . . situation is added incentive to make a move and do it now. I could work a few more years here in Honolulu, pay off the house, then ease onto the beach when I'm ready. I don't feel safe in Philly anymore. My autopsy reports have put a lot of vicious people behind bars throughout the years, and I'd guess about half of them are eligible for parole by now."

"That's because you're good at your job." Brennan, his adrenaline spent, slumped on the sofa. "I can't blame you, Pete. I'm thinking of making a move myself, starting over somewhere new. Maybe Julia had the right idea when she returned to Florida. Make sure that condo comes with a spare bedroom, just in case."

"My door is always open for you, Dan. You know that. Speaking of the missus, here she comes. I gotta run. Talk to you soon." Pete hung up before Brennan could say good-bye.

"I certainly hope so, Pete." He stared at the blank phone. "I hope so." He tossed his new cell on the coffee table. A wave of fatigue made his shoulders sag, and he debated sleeping on the lumpy old couch overnight. His back and hips would scream at him in the morning. Besides, he had things to do. He hadn't worked an all-nighter in a long time, but if tomorrow went as planned, this could be his last one ever. Step one: Get off the damned couch.

For inspiration, he dragged a kitchen chair and wooden TV tray into Elle's bedroom, dumped the attaché full of files onto her bed, and spread them in an evenly spaced line. Six decades-old murders, all meticulously investigated and solved by an eighteen-year-old amateur.

If the Philadelphia PD was going to take Cassie's work seriously, the cases needed to be compiled into traditional police reports. Stark black and white. Plain typed text with addenda for the evidence. Irrefutable logic. It was his last professional hurrah and the least he could do to atone for Erin's unresolved case. Cassie's consolation prize, as she'd so astutely called it.

He plugged in his faithful percolator and tore up two hunks of Italian bread in case the crow decided to make an appearance. The coffee and his laptop went on the tray; the crumbs sat on the sill. He was ready. He grabbed a random folder. Henry's. How fitting. The first case he and Cassie had discussed.

The baby-faced undercover agent had been set up and ambushed by someone within his department. Brennan knew how the poor schmuck felt. He flipped the folder open to the photo of a bullet-ridden Henry draped over a Plymouth. *Starting off with a bang.* He flinched. Another bad pun. Tom would approve.

He worked through the night, stopping only to refill his mug and take a whizz. In the early hours of the morning, as he was typing the final details of case number six, he succumbed to fatigue. He awoke curled around the folders on Elle's twin bed with no memory of how he'd gotten there. The crow had disappointed him—or so he thought. When he got up and stretched his legs, the bread was gone. A shiny treasure sat in its place.

The frozen window refused to budge. He pushed and pounded on the upper sash with the heels of his hands until the frame gave, cracking open barely enough for him to pinch the small brass disc between two fingers.

A Philadelphia Transportation Company token. Old. For over 175 years, the token had been legal tender on the city's network of trains, buses, and trolleys. One of these babies could take you to Jersey, the burbs, and beyond. When the city finally relinquished the antiquated token system in favor of electronic ticketing in 2016, Brennan mourned.

He turned the heavy coin over in his palm and admired the embossed art. It was a relic now, a gentle reminder from simpler days that life does indeed exist outside the Philadelphia city limits. He squeezed it in his fist. The crow had gifted him an omen, a good one, for a change. He shoved it in his pocket for luck, burying it deep within the fabric, next to Elle's pin.

A shower, shave, and a hearty breakfast of eggs and enough toast to sop up all that coffee restored a sense of normalcy to his morning routine. The dark circles and bags under his eyes hinted at his long night, but he drew the line at makeup. Not that he had any. Aftershave would have to do. At least he'd smell perky.

The sun's first beams crested the Delaware River as he drove to the precinct. The captain always made an appearance at the office on Saturday mornings between nine and ten. Whether it was just that—an appearance—versus actual work, he had no idea. He didn't care either way. As long as she was there.

He stopped at security first. Frank, a long-since retired mentor, watched the cameras most every Saturday—a tedious part-time job that got him away from his equally tedious wife. Brennan texted him from outside the door.

Can you let me in? I forgot my badge.

The door popped open before he'd hit send.

Frank, the corners of his eyes creased with age and amusement, hiked himself out of his chair. "You know I can see you, right?" He hitched his thumb at the array of monitors covering half the wall.

"I was counting on it." Brennan deleted his text. "How's life?"

"Meh." Frank fluttered his hands in true Italian fashion. "Getting old sucks, but it's better than the alternative." He plopped in the rolling chair and winced. "Even with a bum hip. Doc says it needs replacing, but then who'd watch over youse guys for me?"

His deep belly laugh filled the drab room with warmth. Brennan smiled. "It wouldn't be the same without ya, Frank."

"Have a seat." The old man patted the chair next to his own. "I know why you're here."

Brennan flushed. "You heard."

"I may work part-time, but I get full-time gossip. The footage from yesterday is gone—copied and erased before they carted poor Jim out the door. The guy who worked yesterday said he had a steady stream of visitors—Internal Affairs, the troopers, Captain Mattern. Everyone was asking for it. Internal Affairs got here first. They got the goods. The rest of 'em got nothing."

Brennan stared at the flickering screens. "I figured as much. I guess I was hoping—"

"That maybe he'd blabbed about what he saw to old Frank?" Frank leaned forward in his chair. "You bet your sweet ass he did. He was able to trace Jim from the time he arrived at the precinct until the cameras went wonky in the basement. Been trying for years to get them to upgrade the wiring down there. Anyhow, Jim had two large escorts in three-piece suits. Let them in with his badge."

"Under duress?"

"I assume. Those same guys, looking a little less put-together, walked out twenty minutes later—without Jim."

"Did he . . ." Brennan shifted in the uncomfortable seat. "Did he say anything about me?"

"He did. You were already in the basement when they arrived. You were still in the basement when they left. Came up, went back down later, found Jim." The corners of Frank's eyes crinkled, and his mouth curved into a kind smile. "You're gonna be all right, kid."

"How do you know that? I'm not a kid anymore, Frank."

"I know. And I'm not as old and senile as I seem."

Brennan navigated the maze of tunnels and corridors connecting the precinct's separate buildings until he reached the office shortly after nine. He loitered in the entry. The communal space was always bustling, but since Brennan was a senior detective who rarely worked weekends, most of its current occupants were unfamiliar. Except for the captain. He appreciated her dedication to routine.

Hunched over a stack of papers and pen in hand, she appeared oblivious to his approach. He strode across the room, rapped on the glass with his knuckles, and walked right in.

Her head jerked; her surprised expression quickly turned to a scowl. She glanced through the glass and back at him. "I thought I told you to stay away."

"Don't worry. I'll be brief. In and out like a ninja." He dropped the stack of six folders on her desk. "These murder cases have been on ice for eighty years. Cassie McConnell changed that. I respect and concur with her assessments. Included are official requests to reopen the cases and the detailed evidence and methodology used to identify the correct perp."

She set her pen on her desk. "Excuse me?"

"Open one. You'll see."

Henry's file was on top. She flipped the cover and spent a moment browsing his report. "Some of the department's best minds have worked on these cases over the years, including my mentor. You expect me to believe a mentally ill child with a silver spoon in her mouth solved them from the comfort of her cushy bedroom?"

"First of all, Cassie's an adult, not a child. Secondly, she has a unique set of skills. And lastly, I told you I validated them myself. They're solved. Period."

"What kind of skills?"

"She's a super-recognizer. I told you that before. The FBI uses people like her to pick suspects out of a crowd after a riot."

"I know what a super-recognizer is and how they're used, Detective. I also know that less than two percent of the world's population possesses that skill."

"Yeah? Good for you. Aren't you smart? She also talks to dead people. Well, photos of dead people, to be exact." What the hell. May as well burn all the bridges on his way out the door.

She blinked. "Dead people. She talks to dead people. Because, I mean, why not? Of course, she does. By dead people, you do mean ghosts, yes?"

"Sure."

"Detective—"

He held up his hand and pulled an additional sheet of paper from the attaché. "This is my resignation, effective immediately. Bust Ryan McConnell and give these cases the attention they deserve and you'll never hear from me again. And while I can't speak for Pete, rumor has it he's planning to resign and relocate in the immediate future."

The captain massaged her forehead. "That would be a great loss for the department."

"You wanted everything wrapped up. Here's your nice little bow." He thrust the resignation letter into her hands. "Are we good?"

"You didn't put anything in these reports about ghosts, did you?"

"Of course not."

"Then we're good." She stood. "It's been a pleasure—"

"Save it. Save it for the cameras."

CHAPTER

35

November 13th
7th Journal Entry

R uth was furious with me. I'd never seen her act like that before. With Paul, maybe, but never with me. She paced the room, her bustle swishing a miasma of ghostly vapors in her wake. My crime? I brought a foreigner into the photo room. Elle.

"I could understand if you wanted to hang a picture of your mother. She belongs here. But a child, Cassandra? His child? How dare you? I've told you before—this room is our temple, my home."

"It's Pap's house, not yours."

The pacing abruptly stopped. The vapors swelled into a dense fog that rose from the tips of her white-slippered toes to the veil on her head. The silence was crushing.

My defiance brought consequences. The lights dimmed; ice crystals formed on the wallpaper, the windows, the piano's ebony keys.

Her pale lips didn't move, yet her voice hammered inside my skull and from behind the walls as it had the first time I heard her speak six years ago, almost to the day. "You will not speak of him in this room. In fact, you'll speak of no man within this room—not your pap, nor your detective friend, no man. Is that clear?"

"You can't tell me what to do. You're supposed to be my friend, Ruth, not my mother. I'm not a child anymore."

"No." The word stretched into a low hiss, like a punctured tire slowly deflating on a cold winter's day. "You're not a child anymore, are you Cassandra?"

She stepped backward into the wall, disappearing into a faded, creased photo next to her unlucky groom. "Pity, isn't it?"

CHAPTER

36

Brennan stood shivering outside the library's revolving glass door and wondered where the time had gone. How long had it been since he returned Elle's last overdue book—a week? Two? He'd sworn after that he wouldn't set foot in the library again, but damn, it was cold out here.

If Cassie didn't get here soon . . .

He glanced at his phone. She was late. An orange ribbon, likely torn from a harvest wreath, fluttered down the street. He sighed. November had passed in a blur. He knew returning to work after Elle's death would be a challenge. He never expected it to result in his unemployment.

She rounded the corner and waved, an apologetic smile on her face. "So sorry. I overslept. I didn't feel great after last night's seizure, and then Ruth was chatty. She gets like that sometimes." She paused. "She doesn't like you, you know."

Brennan's stomach tightened as he imagined Elle's picture, all joy and smiles, hanging next to Ruth's gloomy black-and-white photo. He quickly changed the subject. "Do you think your pap is up for this today? How's he doing?"

"His hip is doing great. His breathing—not so much. But it doesn't matter. We have to tell him today before something shows up in the papers. He reads it every day, as you might expect. My father was already gone when I got up this morning, so you don't have to worry about his stupid restraining order." She fiddled with her wool beret. "I want to apologize for last night."

"For what?"

"For my . . . attitude, I guess you'd call it. My personality changes after my seizures. Thank God it's temporary."

"You have no reason to apologize for a medical condition you can't control."

"That's not what my father says."

"He of all people should know better."

They walked at a brisk pace, driven by the cold, stiff breeze. Brennan blew on his hands. The first two weeks of the month had been chilly, the coldest November in recent memory. Or maybe it was his mood. "I quit my job this morning."

Cassie stopped abruptly. The man behind her swerved to avoid contact and glowered at her as he passed. "Why?"

"It's complicated. But I turned in your cold cases first. My boss, er, Captain Mattern, assured me she'll see them through."

"That's why you needed them last night."

"Yes."

They lapsed into silence.

Pavement yielded to cobblestone, and they slowed their pace. Cassie, her expression pensive, pulled a key chain from her pocket and paused on the front steps. "Did you quit because of my mom's case? Because of us?"

"Partly. As I said, it's complicated. I'm not sure I understand it myself. I just knew it was time. Time for a change. Time to try something new."

Cassie turned the key, stepped over the threshold, and stopped. "Do you smell something?" She tilted her head and sniffed.

Brennan followed suit, puzzled by the strange but vaguely familiar acrid scent. His mother had been an x-ray technician back in the days when they still used film and chemical developers. The foyer smelled like a darkroom, heavy with chemicals, must, and smoke.

"Wait outside." He ran to the library, but the fireplace was cold. A gray cloud wafted down the multilevel staircase.

Cassie had already rounded the first-story landing. "Pap!"

Brennan hurdled the stairs two at a time. "I thought I asked you to wait outside."

"It's my house." She reached the bedroom at the top of the third flight of stairs and pounded on the door. "Pap!" The door flew open. The bedroom was empty.

Brennan, panting, arrived by her side. Thin tendrils of smoke floated near the ceiling. They twirled and twined down the hallway, dimming the overhead lights and beckoning their audience to the photo room.

Cassie stared at the door. "It's unlocked."

"I thought you had the only key."

"I do, but I leave it in the jewelry box in my bedroom when I'm not home. Pap must've taken it."

They exchanged worried looks and walked the long hallway together. Brennan pressed his palm against the door. "It doesn't feel hot. Step back, just in case." He cracked the door open an inch, expecting a surge of black smoke. Nothing. "Mr. Dolan? Are you in there?" He peered around the corner and stepped inside.

The normally frigid room was warm and toasty. A thick, sooty haze hung near the ten-foot-high ceiling, but nothing was ablaze.

Dolan was nowhere to be found. Brennan crossed the parquet floor toward the fireplace, but Cassie called him back, her voice tight and strange.

"Detective Brennan." Eyes wide, she stood in front of where the vintage photos should be. The wall was bare. Faint dark smudges, eighty years of accumulated dust and grime, outlined their previous positions. Only tiny bits of yellowed tape remained.

Brennan brushed his fingers over the empty wall. "He burned them. The bastard burned them all." He turned to the fireplace where a pile of ash still smoldered. "Are their voices still here or did he destroy the connection too? Can you hear them?"

Cassie mutely shook her head.

"Not even Ruth?"

Cassie remained silent.

"What about my daughter?" He stared into the glowing embers. "If I bring you another photo of Elle, can you still talk to her? Your ability—is it you or this room or the photos themselves?"

"I don't know." Her voice quivered. "I just don't hear her anymore."

"It's gotta be you. You talked to her at the cemetery, right?" He ran his hands over his head.

"I didn't actually—"

"I should've asked you to tell her I love her. I love her so much." He paced the smoky room, leaving footprints in the dust. "I didn't realize last night would be my only chance. If I had known—"

"Dan."

He spun on his heel, his agitated brain somehow registering her unexpected use of his given name. "What?"

"She knows how much you love her." She stared into his eyes, her gentle voice as soft and soothing as a warm blanket. "Trust me. She knows."

His breath caught in his throat. "Can you try again, please? One more time. Please."

Cassie closed her eyes and covered them with her palms.

Brennan held his breath.

She shook her head. "Nothing. It's so quiet. It's never been so quiet." She lowered her hands. "Maybe they've moved on."

His lower lip trembled. "Do you think that's what happened to Elle? Do you think she went . . ." He choked on a sob. ". . . to heaven?"

"I hope so," Cassie whispered. Her eyes welled with tears. "I'm sorry I don't have all the answers. I don't have any answers."

He grabbed the poker and foraged through the ashes, flipping charred bits of paper in a desperate search for any remnant of his daughter's smiling face. The embers popped. Sparks drifted and flashed like fireflies in the gray air.

A square scrap of photo paper, its surface bubbled and black, held a familiar image. An arm clad in a long white sleeve with pearl buttons. A pale hand holding a bouquet.

Ruth.

He threw the poker against the stone heart in disgust and conceded defeat. The anguish on Cassie's face matched his own.

A steady stream of tears dripped off her cheeks and onto the sooty floor. She sniffled. "I wanted the voices to stop, but not yet. I wasn't done. I was supposed to help them. And Ruth . . . Ruth was my only friend." She clasped her hand over her mouth and wept.

"She's not your only friend." He moved to place his hand on her quivering shoulder. A deep, phlegmy cough stopped him in his tracks. He twirled and reached for his gun.

"Put that thing away." Dolan's walker, overburdened by an oxygen tank and a saddlebag laden with newspapers and inhalers, barely cleared the open door. Wheezing from the smoky air, he leaned heavily on the walker's aluminum arms and pushed its stubborn wheels forward. It creaked with each slow step. "She was never your friend, Peach. It was a lie, an eighty-year-old plot for revenge. It was Ruth. Ruth murdered your mother."

Cassie and Brennan stood in stunned silence while Dolan worked his way, inch by painful inch, into the room. His energy spent, he plopped onto the nearest sheet-covered chair. A plume of silver dust, residue from the scorched vintage photos, swirled into the air. The glittery flakes sparkled in the filtered light before settling to the floor.

Brennan recovered first. "Revenge against who, Mr. Dolan?" His eyes challenged Dolan to reveal his murderous past. "That's a wild claim from someone who once told me not to believe Cassie's stories. Ryan McConnell killed Erin. You said so yourself. Based on my investigation, I agree."

"Ryan helped. He drugged her up thinking it was only a matter of time before she fell on her own. But Ruth gave the final push. Doesn't mean Ryan shouldn't go to jail for it though. Or worse. Someone has to pay for killing my grandbaby. May as well be him."

Cassie, still dazed, drifted into the chair nearest her pap. "You know Ruth?"

"In life, she was a cold-blooded killer, Peach, and bloodlust never dies. She's tried to kill me more times than I can count. Every night, her icy fingers wrap around my throat, but she's never been strong enough to finish the job. Took her eighty years to learn how to become more than a voice. A few more, and she'd have the run of the house. Knocking me down the stairs was the final straw. I had to burn these photos. I learned my lesson the hard way, in an Okinawa prison camp. The human spirit can't be jailed, but it can be destroyed." He grasped the chair's arms with fingers as blue as his lips. "Their voices haunt me too. We can't both be crazy. But I didn't want you to believe they were real. I'd hoped you'd chalk them up to your seizures and somehow move on, as I did."

"I've always known they were real. But now I don't know if anything they said was true." Cassie's lower lip trembled. "She lied to me. Why would she do that?"

"Ruth aimed to take everything from me. She almost did. Vengeance festers with time." He reached between his walker's rails to clasp Cassie's hand. "Locking the photo room wasn't enough. I know that now. But I never thought she'd use you the way she did, and I didn't realize how much stronger she'd become until she killed my Erin. I should've burned those goddamned photos long ago. Nothing good comes from reliving the past. But I couldn't bring myself to sever that link."

Brennan scowled. "Because bloodlust never dies. Those photos were your trophies. Tell her the truth, Dolan. The whole truth, not just the convenient parts." He crossed the room to hover beside the old man.

Dolan ignored him. He released Cassie's hand. "One day I forgot to set the lock, and the rest is history. By that time, it was too late." His gruff demeanor melted away, and his shoulders, shrouded in an oversized brown cardigan, sagged. "Everything that's happened since— your seizures, your mother's death—is my fault. Forgive me, Peach."

Cassie uttered a strangled sob, shuddered, and slowly rocked in her chair. Inner turmoil as movement. Pain as energy. Agitation as rhythm. Brennan warily eyed her anguished face, watching for telltale signs of an oncoming seizure.

Her rocking accelerated. Brennan inched closer to her chair. "But something good did happen. She's cracked decades-old cold cases I never would've been able to solve myself. And soon, those cases will be reopened and officially resolved."

Dolan shrugged. "So what? The murderers are dead now, their crimes long forgotten."

"Not all of them." Brennan's jaw tightened, and he locked eyes with Dolan.

Cassie jumped to her feet. "Their families haven't forgotten. The victims haven't, either. They have children, grandchildren, great-grandchildren, like myself. They want closure. They asked me to help them find peace. And look what you've done." She swept her arm toward the fireplace.

The roar of an engine shook the windows, then abruptly disappeared. The front door creaked and slammed.

Cassie scowled. "Great. Father's home early."

"Fine and dandy." Dolan leaned back in the chair. "Go get your daddy, Peach. Tell him I want to talk about Erin's inheritance money. That should get his ass moving in a hurry."

Cassie bit her bottom lip. "What are you going to do?"

The old man removed the saddlebag from his walker and placed it in his lap. "We're gonna sit and talk awhile. Talk like the dirty old men we are."

"Father's not old."

"But he's sure as hell dirty. Go on now. Detective Brennan will keep me company until you come back, won't you, Detective?"

Brennan's eyes narrowed. "You can count on it, sir."

CHAPTER

37

The sound of Cassie's footsteps faded down the stairs, replaced by
the distant murmur of voices from the foyer below. Dolan pulled
a photo from the saddlebag's outer pocket and laid it on the end
table for Brennan to see. Three generations of Dolans—Cassie, Erin,
Leland, and a woman Brennan assumed was Leland's wife—smiled at
him through the unknown photographer's lens.

Brennan studied the old man's craggy face, searching for hints to
his game. The once shrewd and ruthless businessman didn't seem the
type to put much stock in the supernatural world of voices from beyond the grave and murderous apparitions. Yet here they were, with
Dolan claiming a ghost murdered his granddaughter and Brennan
debating if the old man was senile, criminally insane, or diabolically
clever.

The faint smile on Dolan's face hinted at silent machinations beyond the capacity of a senile brain. As far as insanity, eighty years of

staring at photos of dead people may have succeeded in doing what a brutal world war could not—breaking Dolan's mind. Brennan didn't think so. Which meant the old man was diabolically clever.

"I know what you're thinking." Dolan's eyes were shut, but despite the faint curve to his pale, blue lips, he looked far from relaxed. Oxygen hissed from the tube in his nose. His chest expanded like a barrel with each labored breath. All that effort just to breathe. Dolan was worth a fortune; such a shame money can't buy breath.

Brennan shook his head. "I doubt it. Or should I add telepathy to your long list of talents? I mean, really—what kind of psychopath blames a ghost to stay in an eighteen-year-old's good graces? You're feeding into her delusions."

Dolan laughed, an unpleasant, phlegmy sound somewhere between a cough and a seal's bark. "Respect, boy. I'm not your average criminal. War sanctioned. Medaled. Vetted, if you'll pardon the lousy pun." He chuckled, pausing to catch his breath afterward. "You wanted my deathbed confession. Here it is: Every one of those four people, Ruth especially, got what they deserved. If you could've seen what she did to those men, you'd pin me another medal. Each one was worse than the last. She's the monster, not me. I could've drunk myself into oblivion like most of my pals. Instead, I channeled my pain for the public good. Since then, I've paid for my crimes in ways you can't even imagine."

"I don't have to imagine. I saw Erin lying in a pool of blood on the steps. I saw her again lying on a slab in the morgue. I've seen Cassie foam at the mouth while she seizes. Was your vigilante justice worth it?"

The old man's lids flew open. The furious glint in his eyes gave Brennan pause, and he stepped out of reach. The war-ravaged vet was old and feeble now, but he was still the legendary Leland Dolan.

The angry spark flickered, then disappeared. Anguish took its place, the depths of which made Brennan regret his harsh words. Almost. Not really.

Dolan inhaled a wheezy, whistling breath. "I have a final mission, Detective, and that's to make damned sure Cassie gets the life she deserves. She's a good girl, my peach. Smart, level-headed, a fine judge of character. This curse of ours is not her fault. I see a lot of me in her, the good parts, before the war destroyed whoever I was meant to be. Ryan thinks he's getting Erin's share of the Dolan family fortune. But since she preceded me in death, to use the legal term, her money returns to the Dolan trust, and I've willed everything to Cassie. Sure as I'm sitting here, he'll kill her for it once I'm gone. He'd do it now, but he knows better."

"He'd kill his own daughter?" Brennan's words rang hollow even to himself.

"Of course he would. You've seen worse, I'm sure."

What could be worse than a father killing his only child? Brennan swore he heard Elle giggle. He swiveled his head, staring first at the fireplace, then at the wall where the photos once hung. His daughter's smiling face, her cheeks rosy and flushed with life, floated before him. He raised his arm, and the specter grew wan and gray before fading into the soot-filled air. A cinder popped, releasing a flurry of sparks and ash.

He dropped his arm and paced between the hearth and the piano. "I can't help you, if that's what you're about to ask." The floorboards groaned his distress. "I can't prove Ryan killed Erin. For one thing, I'm no longer a cop. Secondly, I don't have enough evidence to even prove she was murdered—by a ghost, human, or otherwise. As far as the law is concerned, Erin was under the influence and fell down the steps. End of story."

"I know." Dolan acknowledged the detective's dilemma with a barely perceptible nod. "Help Cassie instead. She likes and respects you. Watch over her when I'm gone. It makes me feel better to know she won't be alone."

The elevator dinged, and heavy steps approached from the hall. Dolan's anguished expression melted into an inscrutable mask. He relaxed his hands into his pockets, but his eyes remained hyperalert, focused. *Like a soldier ready for battle.* Brennan's stomach tightened, and he shifted his position toward the empty photo wall, where the padlock still rested against the expensive baseboard molding. No way would he allow anyone between him and the door.

Ryan McConnell strode into the room. He grimaced at the vinegary odor—and Brennan. "For the love of God, Leland, what were you thinking? You know how volatile old photos can be, not to mention that the flue in this room probably hasn't been cleaned in fifty years. And your oxygen tank—you could've set yourself on fire and burned the place to the ground."

Cassie, her face drawn and tight, lingered in the doorway.

"Have a seat, Ryan." Dolan nodded at the chair an arm's-length away, angled, like his, to face the fire.

McConnell eyed Brennan. "He's not supposed to be here."

Dolan scowled. "It's my house. I can invite—and evict—anyone I please. I asked Detective Brennan here to be my witness."

Brennan flashed a sunny smile.

The doctor's jaw tightened. He turned to Dolan. "Cassie said you wanted to talk about Erin's inheritance. I'd consider that a family affair, wouldn't you?" He aimed a pointed look at Brennan and cocked his head toward the door.

Brennan held his position. "Witness, bodyguard . . . take your pick. I'm staying."

"Sit down, Ryan." Dolan's voice thundered in the sparsely furnished room.

Ryan yanked off the chair's filthy white sheet. The resulting cloud of dust triggered Dolan's cough, and the old man hacked until he turned red in the face.

"Be a dear, will you, Peach . . ." he wheezed, "and bring me a cup of hot tea with a wee shot of whiskey? Use the good stuff. It's a special day."

Cassie hesitated. Her gaze flitted from her father's tense expression to Dolan's placid one. Her pap's cough returned, and her forehead furrowed with worry. "Okay. I'll be right back." She hurried from the room. The grandfather clock tolled the hour, masking her footsteps. Downstairs, a cabinet slammed and china rattled.

Dolan pulled an inhaler and an ornately embroidered handkerchief from the saddlebag in his lap. He took two deep inhalations of the medication and wiped his mouth. His breathing slowed. "There now. Just us men. And you too, Ryan." His eyes twinkled with devilish amusement. Brennan stifled a grin.

The color rose in McConnell's cheeks. "Listen, you crazy old bastard, Erin's gone, and she was the only thing standing between you and a nursing home. We'd been considering it since you had your stroke."

"You'd been considering it. Erin told me what you wanted to do. A nursing home is not a prison. You can't involuntarily commit someone, isn't that right, Detective Brennan?"

"I'm the doctor here." McConnell crossed his arms. "And you absolutely can if the person is deemed mentally incompetent. You're crazy, Cassie's crazy . . . I've made sure my colleagues and confidantes have heard every sad detail. It won't be hard to convince the right people to sign the paperwork." He leaned forward and lowered his voice. "It's been nothing but ghost stories and pseudoseizures around here for the last six years. No more. I don't need to play nice anymore."

Dolan stuffed his handkerchief back in the saddlebag and smiled. "Neither do I."

The blast rattled the stained-glass windows. Red splinters of light ricocheted around the room like laser beams. Brennan ducked against the wall, shielded his face with one forearm, and pulled out his gun. Bits of fallen plaster peppered his head and neck. Swirling dust and grit blinded him and choked his breath. Eyes watering, he coughed and blinked until the room swam back into view.

Ryan McConnell, hands pressed over a gaping hole in his liver area, spent his last few seconds trying to run. He never made it out of the chair. He rolled over the armrest, tipping the vintage chair onto its side, its curvy legs splintering and splaying skyward. Dark blood seeped into the parquet floor's scratches and seams, producing a geometric pattern that grew with alarming speed. Tattered ribbons of fabric, the remnants of Dolan's saddlebag, dangled from the walker.

Dolan held the gun at eye level, rotating it so Brennan could see. "Colt nineteen eleven. Standard issue. I was supposed to turn it in after the war, but I didn't. It's been my most loyal companion. It's a heavy bugger now that I'm old." His hand trembled. "Too old."

Brennan slowly rose to his feet. He stretched out his hand. "Put it down, Dolan. Cassie's coming. She doesn't need to see this." He inched toward the exit.

The old man nodded. "Shut the door behind you. Make sure the newspapers get it right. Tell them everything they need to know." He raised the gun to his temple. "And nothing they don't."

The second blast deafened Brennan's ears and painted Dolan's sheet-covered chair a stomach-churning blend of red and gray. Brennan's mind reeled. Leland Dolan—photo thief, escape artist, war hero, media mogul, and serial-killing bastard—was dead.

Cassie's screams pierced his muffled hearing. A glass shattered in the kitchen. The teapot whistled. Her footsteps pounded on the stairs.

Brennan staggered from the room, slamming the door behind him. Cassie rounded the landing and caught her toe on the top step. She stumbled, recovered, and sprinted down the hall in a dead run.

He caught her around the waist before she could reach the door. "Don't go in there."

"What happened? Oh my God, oh my God." She hyperventilated, gasping for air and staring wild-eyed over his shoulder at the door. Her breathing suddenly slowed. "I know."

Behind him, something clicked. He raised his hands and slowly turned to stand by Cassie, partially shielding her body with his own. Nothing. The door remained shut; the air grew frigid. He shivered.

Cassie exhaled a long, frosty breath. "I know." Her pupils dilated.

He grabbed her by the shoulders. "No. Not now. Cassie, look at me."

She seemed to stare straight through him, through the thick wooden door as well, into the photo room and beyond. Her blank expression changed in slow motion. Her eyes widened in horror; her mouth formed a silent O. She stretched out both hands, fingers writhing as if desperately trying to grasp something just beyond her reach.

A faint noise, like that of a swing creaking on a pair of rusty metal chains, echoed from within the photo room. He gasped. "Dolan?" There was zero chance the old man survived, even if he was the legendary Leland Dolan. Not a gunshot to the head. No way.

Cassie moaned.

He stepped between her and the door and pounded it with his fist. "Dolan!" Nothing. "Ruth, is that you? Let her go, you bitch. Let her go!" He rattled the brass knob. The heavy wooden door wouldn't budge. The photo room was locked—from the inside.

A jolt of searing pain stung his hand. He swore and yanked it away. The faint blush of a first-degree burn reddened his palm. He massaged it with his thumb. "Ruth, you open this goddamned door right now." Jesus Christ, what was he saying? What if she did? What was he gonna do? He had no idea.

Cassie brushed by his elbow and placed her palms flat against the door. She leaned her forehead against the polished wood and closed her eyes. A single tear trickled down her pale cheek. "It's not Ruth. It's Pap. He just wanted to say goodbye."

Like his granddaughter, Leland Dolan was buried on a clear sunny day marred by the brutal cold. Unlike Erin's, the funeral was a private affair, lacking in audience and spectacle. Cassie decreed it. Brennan commended her choice. Dolan would've hated the morbid gawkers, the crowd of faux mourners, the ex-business partners expressing sympathy while snickering under their breath. His Purple Heart rested with him in his coffin along with a snippet of Cassie's red hair—and a handful of photos.

Brennan shivered and pulled his jacket tighter around his neck. The past two weeks had been stressful on multiple fronts. The murder-suicide brought unwanted attention to the McConnell family, prompting the police to rush their operation's timeline. The Organized Crime Unit swooped in and busted the Irish mob in a well-coordinated sting. Beck and his cronies landed in jail—until they posted millions in bail—and the city enjoyed a media circus unlike any they'd seen in years. Chief Mattern made her rounds on the local news channels, accepting the praise the commissioner lavished upon her with gracious aplomb and offering the frenzied city a calm, steady hand. She'd already offered Brennan his job back; he'd already refused.

Somewhere, Leland Dolan, the old newsman, was chortling with glee.

The priest gave his final blessing and sprinkled the casket with holy water. Brennan inched closer to Cassie, offering his silent support during the brief service. Despite losing both parents and her beloved pap over such a short time, she didn't seem to need it. Throughout the whirlwind of drama, Cassie remained serene. Reporters choked the cobblestone streets around Dolan Mansion, feasting off the poor-little-rich-girl story like hyenas stripping a gazelle. With her seizures in remission for the first time in years, she stepped into the spotlight and played the media like a pro. Brennan wasn't surprised. She'd learned from the best—media mogul, Leland Dolan.

Yesterday, she'd dumped Ryan's ashes on the ground under her mother's treasured white rose bush—the one in the center of the maze. Fertilizer, she explained, without a touch of irony. Again, Brennan approved. He'd met a lot of victims in his career. Cassie was not one of them. She had too much of her pap in her. She was going to be okay. Someday, he'd have to tell her that her pap was a serial killer on par with Ruth. But that day could wait. Besides, he suspected that somewhere in the back of her hyper-observant mind, she already knew.

"I'm thinking of selling the house," she said, from the backseat of the limo as the cemetery faded from sight.

"Makes sense. It's a lot of space for one person. A lot of memories too. Good and bad." He'd only seen the bad, but there had to have been some good ones somewhere along the line.

"It's been in the Dolan family for four generations. I'd hate to see it demolished and something ugly put in its place." The limo passed a razor-wired parking lot, and she pointed. "Like that."

"I doubt that would happen. Not in your neighborhood. But don't rush into anything. There's no hurry to decide. It's been a hell of a month. Take some time to regroup."

They turned a corner, and the scenery changed to the brick row houses and tony mansions of Society Hill.

She smiled. "On the other hand, I'm thinking of starting my own business, and the mansion would make an impressive office. Entrepreneurship runs in the Dolan family, you know." She cast him a sideways look. "I might need a partner. Got any plans?"

"I'm working on it."

Her smile widened. "That means no."

"It means I'm workin' on it." He flashed a lopsided grin. "What kind of business?"

She laughed until the black tweed cap bounced on her head. "I knew you couldn't resist. Stay tuned. I'm still hammering out the details."

The wide asphalt street changed to the narrow cobblestone alleys of Society Hill. The limo glided to a stop two blocks from the mansion and put on its flashers. The driver opened Cassie's door.

Brennan peered through the windshield at the dozens of cars illegally parked along the narrow road. "Looks like the vultures are still circling. Do you want me to run interference and clear a path to the front door for you?"

"No, I'll be fine. I've been sneaking in through the back gate. The neighbors are highly protective of the alley. They've been keeping it reporter-free—more for themselves than for me, but whatever works."

An awkward silence ensued.

Brennan cleared his throat. "You know how to reach me. The holidays are coming up fast. It's a tough time of year for someone to be alone. Trust me—I know. Text me if you need anything, or if you want to go out for ice cream—"

Cassie burst into laughter.

He grinned. "Sorry. But at your age, you could be my daughter."

"I could be your daughter. I think I'd like that." She reached under the limo's cushy seat and withdrew an envelope. She handed it to Brennan. "Before I go, I thought you might like to see this. It came in the mail yesterday."

The nine-by-twelve-inch manila envelope lacked a return address. The postmark was smudged beyond legibility. He turned it over in his hands. Thick, high-quality paper, no watermark . . . "What's inside?"

"Open it and see."

The top of the envelope had been slit by a letter opener—or a very sharp knife. Cassie's demeanor changed from relaxed to sober. A sudden sense of trepidation raised the hair on his arms. He slipped his fingers inside the envelope and extracted a single item—a black-and-white photo. It was old, like the ones in the photo room, but not quite as old. A woman in a bell-bottom jumpsuit stood next to a skinny young man in uniform. Their smiles appeared forced; their eyes, sad. A battleship loomed in the background.

He flipped the photo over. The ink was faded and smudged, but he could discern a faint date and two words: *1968, New Jersey.* "Who are they?"

Cassie shrugged and lightly stroked the photo's crinkled surface. "She wouldn't say."

EPILOGUE

December 27th
8th Journal Entry

A single black-and-white photo can damage a woman's mind if the image is powerful enough. I now know to be careful. Experience is a powerful ally, pain a costly deterrent. I never want to experience that degree of pain again.

I can't resist. I tack her picture in the middle of the photo room's empty wall and wait. The cleaners have come and gone; the stained furniture has long been removed. The air still smells of soot and blood. At first, I blame the mansion's poor ventilation. The reality? It's the parquet floor. All those gaps and grooves, clinging to molecules of memory.

When the waiting drags on too long, I sit at the piano and play the songs Ruth taught me. "Clair de Lune." "Moonlight Sonata." That nameless Russian dirge in D minor that always makes me cry.

The tears don't help, and my playing gets sloppier and more discordant. But it doesn't matter. The lead-glass windows and a thick layer of snow on the slate roof cocoons the sound. No one outside these walls hears what I hear. I'm the music box in my own little snow globe.

After the silver glitter settles and the final notes sink to the floor, I sit. I wait. I listen. And I am rewarded.

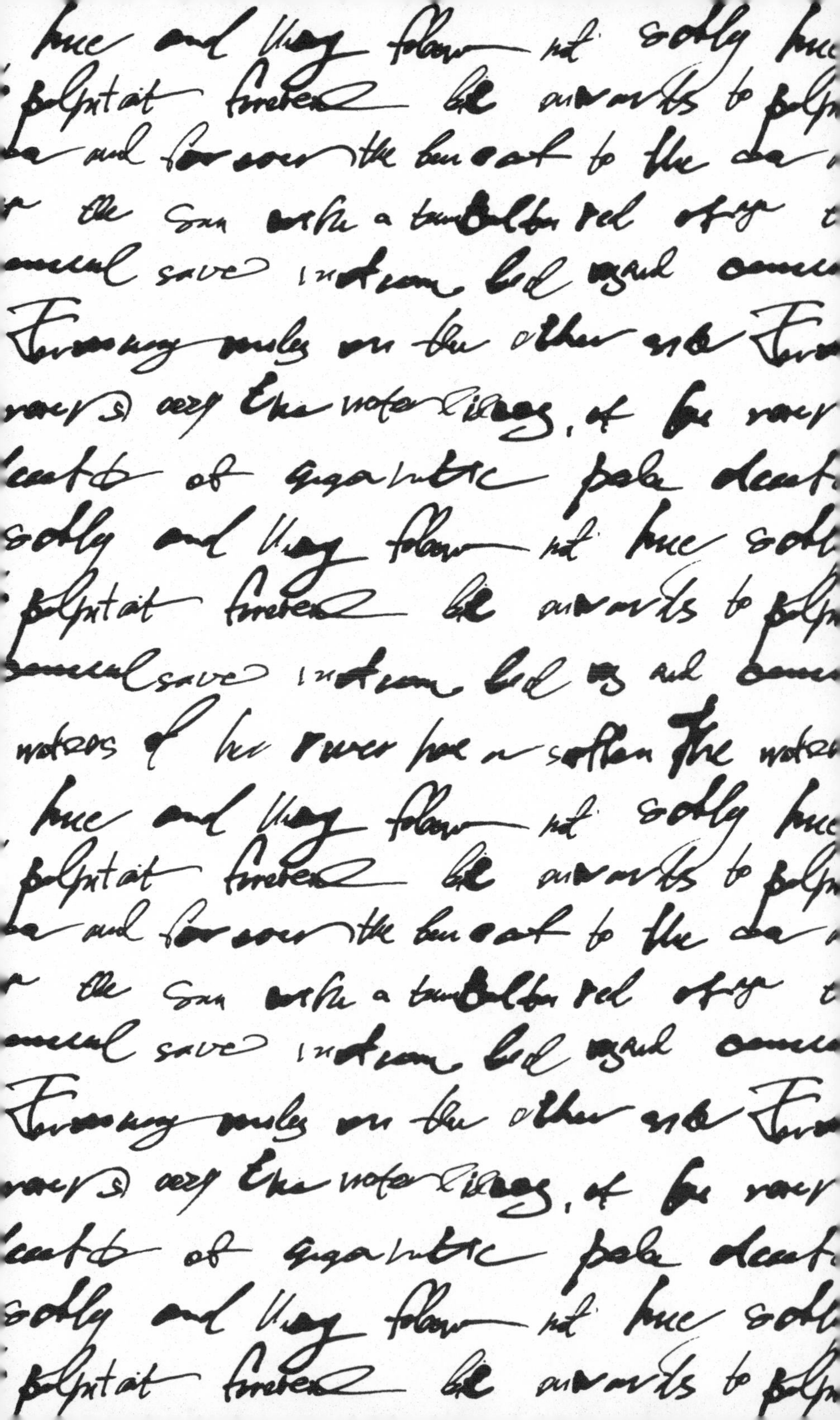

ACKNOWLEDGMENTS

A hearty thanks to:
My editor, Helga, for her wise and steady hand.
The entire CamCat family for their enthusiastic support.
My agent, Lucienne, for her industry prowess.
My writing community of betas, critique partners, and friends.
You know who you are. I cherish you all.
And lastly, to my readers. I do this for you. The best compliment a
writer can receive is a five-star review.

ABOUT THE AUTHOR

J. L. Delozier submitted her first story, handwritten in pencil on lined school paper, to Asimov's magazine while still in junior high school. Several years later, she took a creative writing elective at Penn State and was hooked. She received her BS and MD degrees in six years, which was followed by the blur of internship, residency, and the launch of her medical career. But she never forgot her first love. From the deductive reasoning of Sir Arthur Conan Doyle to the cutting-edge science of Michael Crichton, she remains inspired by facts that lie on the edge of reality: bizarre medical anomalies, new genetic discoveries, and anything that seems too weird to be true.

Dr. Delozier's 2016 debut thriller, *Type and Cross*, was nominated for a Best First Novel Award by the International Thriller Writers organization. *Storm Shelter* followed, and *Blood Type X* completed the trilogy in 2019. Her fourth novel, *Con Me Once*, won a Silver Falchion Award. Her short fiction has won an Omega Award and appeared in

Artemis Journal, The Pittsburgher, Thriller Magazine, Retreats from Oblivion, and the anthologies *Noirville: Tales from the Dark Side* and *Writers Crushing COVID-19.* A retired Associate Clinical Professor of Medicine at Penn State, she lives in Pennsylvania with her husband and feline twins. See more at www.jldelozier.com.

If you liked

J. L. Delozier's *The Photo Thief,*

you'll enjoy

K. L. Murphy's *Her Sister's Death.*

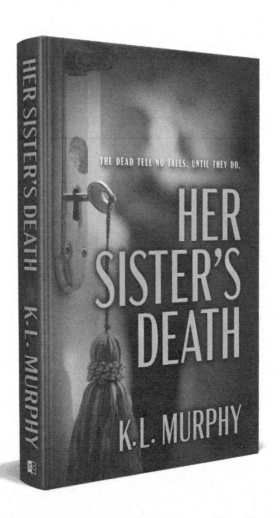

PRESENT DAY

CHAPTER

1

VAL

Monday, 9:17 a.m.

O nce, when I was nine or maybe ten, I spent weeks researching a three-paragraph paper on polar bears. I don't remember much about the report or polar bears, but that assignment marked the beginning of my lifelong love affair with research. As I got older, I came to believe that if I did the research, I could solve any problem. It didn't matter what it was. School. Work. Relationships. In college, when I suspected a boyfriend was about to give me the brush-off, I researched what to say before he could break up with me. Surprisingly, there are dozens of pages about this stuff. Even more surprising, some of it actually works. We stayed together another couple of months, until I realized I was better off without him.

He never saw it coming.

When I about to get married, I researched everything from whether or not we were compatible (we were) to our average life expectancy based on our medical histories (only two years of difference). Some couples swear they're soul mates or some other crap, but I consider myself a little more practical than that. I wanted the facts before I walked down the aisle. The thing is, research doesn't tell you that your perfect-on-paper husband is going to prefer the ditzy receptionist on the third floor before you've hit your five-year anniversary. It also doesn't tell you that your initial anger will turn into something close to relief, or that all that perfection was too much work and maybe the whole soul mate thing isn't as crazy as it sounds. If you doubt me, look it up.

My love of research isn't as odd as one might think. My father is a retired history professor, and my mother is a bibliophile. It doesn't matter the genre. She usually has three or more books going at once. She also gets two major newspapers every day and a half dozen magazines each month. Some people collect cute little china creatures or rare coins or something. My mother collects words. When I decided to become a journalist, both my parents were overjoyed.

"It's perfect," my father had said. "We need more people to record what's going on in the world. How can we expect to learn if we don't recognize that everything that happens impacts our future?" I'd had to fight the urge to roll my eyes. I knew what was coming, but how many times can a person hear about the rise and fall of Caesar? The man was stabbed to death, and it isn't as though anyone learned their lesson. Ask Napoleon. Or Hitler. My dad was right about one thing though. History can't help but repeat itself.

"Darling," my mother had interrupted. "Val will only write about important topics. You know very well she is a young lady of principle." Again, I'd wanted to roll my eyes.

Of course, for all their worldliness, neither of my parents understand how the world of journalism works. You don't walk into a newsroom as an inexperienced reporter and declare that you will be writing about the environment or the European financial market or the latest domestic policy. The newspaper business is not so different from any other—even right down to the way technology is forcing it to go digital. Either way, the newbies are given the jobs no one else wants. Naturally, I was assigned to obituaries.

After a year, I got moved to covering the local city council meetings, but the truth was, I missed the death notices. I couldn't stop myself from wondering how each of the people had died. Some were obvious. When the obituary asks you to donate to the cancer society or the heart association, you don't have to think too hard to figure it out. Also, people like to add that the deceased "fought a brave battle with [fill in the blank]." I've no doubt those people were brave, but they weren't the ones that interested me. It was the ones that seemed to die unexpectedly and under unusual circumstances. I started looking them up for more information. The murder victims held particular fascination for me. From there, it was only a short hop to my true interest: crime reporting.

The job isn't for everyone. Crime scenes are not pretty. Have you ever rushed out at three in the morning to a nightclub shooting? Or sat through a murder trial, forced to view photo after photo of a brutally beaten young mother plastered across a giant screen? My sister once told me I must have a twisted soul to do what I do. Maybe. I find myself wondering about the killer, curious about what makes them do it. That sniper—the one that picked off the poor folks as they came out of the state fair—that was my story. Even now, I still can't get my head around that guy's motives. So, I research and research, trying to get things right as well as find some measure of understanding. It doesn't always work but knowing as much as I can is its own kind of answer.

Asking questions has always worked for me. It's the way I do my job. It's the way I've solved every problem in my life. Until now. Not that I'm not trying. I'm at the library. I'm in my favorite corner in the cushy chair with the view of the pond. I don't know how long I've been here. How many hours. My laptop is on, the screen filled with text and pictures. Flicking through the tabs, I swallow the bile that reminds me

I have no answer. I've asked the question in every way I can think of, but for the first time in my life, Google is no help. Why did my sister— my gorgeous sister with her two beautiful children and everything to live for—kill herself? Why?

Sylvia has been dead for four days now. Actually, I don't know how long she's been dead. I've been told there's a backlog at the ME's office. Apparently, suicides are not high priority when you live in a city with one of the country's highest murder rates. I don't care what the reason is. I just want the truth.

While we wait for the official autopsy, I find myself reevaluating what I do know.

Her body was discovered on Thursday at the Franklin, a "Do not Disturb" sign hanging from the door of her room. The hotel claims my sister called the front desk after only one day and asked not to be disturbed unless the sign was removed. This little detail could not have been more surprising. My sister doesn't have trouble sleeping. Sylvia went to bed at ten every night and was up like clockwork by six sharp. I have hundreds of texts to prove it. Even when her children were babies with sleep schedules that would kill most people, she somehow managed to stick to her routine.

Vacations with her were pure torture.

"Val, get up. The sun is shining. Let's go for a walk on the beach." I'd open one eye to find her standing in the doorway. She'd be dressed in black nylon shorts and neon sneakers, bouncing up and down on her toes. "I promise I won't run. We'll just walk."

Tossing my pillow at her, I'd groan and pull the covers over my head.

"You can't sleep the day away, Val." She'd cross the room in two strides and rip back the sheets. "Get up."

In spite of my night-owl tendencies, I'd crawl out of bed. Sylvia had a way of making me feel like if I didn't join her, I'd be missing out on something extraordinary. The thing is, she was usually right. Sure, a sunrise is a sunrise, but a sunrise with Sylvia was color and laughter and tenderness and love. She had that way about her. She loved mornings.

I tried to explain Sylvia to the police officer, to tell him that hanging a sleeping sign past six in the morning, much less all day, was not just odd behavior but also downright suspicious. He did his best not to dismiss me outright, but I knew he didn't get it.

"Sleeping too much can be a sign of depression," he'd said.

"She wasn't depressed."

"She hung a sign, ma'am. It's been verified by the manager." He'd stopped short of telling me that putting out that stupid sign wasn't atypical of someone planning to do what she did. Whatever that's supposed to mean.

The screen in front of me blurs, and I rub my burning eyes. There are suicide statistics for women of a certain age, women with children, women in general. My fingers slap the keys. I change the question, desperate for an answer, any answer.

A shadow falls across the screen when a man takes the chair across from me, a newspaper under his arm. My throat tightens, and I press my lips together. He settles in, stretching his legs. The paper crackles as he opens it and snaps when he straightens the pages.

"Do you mind?"

He lowers the paper, his brows drawn together. "Mind what?"

"This is a library. It's supposed to be quiet in here."

He angles his head. "Are you always this touchy or is it just me?"

"It's you." I don't know why I say that. I don't even know why I'm acting like a brat, but I can't help myself.

Silence fills the space between us as he appears to digest what I've said. "Perhaps you'd like me to leave?"

"That would be nice."

He blinks, the paper falling from his hand. I'm not sure which of us is more surprised by my answer. I seem to have no control over my thoughts or my mouth. The man has done nothing but crinkle a newspaper, but I have an overwhelming need to lash out. He looks around, and for a moment, I feel bad.

The man gets to his feet, the paper jammed under his arm. "Look, lady, I'll move to another spot, but that's because I don't want to sit here and have my morning ruined by some kook who thinks the public library is her own personal living room." He points a finger at me. "You've got a problem."

I feel the sting, the well of tears before he's even turned his back. They flood my eyes and pour down over my cheeks. Worse, my mouth opens, and I sob, great, loud, obnoxious sobs. I cover my face with my hands and sink lower into the chair, my body folding in on itself. My laptop slips to the floor, and I somehow cry harder.

"Is she all right?" a woman asks, her voice high and tight.

The annoying man answers. "She'll be fine in a minute."

"Are you sure?" Her gaze darts back and forth between us, and her hands flutter over me like wings, nearing but never touching. I recognize her from the reference desk. "People are staring. This is a library, you know."

I want to laugh, but it gets caught in my throat, and comes out like a bark. Her little kitten heels skitter back. I don't blame her. Who wouldn't want to get away from the woman making strange animal noises?

"Do you have a private conference room?" the man asks. The woman points the way, and large hands lift me to my feet. "Can you get her laptop and her bag, please?"

The hands turn into an arm around my shoulders. He steers me toward a small room at the rear of the library. My fading sobs morph into hiccups.

The woman places my bag and computer on a small round table. "I'll make sure no one bothers you here." She slinks out, pulling the door shut.

The man sets his paper down and pulls out a chair for me. I don't know how many minutes pass before I'm able to stop crying—before I'm able to speak.

"Are you okay now?" I can't look at him. His voice is kind, far kinder than I deserve. He pushes something across the table. "Here's my handkerchief." He gets to his feet. "I'm going to see if I can find you some water."

The door clicks behind him, and I'm alone. The man is gone. My sister, my best friend, is gone, and I'm alone.

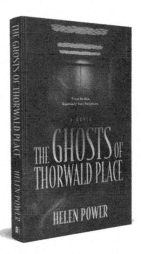
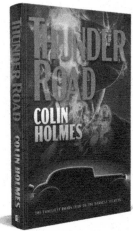